From biting asides to bilious pronouncements, here are more than a thousand quotations arranged A to Z for instant reference to the peeve of your choice. Here's a sampling:

ADVICE TO WRITERS
"Your life story would not make a good book. Don't even try."
—FRAN LEBOWITZ

CHILDREN
"The trouble with children is that they are not returnable."
—QUENTIN CRISP

HAPPINESS
"To be stupid, selfish, and have good health are three requirements for happiness, though if stupidity is lacking, all is lost."
—GUSTAVE FLAUBERT

LYING
"Lying increases the creative faculties, expands the ego, and lessens the frictions of social contacts." —CLARE BOOTHE LUCE

LOVE
"Love is an exploding cigar we willingly smoke." —LINDA BARRY

WOMEN
"Thirty-five is a very attractive age; London society is full of women who of their own free choice remained thirty-five for years."
WILDE

JON WINOKUR is the author ⬚ ⬚ best-selling *The Portable Curmudgeo⬚* ⬚ (all available in Plume editions). He ⬚ ⬚ia.

RETURN OF
THE
PORTABLE
CURMUDGEON

COMPILED AND EDITED BY
JON
WINOKUR

A PLUME BOOK

PLUME
Published by the Penguin Group
Penguin Books USA Inc., 375 Hudson Street, New York, New York 10014, U.S.A.
Penguin Books Ltd, 27 Wrights Lane, London W8 5TZ, England
Penguin Books Australia Ltd, Ringwood, Victoria, Australia
Penguin Books Canada Ltd, 10 Alcorn Avenue, Toronto, Ontario, Canada M4V 3B2
Penguin Books (N.Z.) Ltd, 182–190 Wairau Road, Auckland 10, New Zealand

Penguin Books Ltd, Registered Offices: Harmondsworth, Middlesex, England

Published by Plume, an imprint of Dutton Signet,
a division of Penguin Books USA Inc.
Previously published in a Dutton edition as *The Portable Curmudgeon Redux*.

First Plume Printing, September, 1995
10 9 8 7 6 5 4 3 2 1

 REGISTERED TRADEMARK—MARCA REGISTRADA

The Library of Congress has catalogued the Dutton edition as follows:

The Portable curmudgeon redux / compiled and edited by Jon Winokur.
p. cm.
ISBN 0-525-93489-8 (hc.)
ISBN 0-452-27030-8 (pbk.)
1. Quotations, English.   2. American wit and humor.   I. Winokur, Jon.
PN6083.P48   1992
808.8'2—dc20   92–7692
                                                                CIP

Printed in the United States of America
Original hardcover design by Barbara Huntley

BOOKS ARE AVAILABLE AT QUANTITY DISCOUNTS WHEN USED TO PROMOTE PRODUCTS
OR SERVICES. FOR INFORMATION PLEASE WRITE TO PREMIUM MARKETING DIVISION,
PENGUIN BOOKS USA INC., 375 HUDSON STREET, NEW YORK, NY 10014.

cur•mud•geon/, kər-ˈməj-ən *n* [origin unknown]
1 *archaic:* a crusty, ill-tempered, churlish old man
2 *modern:* anyone who hates hypocrisy and pretense and has the temerity to say so; anyone with the habit of pointing out unpleasant facts in an engaging and humorous manner

Merry Christmas, Fred!

Best wishes, Lorraine

TO WHOM IT MAY CONCERN

CONTENTS

INTRODUCTION 1

WORLD-CLASS CURMUDGEONS 4

QUOTES ON "A" 7

QUOTES ON "B" 18

CATHY CRIMMINS 24
The Anti-Mom

THE CRITICAL CURMUDGEON: Art and Literature 34

QUOTES ON "C" 37

QUOTES ON "D" 58

JOHN WATERS 65
Things I Hate

THE CRITICAL CURMUDGEON: Theater and Film 76

ALEXANDER WOOLLCOTT 86
The Man Who Came to Dinner

WOOLLCOTT SPEAKING 94

QUOTES ON "E" 97

QUOTES ON "F" 103

FRANK ZAPPA 109
Drowning in the News Bath

HAIL TO THE CHIEFS   120

QUOTES ON "G"   129

QUOTES ON "H"   133

LARRY GELBART   140
Stuck on "Angry"

HOORAY FOR HOLLYWOOD   148

OSCAR WILDE   158
Everything to Declare

WILDE ON WOMEN   163

THERE'LL ALWAYS BE AN ENGLAND (ALAS)   166

DAVE BARRY   171
Passages

QUOTES ON "I"   184

QUOTES ON "J"   187

QUOTES ON "L"   190

QUOTES ON "M"   196

FLORENCE KING   206
Go Away

QUOTES ON "N"   216

QUOTES ON "O"   221

JOHN LEO   223
Wanted by the Niceness Police

QUOTES ON "P" 235

QUOTES ON "R" 248

ROBERT BENCHLEY 251
I May Be Wrong . . .

QUINTESSENTIAL BENCHLEY 256

THE CRITICAL CURMUDGEON: Music 259

MARGO KAUFMAN 268
Redhead

QUOTES ON "S" 283

QUOTES ON "T" 289

ABSENT FRIENDS 294

CARRIE FISHER 299
Aghast in Her Own House

QUOTES ON "V" 312

QUOTES ON "W" 314

QUOTES ON "Y" 318

BEDFELLOWS 319

P. J. O'ROURKE 327
Why I Am a Republican

Ye shall know the truth,
and the truth shall make you mad.
ALDOUS HUXLEY

INTRODUCTION

This is the third curmudgeon compilation, a companion to *A Curmudgeon's Garden of Love* and *The Portable Curmudgeon*, the jacket photograph of which showed my face in repose (mistakenly believed by some readers to be a scowl) with the caption: "Winokur has been in a bad mood since 1971." I have since been asked repeatedly whether my disposition has improved. The answer is: no. I am still in a bad mood. And in truth, I had actually been in a bad mood since 1963, but did not think anyone would believe it because in 1963 I was still in high school.

I remain convinced that there is no hope for the human race and that we are in the terminal stages of Life As We Know It. This book is an attempt to amuse myself and others while we're waiting for the last lug nut to fly off the last wheel of civilization. To that end I have written profiles of a few of my favorite world-class curmudgeons (Alexander Woollcott, Oscar Wilde, Robert Benchley), have interviewed a variety of curmudgeonly commentators (Florence King, Frank Zappa, Carrie Fisher, Dave Barry, Margo Kaufman, P. J. O'Rourke, John Leo, Larry Gelbart, Cathy Crimmins, John Waters), and have compiled hundreds of the quotations and anecdotes that have helped preserve my sanity over the past several years.

An odd word, *curmudgeon*. Its origin is unknown, but it may descend from an old Scottish word that meant: to murmur or mumble. The standard dictionary definition is a "churlish, cantankerous old fellow," and the *Oxford English Dictionary* lists several forms (*cormogeon, cormogion, cormoggian, curmudgion*), traces the word to *cornmudgin*, "concealer or hoarder of corn," adds cupidity to the definition ("an avaricious churlish fellow") and suggests that the first syllable, *cur*, refers to a dog.

Whatever its provenance, *curmudgeon* has come to denote a not unlikable grouch, an astute, unsentimental commentator on the human condition. Curmudgeons are mockers and debunkers whose bitterness is a symptom rather than a disease. They cannot stomach pretentiousness or maudlinism. They cannot abide bores, dissemblers, mountebanks, or politicians (but I repeat myself). They snarl at pretense and bite at hypocrisy out of a healthy sense of outrage. They point out unpleasant facts engagingly and humorously. They comfort us with satire.

I was fortunate to have interviewed the late Edward Abbey for *A Curmudgeon's Garden of Love*. He died not long after he wrote this concise treatise on curmudgeonry in *A Voice Crying in the Wilderness*:

I have been called a curmudgeon, which my obsolescent dictionary defines as a "surly, ill-mannered, bad-tempered fellow." The etymology of the word is obscure; in fact, unknown. But through frequent recent usage, the term is acquiring a broader meaning, which our dictionaries have not yet caught up to. Nowadays, curmudgeon is likely to refer to anyone who hates hypocrisy, cant, sham, dogmatic ideologies, the pretenses and evasions of euphemism, and has the nerve to point out unpleasant facts and takes the trouble to impale these sins on the skewer of humor and roast them over the fires of empiric fact, common sense, and native intelligence. In this nation of bleating sheep and braying jackasses, it then becomes an honor to be labeled curmudgeon.

My sentiments exactly.

—J.W.
Pacific Palisades, California
December 1991

WORLD-CLASS CURMUDGEONS

EDWARD ABBEY
GOODMAN ACE
FRED ALLEN
WOODY ALLEN
KINGSLEY AMIS
MARTIN AMIS
MATTHEW ARNOLD
RUSSELL BAKER
TALLULAH BANKHEAD
DAVE BARRY
JOHN BARRYMORE
JOHN BARTH
ORSON BEAN
LUCIUS BEEBE
SIR THOMAS BEECHAM
MAX BEERBOHM
ROBERT BENCHLEY
AMBROSE BIERCE
ROY BLOUNT, JR.
DANIEL J. BOORSTIN
JIMMY BRESLIN
DAVID BRINKLEY
BROTHER THEODORE
HEYWOOD BROUN

RITA MAE BROWN
LENNY BRUCE
WILLIAM F. BUCKLEY, JR.
HERB CAEN
TRUMAN CAPOTE
AL CAPP
CARROLL CARROLL
NICOLAS CHAMFORT
G. K. CHESTERTON
E. M. CIORAN
JOHN CLEESE
MARC CONNELLY
CATHY CRIMMINS
QUENTIN CRISP
EDWARD DAHLBERG
BETTE DAVIS
PETER De VRIES
LINDA ELLERBEE
CHRIS ELLIOTT
HARLAN ELLISON
JOSEPH EPSTEIN
JULES FEIFFER
W. C. FIELDS
CARRIE FISHER

JOHN FORD
GENE FOWLER
ANATOLE FRANCE
ROBERT FROST
PAUL FUSSELL
LARRY GELBART
EDWARD GOREY
LEWIS GRIZZARD
BEN HECHT
TONY HENDRA
BUCK HENRY
ALFRED HITCHCOCK
CHRISTOPHER
  HITCHENS
HENRIK IBSEN
HAROLD L. ICKES
MOLLY IVINS
CLIVE JAMES
SAMUEL JOHNSON
ERICA JONG
BEN JONSON
ALICE KAHN
GEORGE S. KAUFMAN
MARGO KAUFMAN
ALEXANDER KING
FLORENCE KING
TONY KORNHEISER
KARL KRAUS

STEPHEN LEACOCK
FRAN LEBOWITZ
STANISLAW J. LEC
TOM LEHRER
JOHN LEO
DAVID LETTERMAN
OSCAR LEVANT
BEA LILLIE
WILLIAM LOEB
PHILLIP LOPATE
HERMAN MANKIEWICZ
SAMUEL MARCHBANKS
DON MARQUIS
GROUCHO MARX
MARY McCARTHY
COLIN McENROE
H. L. MENCKEN
DENNIS MILLER
HENRY MILLER
JESSICA MITFORD
NANCY MITFORD
WILSON MIZNER
HENRY MORGAN
ROBERT MORLEY
MALCOLM MUGGERIDGE
MARTIN MULL
VLADIMIR NABOKOV
GEORGE JEAN NATHAN

FRIEDRICH WILHELM
  NIETZSCHE
RALPH NOVAK
P. J. O'ROURKE
GEORGE ORWELL
CAMILLE PAGLIA
DOROTHY PARKER
S. J. PERELMAN
J. B. PRIESTLEY
PRINCE PHILIP
JOE QUEENAN
FRANK RICH
ANTOINE DE RIVAROL
ANDY ROONEY
HOWARD ROSENBERG
MIKE ROYKO
HUGHES RUDD
RITA RUDNER
HORACE RUMPOLE
BERTRAND RUSSELL
MORT SAHL
DELMORE SCHWARTZ
ARTIE SHAW
GEORGE BERNARD SHAW
HARRY SHEARER
WILFRID SHEED
IAN SHOALES
JOHN SILBER

JOHN SIMON
GLORIA STEINEM
AUGUST STRINDBERG
TAKI
  THEODORACOPULOS
HUNTER THOMPSON
JAMES THURBER
CALVIN TRILLIN
MARK TWAIN
GORE VIDAL
VOLTAIRE
NICHOLAS
  VON HOFFMAN
ERIC VON STROHEIM
JOHN WATERS
EVELYN WAUGH
CLIFTON WEBB
ORSON WELLES
IAN WHITCOMB
T. H. WHITE
OSCAR WILDE
BILLY WILDER
GEORGE WILL
EDMUND WILSON
ALEXANDER
  WOOLLCOTT
JONATHAN YARDLEY
FRANK ZAPPA

QUOTES ON "A"

————ACADEME————

Academe, *n*. An ancient school where morality and philosophy were taught.   AMBROSE BIERCE

————ACADEMY————

Academy, *n*. (from academe). A modern school where football is taught.   AMBROSE BIERCE

————ACTING————

It is the most minor of gifts and not a very high-class way to earn a living. After all, Shirley Temple could do it at the age of four.

KATHARINE HEPBURN

Acting is like roller skating. Once you know how to do it, it is neither stimulating nor exciting.

GEORGE SANDERS

I love acting. It is so much more real than life.

OSCAR WILDE

————ACTION————

Actions lie louder than words. CAROLYN WELLS

The basis of action is lack of imagination. It is the last resource of those who know not how to dream.
OSCAR WILDE

ACTORS

The physical labor actors have to do wouldn't tax an embryo.
NEIL SIMON

If there's anything unsettling to the stomach, it's watching actors on television talk about their personal lives.
MARLON BRANDO

Scratch an actor—and you'll find an actress.
DOROTHY PARKER

ADVERSARIES

In all matters of opinion, our adversaries are insane.
OSCAR WILDE

ADVERTISING

Advertising is a valuable economic factor because it is the cheapest way of selling goods, especially if the goods are worthless.
SINCLAIR LEWIS

Time spent in the advertising business seems to create a permanent deformity like the Chinese habit of foot-binding.
DEAN ACHESON

ADVICE TO WRITERS

Your life story would not make a good book.
Don't even try.   FRAN LEBOWITZ

ADOLESCENCE

You don't have to suffer to be a poet; adolescence
is enough suffering for anyone.   JOHN CIARDI

AGENT

An agent is a guy who's sore because an actor gets
ninety percent of what he makes.
                                   ALVA JOHNSTON

AGING

It is after you have lost your teeth that you can
afford to buy steaks.   PIERRE AUGUST RENOIR

As you get older, the pickings get slimmer, but
the people don't.   CARRIE FISHER

AGREEMENT

The fellow that agrees with everything you say is
either a fool or he is getting ready to skin you.
                                   KIN HUBBARD

If you can find something everyone agrees on, it's wrong. MO UDALL

ALCOHOL

Alcohol is a very necessary article. . . . It enables Parliament to do things at eleven at night that no sane person would do at eleven in the morning.

GEORGE BERNARD SHAW

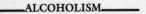

ALCOHOLISM

I called a detox center—just to see how much it would cost: $13,000 for three and a half weeks! My friends, if you can come up with thirteen grand, you don't have a problem yet!

SAM KINISON

AMERICA

It was wonderful to find America, but it would have been more wonderful to miss it.

MARK TWAIN

The trouble with us in America isn't that the poetry of life has turned to prose, but that it has turned to advertising copy.

LOUIS KRONENBERGER

In America everything goes and nothing matters. While in Europe nothing goes and everything matters.
PHILIP ROTH

Everyone has a right to a university degree in America, even if it's in Hamburger Technology.
CLIVE JAMES

To have a license number of one's automobile as low as possible is a social advantage in America.
ANDRÉ MAUROIS

The trouble with America is that there are far too many wide-open spaces surrounded by teeth.
CHARLES LUCKMAN

Some American delusions:
1. That there is no class-consciousness in the country.
2. That American coffee is good.
3. That Americans are businesslike.
4. That Americans are highly sexed and that red-heads are more highly sexed than others.
W. SOMERSET MAUGHAM

The United States is a nation of laws: badly written and randomly enforced.
FRANK ZAPPA

America's one of the finest countries anyone ever
stole.   BOBCAT GOLDTHWAITE

> It is absurd to say that there are neither ruins nor
> curiosities in America when they have their moth-
> ers and their manners.   OSCAR WILDE

What a pity, when Christopher Columbus discovered America, that he ever mentioned it.
                                          MARGOT ASQUITH

> Perhaps, after all, America never has been discov-
> ered. I myself would say that it had merely been
> detected.   OSCAR WILDE

The thing that impresses me most about America
is the way parents obey their children.
                                          DUKE OF WINDSOR

> In America, health is not regarded as a right, but
> as a commodity to be bought and sold just like
> anything else. There are places where an ambu-
> lance team will investigate your financial health
> before it will have any truck with your physical
> health.   WILLIAM GOLDING

In modern-day, new-age America, generally speaking, folks would prefer that your dog vomit on the
new Karastan than that you ignite a Don Diego

Lonsdale in their presence. In their vicinity. In their lifetime.   BRUCE MCCALL

There are three social classes in America: upper middle class, middle class, and lower middle class.
MISS MANNERS (JUDITH MARTIN)

Our national flower is the concrete cloverleaf.
LEWIS MUMFORD

The trouble with this country is that there are too many people going about saying, "The trouble with this country is—"   SINCLAIR LEWIS

——AMERICAN CARS——

All American cars are basically Chevrolets.
HERB CAEN

——AMERICAN MALES——

Eternal boyhood is the dream of a depressing percentage of American males, and the locker room is the temple where they worship arrested development.   RUSSELL BAKER

——AMERICANS——

Americans detest all lies except lies spoken in public or printed lies.   ED HOWE

Whatever else an American believes or disbelieves about himself, he is absolutely sure he has a sense of humor. E. B. WHITE

An Anglo-Saxon relapsed into semi-barbarism.
BAYARD TALOR

Food, one assumes, provides nourishment; but Americans eat it fully aware that small amounts of poison have been added to improve its appearance and delay its putrefaction. JOHN CAGE

When good Americans die they go to Paris; when bad Americans die they go to America.
OSCAR WILDE

You may be sure that the Americans will commit all the stupidities they can think of, plus some that are beyond imagination. CHARLES DE GAULLE

Americans have an abiding belief in their ability to control reality by purely material means . . . airline insurance replaces the fear of death with the comforting prospect of cash. CECIL BEATON

Americans will put up with anything provided it doesn't block traffic. DAN RATHER

Americans adore me and will go on adoring me
until I say something nice about them.

GEORGE BERNARD SHAW

If you surveyed a hundred typical middle-aged
Americans, I bet you'd find that only two of them
could tell you their blood types, but every last one
of them would know the theme song from *The
Beverly Hillbillies*.

DAVE BARRY

ANTS

Ants are so much like human beings as to be an
embarrassment. They farm fungi, raise aphids as
livestock, launch armies into war, use chemical
sprays to alarm and confuse enemies, capture
slaves, engage in child labor, exchange information
ceaselessly. They do everything but watch
television.

LEWIS THOMAS

APPPEAL

An appeal is when you ask one court to show its
contempt for another court.

FINLEY PETER DUNNE

APPRECIATION

Appreciation is a wonderful thing: it makes what
is excellent in others belong to us as well.

VOLTAIRE

ARCHITECTURE

The art of how to waste space. PHILIP JOHNSON

ARGUMENT

It is not necessary to understand things in order to argue about them.

CARON DE BEAUMARCHAIS

It is only the intellectually lost who ever argue.

OSCAR WILDE

ART CRITICS

[The] tendency to degenerate into a mere mouthing of meaningless words seems to be peculiar to so-called art criticism. . . . Even the most orthodox of the brethren, when he finds himself before a canvas that genuinely moves him, takes refuge in esoteric winks and grimaces and mysterious gurgles and belches. H. L. MENCKEN

No degree of dullness can safeguard a work against the determination of critics to find it fascinating. HAROLD ROSENBERG

ARTIFICIAL INTELLIGENCE

The real problem is not whether machines think but whether men do. B. F. SKINNER

ASTROLOGY

I don't believe in astrology. The only stars I can blame for my failures are those that walk about the stage. NOEL COWARD

ASTRONAUTS

Rotarians in outer space. GORE VIDAL

AUTHOR

A fool who, not content with having bored those who have lived with him, insists on tormenting the generations to come. MONTESQUIEU

QUOTES ON "B"

BABIES

One cannot love lumps of flesh, and little infants are nothing more.   SAMUEL JOHNSON

An ugly baby is a very nasty object, and the prettiest is frightful when undressed.

QUEEN VICTORIA

If you were to open up a baby's head—and I am not for a moment suggesting that you should—you would find nothing but an enormous drool gland.   DAVE BARRY

BABY BOOMERS

I'm trying very hard to understand this generation. They have adjusted the timetable for childbearing so that menopause and teaching a sixteen-year-old how to drive a car will occur in the same week.

ERMA BOMBECK

BAGPIPES

I understand the inventor of the bagpipes was inspired when he saw a man carrying an indignant, asthmatic pig under his arm. Unfortunately, the man-made sound never equalled the purity of the sound achieved by the pig.   ALFRED HITCHCOCK

BALLET

I don't understand anything about the ballet; all I know is that during the intervals the ballerinas stink like horses.   CHEKHOV

BANK

Except for con men borrowing money they shouldn't get and the widows who have to visit with the handsome young men in the trust department, no sane person ever enjoyed visiting a bank.
MARTIN MAYER

Banking establishments are more dangerous than standing armies.   THOMAS JEFFERSON

BEES

Did you know the male bee is nothing but the slave of the queen? And once the male bee has—how should I say—serviced the queen, the male dies. All in all, not a bad system.
CLORIS LEACHMAN on
"The Mary Tyler Moore Show"

BICYCLISTS

The people I see on bicycles look like organic-gardening zealots who advocate federal regulation of bedtime and want American foreign policy to

be dictated by UNICEF. These people should be
confined.   P. J. O'ROURKE

———————BILLS———————

It is only by not paying one's bills that one can
hope to live in the memory of the commercial
classes.   OSCAR WILDE

———————BIRTH———————

Birth, *n.* The first and direst of all disasters.
                                           AMBROSE BIERCE

BLASPHEMER'S PRAYER

All I ask of Thee, Lord
Is to be a drinker and a fornicator
An unbeliever and a sodomite
And then to die.   CLAUDE DE CHAUVIGNY

———————BLESSINGS———————

What a blessing it would be if we could open and
shut our ears as easily as we open and shut our
eyes!   G. C. LICHTENBERG

———————BLONDES———————

That gentlemen prefer blondes is due to the fact
that, apparently, pale hair, delicate skin and an

infantile expression represent the very apex of
frailty which every man longs to violate.

ALEXANDER KING

BORE

Every improvement in communication makes the
bore more terrible. FRANK MOORE COLBY

It's so much easier to pray for a bore than to go
and see one. C. S. LEWIS

A healthy male adult bore consumes each year one
and a half times his own weight in other people's
patience. JOHN UPDIKE

You must be careful about giving any drink whatsoever to a bore. A lit-up bore is the worst in the
world. DAVID CECIL

BOSTON

When I go abroad I always sail from Boston because it is such a pleasant place to get away from.
OLIVER HERFORD

BRAN

You do live longer with bran, but you spend the
last fifteen years on the toilet. ALAN KING

_____BUG SPRAY_____

There is no record of one single bug dying from a household bug spray. Most sprays will cause a bug to lie quietly for about forty-five seconds, after which the bug will spring up feeling renewed, refreshed, chemically mutated, and therefore able to fly at supersonic speeds and inject previously unknown poisons into the person who sprayed it. COLIN MCENROE

_____BUREAUCRACY_____

Bureaucracy defends the status quo long past the time when the quo has lost its status.
LAURENCE J. PETER

There is no passion like that of a functionary for his function. GEORGES CLEMENCEAU

If you are going to sin, sin against God, not the bureaucracy. God will forgive you but the bureaucracy won't. HYMAN RICKOVER

Guidelines for Bureaucrats:
1. When in charge, ponder.
2. When in trouble, delegate.
3. When in doubt, mumble. JAMES H. BOREN

A bureaucrat is a Democrat who holds some office
that a Republican wants.   ALBEN W. BARKLEY

> Bureaucrats write memoranda both because they
> appear to be busy when they are writing and be-
> cause the memos, once written, immediately be-
> come proof that they were busy.
>
> CHARLES PETERS

The only thing that saves us from the bureaucracy
is inefficiency. An efficient bureaucracy is the
greatest threat to liberty.   EUGENE MCCARTHY

> Hell hath no fury like a bureaucrat scorned.
>
> MILTON FRIEDMAN

———BUSINESSMEN———

I find it rather easy to portray a businessman.
Being bland, rather cruel and incompetent comes
naturally to me.   JOHN CLEESE

> The human being who would not harm you on
> an individual, face-to-face basis, who is charitable,
> civic-minded, loving and devout, will wound or
> kill you from behind the corporate veil.
>
> MORTON MINTZ

CATHY CRIMMINS

The Anti-Mom

JW: *You've been a mother for how long now, eighteen months?*
CC: Twenty and a half months, but who's counting?
JW: *Don't you like it?*
CC: Let's just say I'm not going gentle into that good nitey-nite. When they were giving out mothering skills, I was probably at the movies. I never even learned to cut fruit into pieces. Ever since Kelly could sit up, I've given her a whole apple. She just

chews on it and spits it out on the floor and I just sort of vacuum it up later. For most mothers, day care is a problem. I'm looking for night care, too. Actually, I'm looking for a boarding day-care center. My friends have taken to calling me "The Anti-Mom." You're talking to me on a bad day: I was up driving the Schuylkill Expressway at three o'clock this morning trying to put my insomniac child to sleep.

JW: *I gather from some of the things you've written that you didn't enjoy pregnancy, either.*

CC: Being pregnant makes you feel like an adolescent girl. First, you're constantly embarrassed about your sexuality, because there it is for everybody to see: "Ha ha, look at her, she had sex!" Then there's the raging hormones. You're crying one day, laughing the next. You feel ugly and worthless and desperate. If you hated adolescence, I'd advise skipping pregnancy.

But the worst are the Maternity Police. I tell women not to let anybody know they're pregnant until they absolutely must, until they throw up over their boss's desk, because once people realize you're pregnant, the Maternity Police descend on you. You can't smoke, you can't drink, you can't stand there and watch somebody spray a bug dead. I resented that, and I used to sit around in bars drinking a glass of wine just to see how many people would accost me.

And people give you books. My favorite is *Thank You, Dr. Lamaze*, written by Marjorie Karmel, the first American woman to try the Lamaze method. She was always visiting her friends and having martinis in the afternoon while they discussed how in the world they were going to find a doctor who would deliver the baby naturally. They would have three or four cocktails and I thought, This method is for me! You sip a glass of Chablis as you go into labor!

JW: *What about those warnings against drinking while you're pregnant: "When you take a drink, your baby takes a drink . . . "*

CC: Not a bad idea—somebody to drink with. This stuff is taken to absurd extremes: While I was pregnant I went into a store to buy a pack of cigarettes *for a friend of mine* who was out in the car, and I had to endure a lecture about smoking and pregnancy. It infuriated me.

With my decadent bent, I was a strange candidate for the whole natural childbirth routine. And I've always been a chicken. I would cry hysterically whenever Al pinched my legs during the exercise to simulate labor contractions. He doubted that I could make it through, but I did.

I had an insane desire to give birth in a really groovy fashion. Guess I'm a child of the sixties in that way. Hospitals weren't good enough for me, so I tried this little "birth center" at which you're supposed to write a "birth plan" and "center" yourself. I had "Jacuzzi labor," that's how groovy I am.

The biggest drawback with the birth center is that they make you dispose of your own placenta. They discuss it with you beforehand, so we debated with our friends what we should do with it. One person suggested we drive to the nearest Roy Rogers and throw it in the Dumpster. The birth center suggested planting a tree with the afterbirth under it. We finally compromised: we weren't living at our house because we were renovating (which is another maternity-related illness), so we couldn't plant a tree. So we put it in the freezer. (I never looked at it. The midwife kept trying to get me to look at it, but I said, "No, thanks, I'll just look at my baby here, okay?") I would show visitors the baby and Al would show them the frozen placenta. We thought of it as a sort of evil twin of our daughter (she has my last name, but the placenta had Al's last name—I promised him). Al finally buried the thing in our backyard when we moved back into the house, but we didn't know what the correct procedure was, whether we should have defrosted it in the microwave first or not, so we buried it frozen. It was a simple ceremony.

JW: *And now that the baby's almost two years old, how has motherhood changed you?*

CC: Aside from sleep deprivation as a way of life, I haven't really changed at all. I still hate children as I always have and always will, and I don't know why I did this.

JW: *Why you had a baby?*

CC: Right. I haven't the foggiest notion. I was apparently acting out some biological imperative. A friend of mine says I don't have a single maternal bone in my body, and he's amazed by it because his wife breast-fed their kids until they were twenty years old. But . . . children irritate me. They get up very early, they're loud, they interrupt, they think they're more important than you. They prevent you from being a child: My little girl has already broken all of my toys. Just this morning I was watching her play with a book of matches, and I said to Al that I should open "Mrs. Cathy's Day Care Center" with open scissors and all the other dangerous things our child seems to find around the house. When she was very small I liked to give her things to play with that would gross other people out, things that *she* just saw as objects. There was a big rubber rat, and a rubber snake. I also liked dressing her in black. My mother was pretty freaked out by that. "Why don't you put a little beret on her and send her to sit in a café in Paris?" she said.

JW: *I've never seen a baby dressed in black.*

CC: My mother was pushing Kelly down the street in her little town and she had on a little black stretchy thing—this was when she was about six months old—and little kids came up and asked, "Is that a *baby*?" They didn't know that babies could look like that. She looked like Yul Brynner in *The King and I*. That's how I'd dress if I were a baby.

JW: *Why did you name her Kelly?*

CC: It's my mom's maiden name. Otherwise it borders dangerously on being a bimbo name. Have you ever noticed that bimbo strain of Kellys? There's a bimbo strain and a tomboy strain. It's sort of soap opera-bimbo-name territory. It's what *I* was supposed to be named, actually. So, I'm just recreating myself, since it would have been rude to name her Cathy Crimmins, Jr.

JW: *Maybe recreating yourself is a reason for having a baby.*

CC: Maybe. I've been working on a list of why people have children. I think about it when I'm up in the middle of the night with Kelly. I think, Wait a minute: People have done this for *centuries*? It's hard for me to believe. So I have a list of reasons for having children. One of them is an attraction to Velcro—

JW: *Sorry?*

CC: All the little kiddie things are made with Velcro so you don't have to tie anything anymore. I also think people have babies because they secretly long for celibacy, or they want to dispose of income without actually dealing with insurance agents or bankers.

Now that I've had one I think there should be a moratorium. There are just too many people already. Most other things on the planet reproduce and then die right away. I think it would be much better if you just crawled away and died. You *flowered*, and that would be it. My paternal grandmother died in childbirth, and it's not a bad idea. You miss an awful lot of work that way.

JW: *What's the connection between having a baby and remodeling?*

CC: Remodeling is a mental illness of late pregnancy. It's the nesting instinct. The month before my daughter was born, we had to move out of the house because it was in the demolition stage. When they demo'ed it they discovered that *everything* was wrong with the house. The weight-bearing walls didn't bear weight, the whole house was resting on the sewer pipe so that *any minute* there could be sewage oozing through the floorboards. I was two hundred pounds pregnant, bouncing over planks and saying things like, "Oh, I don't know, I think the vanity should go *there*." I'll never forget the plumber who said—and this is a metaphor for my entire life from then on—the guy said to me, "Geez, Cath, you had a nice house but it turned to shit." That's how I've felt about my life ever since then, basically. I mean, why did I do this? We renovated because I wanted to keep my office, otherwise it would have had to become the baby's room. So right from the start we were in conflict: "You can't have my office. You can have my body, but you can't have my office." The contractors would work for maybe an hour and then they would go away— I assume they were off drinking somewhere—it was like they had beamed up to another planet. They would leave their chain saws all over the stairs and just disappear for days. I would be calling the guy constantly, and when he finally got back to me he would say, "I had very, very personal problems." That was always his excuse: "Very, very personal problems."

JW: *Were there any positive experiences at all?*

CC: Well, we had a Jewish plumber who was great, but he emigrated to Israel. I often wish I had gone with him.

JW: *Do you like living in Philadelphia?*

CC: Philadelphia is comfortable. It allows me to fulfill my own mediocrity. It kind of reminds me of Rutgers University, where Ozzie Nelson was one of our wonderful alums. Well, Paul Robeson was, too. (Ozzie Nelson and Paul Robeson are not often mentioned in the same breath.)

What's nice about Philly is you can be a big fish in a small pond—which is great for immediate gratification—and you can still get to New York quickly. I recently interviewed a local bureaucrat who talked about Philadelphia like it's a town house development: "For me, personally, it's ideally located. It's close to my friends in New York, to my friends in Washington, it's affordable." These are not things for a city to brag about. "Affordable" should be groceries or Toyotas, not cities. I probably resent that attitude even more because in an "affordable" city I live way beyond my means. I'd be in big trouble if I lived in a city that wasn't "affordable."

JW: *Have you considered moving?*

CC: I *dream* of escaping Philadelphia someday, although I had the chance once and didn't take it. I could have moved to the West

Coast and I probably should have, because I think I'm working in a dead form. I should be working in television, I think, but I don't know if I'd fit into that world.

JW: *A "dead form"?*

CC: As a writer I've come up against a kind of wall that is starting to exist in America, which is that . . . there's hardly anything left to parody. Almost anything you try to do satirically comes true within a few months. Life in late twentieth-century America is just so fucking funny to begin with, so disjointed, so bizarre, so alienating, that there's nothing left to make fun of.

JW: *Then what's a satirist to do?*

CC: Move to another planet? It's really frightening. I tried *not* writing humor, but I'm like a drug addict. I end up doing these little ribs which become more and more esoteric, and that drastically reduces your audience. I've had people come up to me at book signings and say, "My friend and I have a bet on. Is this a funny book or a serious book?" What can you say? I was brought up to be polite. (My mother was there when I had the baby—she said she couldn't believe that I said "please" and "thank you" during the final stages of labor. "Please get this baby out of me, *please!*" were my final words.) So when someone asks if the book is supposed to be serious or humorous, I'm too polite to say, "You fucking idiot, don't you know that this is a *joke?*" It's happening to me more and more. Almost everything I write, somebody takes seriously.

JW: *You've written of your aversion to euphemisms. Have you collected any new ones since you've become a mother?*

CC: Yes, there's *play yard*—play pens are no longer cool. You don't have a play *pen* for a kid because a pen suggests imprisonment. *Care giver* sounds like some kind of caretaker, like you have some huge estate, when actually a care giver is a baby sitter you're paying five bucks an hour. And then there are all those euphemisms for disabilities: *physically challenged, differently abled*—of which a friend of mine who is disabled says, "How am I 'differently abled'? Like, my unique ability is that without a wheelchair I have to drag myself across the floor?" And I've always thought that *special children* is kind of sad, and it disturbs me when the parents of retarded children say, "God gave me this special child because He wanted to test me."

JW: *If you had your druthers, how would your life be different?*

CC: I want a cold of my own. I want to get a cold, get really, really sick and be the only person in my house with the cold, so that I can get all the attention. Because every time I get a cold, Al gets a cold and then I can't be sick anymore because his cold is always worse. I just want to be injected with the flu virus and go to a motel with room service for a week.

My other goal in life is someday to write a book that I would actually want to read. It's a horrible thing to say, but that's what I'm working for. I don't know if I'll get there during this decade or the next. You see, everything I've made fun of, I've become. I'm afraid to write about anything because within a year I either have the same problem, or I'm doing it. I have become . . . here's what I have become: a person who has a ceiling-fan repair person. One day when I was waiting for my ceiling-fan repair person, Klaus, I thought, I've hit bottom. How much more complicated can your life be?

Cathy Crimmins' books include Entre Chic: The Mega-Guide to Entrepreneurial Excellence; YAP: The Official Young Aspiring Professional's Fast-Track Handbook; *and* The Secret World of Men: A Girl's-Eye View.

THE CRITICAL CURMUDGEON
Art and Literature

The goitrous, torpid and squinting husks provided by Matisse in his sculpture are worthless except as tactful decorations for a mental home.

PERCY WYNDHAM-LEWIS

Just explain to Monsieur Renoir that the torso of a woman is not a mass of decomposing flesh, its green and violet spots indicating the state of complete putrefaction of a corpse. ALBERT WOLFF

For Mr. Whistler's own sake one ought not to have admitted works into the gallery in which the ill-educated conceit of the artist so nearly approached the aspect of willful imposture. I have seen, and heard, much of Cockney impudence before now; but never expected to hear a coxcomb ask two hundred guineas for flinging a pot of paint in the public's face. JOHN RUSKIN

Klee's pictures seem to me to resemble, not pictures, but a sample book of patterns for linoleum.

SIR CYRIL ASQUITH

For the reader who has put away comic books, but isn't yet ready for editorials in the *Daily News*.
> GLORIA STEINEM on *Valley of the Dolls* by Jacqueline Susann

Too many ironies in the fire.
> JOHN LEONARD on *Two Sisters* by Gore Vidal

This is not at all bad, except as prose.
> GORE VIDAL on *The Winds of War* by Herman Wouk

I regard this novel as a work without redeeming social value, unless it can be recycled as a cardboard box.
> ELLEN GOODMAN on *Message from Nam* by Danielle Steel

It's like going for brain dialysis, this book.
> D. KEITH MANO on *Ancient Evenings* by Norman Mailer

Hope Ryden writes with great affection about the often maligned coyote; unfortunately, she doesn't write about them with great skill.
> CHARLES SOLOMON

An acquaintance told James Thurber that he'd read a French translation of Thurber's *My Life and Hard Times*, adding, "You know, the book is even better in French!" "Yes," replied Thurber, "my work tends to lose something in the original."

John Dollar is a novel by Marianne Wiggins, who is now in hiding because she is married to Salman Rushdie. Allah be praised.   FLORENCE KING

The subtitle of this book is "Some Observations from Both Sides of the Refrigerator Door," which is appropriate, since it could have been written by a cabbage, either before or after conversion to coleslaw.   RALPH NOVAK on *Uh-Oh* by Robert Fulghum

This paperback is very interesting, but I find it will never replace a hardcover book—it makes a very poor doorstop.   ALFRED HITCHCOCK

One never steps twice into the same Auden.   RANDALL JARRELL

I do not think this poem will reach its destination.   VOLTAIRE on Rousseau's "Ode to Posterity"

CAB DRIVERS

Cab drivers are living proof that practice does not make perfect.
HOWARD OGDEN

CALAMITIES

Calamities are of two kinds: misfortunes to ourselves, and good fortune to others.
AMBROSE BIERCE

CALENDARS

Most modern calendars mar the sweet simplicity of our lives by reminding us that each day that passes is the anniversary of some perfectly uninteresting event.
OSCAR WILDE

CALIFORNIA

California reminds me of the popular American Protestant concept of Heaven: there is always a reasonable flow of new arrivals; one meets many—not all—of one's friends; people spend a good deal of their time congratulating one another about the fact that they are there; discontent would be unthinkable; and the newcomer is slightly discon-

certed to realize that now, the devil having been
banished and virtue being triumphant, nothing
terribly interesting can ever happen again.

GEORGE F. KENNAN

CANADA

Canada is a country whose main exports are
hockey players and cold fronts. Our main imports
are baseball players and acid rain.

PIERRE TRUDEAU

Canada is a country so square that even the female
impersonators are women.   RICHARD BENNER

Very little is known of the Canadian country since
it is rarely visited by anyone but the Queen and
illiterate sport fishermen.   P. J. O'ROURKE

Canada has never been a melting pot; more like a
tossed salad.   ARNOLD EDINBOROUGH

In any world menu, Canada must be considered
the vichyssoise of nations—it's cold, half French,
and difficult to stir.   STUART KEATE

Canada is useful only to provide me with furs.

MADAME DE POMPADOUR

Canada is the only country in the world that knows how to live without an identity.

MARSHALL MCLUHAN

For some reason, a glaze passes over people's faces when you say Canada.

SONDRA GOTLIEB

——————CANCER——————

My father died of cancer when I was a teenager. He had it before it became popular.

GOODMAN ACE

——————CAPITAL——————

Capital, *n*. The seat of misgovernment.

AMBROSE BIERCE

——CAPITAL PUNISHMENT——

The big thieves hang the little ones.

CZECH PROVERB

——————CAPITALISM——————

Capitalism is a condition both of the world and of the soul.

FRANZ KAFKA

CARS

Is fuel efficiency really what we need most desperately? I say what we really need is a car that can be shot when it breaks down.　RUSSELL BAKER

CAR ALARMS

They erupt like indignant metal jungle birds, and they whoop all night. They make American cities sound like lunatic rain forests, all the wildlife affrighted, violated, outraged, shrieking. . . . In a neighborhood of apartment buildings, one such beast rouses sleepers by the hundreds, even thousands. They wake, roll over, moan, jam pillows on their ears and try to suppress the adrenaline. Car thieves, however, pay no attention to the noise.

LANCE MORROW

CAREER

My career is a fascist state. I'm the dictator, the chief of police, the head of the army. Anybody who tries to interfere is put up against the wall and shot.　MICHAEL CAINE

CATS

Cat, *n.* A soft, indestructible automaton provided by nature to be kicked when things go wrong in the domestic circle.　AMBROSE BIERCE

I can see stopping a car for a dog. But a cat? You
squish a cat and go on.   JAMES GALLAGHER

> The trouble with a kitten is
> THAT
> Eventually it becomes a
> CAT
> OGDEN NASH

Cats seem to go on the principle that it never
does any harm to ask for what you want.
                JOSEPH WOOD KRUTCH

> The cat is the only non-gregarious domestic
> animal.   FRANCIS GALTON

I am not a cat man, but a dog man, and all felines
can tell this at a glance—a sharp, vindictive glance.
                        JAMES THURBER

> The only good cat is a stir-fried cat.   "ALF"

————CELEBRITY————

A celebrity is a person who works hard all his life
to become well known, then wears dark glasses to
avoid being recognized.   FRED ALLEN

You can't shame or humiliate modern celebrities. What used to be called shame and humiliation is now called publicity. And forget traditional character assassination. If you say a modern celebrity is an adulterer, a pervert, and a drug addict, all it means is that you've read his autobiography.

P. J. O'ROURKE

The nice thing about being a celebrity is that when you bore people, they think it's their fault.

HENRY KISSINGER

A celebrity is one who is known to many persons he is glad he doesn't know.   H. L. MENCKEN

When everyone is somebody, then no one's anybody.   W. S. GILBERT

———CHEERFULNESS———

Early morning cheerfulness can be extremely obnoxious.   WILLIAM FEATHER

———CHILDHOOD———

A happy childhood is poor preparation for human contacts.   COLETTE

Children are given to us to discourage our better emotions.

SAKI

It is almost nicer being a godfather than a father, like having white mice but making your nanny feed them for you.

T. H. WHITE

Humans are the only animals that have children on purpose with the exception of guppies, who like to eat theirs.

P. J. O'ROURKE

A philosopher told me that, having examined the civil and political order of societies, he now studied nothing except the savages in the books of explorers, and children in everyday life.

NICOLAS CHAMFORT

I have been assured by a very knowing American of my acquaintance in London that a healthy young child, well nursed, is at a year old a most delicious, nourishing and wholesome food, whether stewed, roasted, baked or boiled; and I make no doubt that it will equally serve in a fricassee or a ragout.

JONATHAN SWIFT

Perhaps host and guest is really the happiest relation for a father and son.

EVELYN WAUGH

America's gross national product.

FLORENCE KING

Children are cruel, ruthless, cunning and almost incredibly self-centered. Far from cementing a marriage, children more frequently disrupt it. Child-rearing is on the whole an expensive and unrewarding bore, in which more has to be invested both materially and spiritually than ever comes out in dividends. NIGEL BALCHIN

I want to have children and I know my time is running out: I want to have them while my parents are still young enough to take care of them.

RITA RUDNER

Children are satisfied with the stork story up to a certain age because the little fartlings are the world's most crustaceous reactionaries; they don't *want* to know, they don't *want* their preconceived opinions toppled. FLORENCE KING

Never raise your hand to your children; it leaves your midsection unprotected. ROBERT ORBEN

Children today are tyrants. They contradict their parents, gobble their food, and tyrannize their teachers. SOCRATES

My husband and I are either going to buy a dog or have a child. We can't decide whether to ruin our carpet or ruin our lives.   RITA RUDNER

It is no wonder that people are so horrible when they start life as children.   KINGSLEY AMIS

The trouble with children is that they are not returnable.   QUENTIN CRISP

CHILD-PROOF BOTTLE TOPS

Allen Ginsberg said he saw the best minds of his generation destroyed by madness. I have seen the best minds of my generation go at a bottle of Anacin with a ball-peen hammer.

P. J. O'ROURKE

—— **CHILDLESSNESS** ——

Childlessness has many obvious advantages. One is that you need not spend two hundred thousand dollars to send anyone to college, or contribute a similar sum to the retirement fund of a stranger who has decided to become a pediatrician. But the principal advantage of the nonparental life-style is that on Christmas Eve, you need not be struck dumb by the three most terrifying words that the government allows to be printed on any product: "Some assembly required."   JOHN LEO

——CHILD RAISING——

One thing they never tell you about child raising is that for the rest of your life, at the drop of a hat, you are expected to know your child's name and how old he or she is.   ERMA BOMBECK

——CHRISTIAN CHARITY——

The Jews and Arabs should settle their dispute in the true spirit of Christian charity.

ALEXANDER WILEY

——CHRISTMAS——

The prospect of Christmas appalls me.

EVELYN WAUGH

In the United States Christmas has become the rape of an idea.   RICHARD BACH

Christmas is when you have to go to the bank and get crisp money to put in envelopes from the stationery store for tips. After you tip the doorman, he goes on sick leave or quits and the new one isn't impressed.   ANDY WARHOL

There is a remarkable breakdown of taste and intelligence at Christmastime. Mature, responsible grown men wear neckties made out of holly leaves and drink alcoholic beverages with raw egg yolks and cottage cheese in them.   P. J. O'ROURKE

Did you ever notice, the only one in *A Christmas Carol* with any character is Scrooge? Marley is a whiner who fucked over the world and then hadn't the spine to pay his dues quietly; Belle, Scrooge's ex-girlfriend, deserted him when he needed her most; Bob Cratchit is a gutless toady without enough get-up-and-go to assert himself; and the less said about that little treacle-mouth, Tiny Tim, the better.   HARLAN ELLISON

Early in life I developed a distaste for the Cratchits that time has not sweetened. I do not think I was an embittered child, but the Cratchits' aggressive worthiness, their bravely borne poverty, their exultation over that wretched goose, disgusted me. I particularly disliked Tiny Tim (a part always played by a girl because girls had superior powers of looking moribund and worthy at the same time), and when he chirped, "God bless us every one!" my mental response was akin to Sam Goldwyn's famous phrase, "Include me out."

ROBERTSON DAVIES

Adults can take a simple holiday for children and screw it up. What began as a presentation of simple gifts to delight and surprise children around the Christmas tree has culminated in a woman opening up six shrimp forks from her dog, who drew her name.   ERMA BOMBECK

"Merry Christmas, Nearly Everybody!"
OGDEN NASH

————THE CHURCH————

The church is only a secular institution in which the half-educated speak to the half-converted.
W. R. INGE

————CIVILIZATION————

You can't say civilization isn't advancing: in every war they kill you in a new way.   WILL ROGERS

I regard everything that has happened since the last war as a decline in civilization.   A.L. ROWSE

Civilization is the distance man has placed between himself and his excreta.   BRIAN ALDISS

CLASSICAL EDUCATION

The advantage of a classical education is that it enables you to despise the wealth which it prevents you from achieving. RUSSELL GREEN

CLASSICS

Have I uttered the fundamental blasphemy, that once said sets the spirit free? The literature of the past is a bore—when one has said that frankly to oneself, then one can proceed to qualify and make exceptions. OLIVER WENDELL HOLMES, JR.

A classic is something that everybody wants to have read and nobody wants to read.
MARK TWAIN

CLEANLINESS

Cleanliness is almost as bad as godliness.
SAMUEL BUTLER

CLERGYMAN

Clergyman: a ticket speculator outside the gates of heaven. H. L. MENCKEN

The first clergyman was the first rascal who met the first fool. VOLTAIRE

I won't take my religion from any man who never works except with his mouth.   CARL SANDBURG

COCKTAILS

Cocktails have all the disagreeability without the utility of a disinfectant.   SHANE LESLIE

A cocktail is to a glass of wine as rape is to love.   PAUL CLAUDEL

COCKTAIL PARTIES

The cocktail party has the form of friendship without the warmth and devotion. It is the device for getting rid of social obligations hurriedly en masse, or for making overtures toward more serious social relationships, as in the etiquette of whoring.   BROOKS ATKINSON

A hundred standing people smiling and talking to one another, nodding like gooney birds.   WILLIAM COLE

COMMITTEES

Not even computers will replace committees, because committees buy computers.   EDWARD SHEPHERD MEAD

COMMUNICATION

Let us make a special effort to learn to stop communicating with each other, so we can have some conversation. MISS MANNERS (JUDITH MARTIN)

COMMUNISM

Communism is the opiate of the intellectuals.
CLARE BOOTHE LUCE

COMMUNISTS

I never agree with Communists or any other kind of kept men. H. L. MENCKEN

COMPANIONSHIP

I hold that companionship is a matter of mutual weaknesses. We like that man or woman best who has the same faults we have.

GEORGE JEAN NATHAN

COMPUTERS

The computer is a moron. PETER DRUCKER

CONFERENCE

A conference is a gathering of important people who singly can do nothing, but together can decide that nothing can be done. FRED ALLEN

CONGRESS

Ancient Rome declined because it had a Senate; now what's going to happen to us with both a Senate and a House?   WILL ROGERS

CONGRESSMEN

A flea can be taught everything a congressman can.   MARK TWAIN

A palm-pounding pack of preening pols.
          WILLIAM SAFIRE

Eighty percent were hypocrites, eighty percent liars, eighty percent serious sinners . . . except on Sundays. There is always boozing and floozying. . . . I don't have enough time to tell you everybody's name. WILLIAM "FISHBAIT" MILLER

Reader, suppose you were an idiot. And suppose you were a member of Congress. But I repeat myself.   MARK TWAIN

CONSCIOUSNESS

I used to wake up at 4 A.M. and start sneezing, sometimes for five hours. I tried to find out what sort of allergy I had but finally came to the conclusion that it must be an allergy to consciousness.
          JAMES THURBER

———CONSERVATIVES———

They define themselves in terms of what they
oppose.   GEORGE WILL

———CONSISTENCY———

Consistency is a paste jewel that only cheap men
cherish.   WILLIAM ALLEN WHITE

Consistency requires you to be as ignorant today
as you were a year ago.   BERNARD BERENSON

———CONSTITUTION———

Our Constitution protects aliens, drunks and U.S.
senators.   WILL ROGERS

———CONTENTMENT———

Contentment is, after all, simply refined
indolence.   RICHARD HALIBURTON

Who is rich? He that is content. Who is that?
Nobody.   BENJAMIN FRANKLIN

———COOKBOOKS———

Cookbooks . . . bear the same relation to real
books that microwave food bears to your
grandmother's.   ANDREI CODRESCU

COOKS

It is no wonder that diseases are innumerable: count the cooks.　　　　　　SENECA

COPY EDITOR

It is wonderful that our society can find a place for the criminally literal-minded.　ALICE KAHN

CORPORAL PUNISHMENT

Let's reintroduce corporal punishment in the schools—and use it on the teachers.

P. J. O'ROURKE

COSMETIC SURGERY

What does it profit a seventy-eight-year-old woman to sit around the pool in a bikini if she cannot feed herself?　　　ERMA BOMBECK

Anyone who gives a surgeon six thousand dollars for "breast augmentation" should give some thought to investing a little more on brain augmentation.　　　MIKE ROYKO

I have a professional acquaintance whose recent eyelid job has left her with a permanent expression

of such poleaxed astonishment that she looks at
all times as if she had just read one of my books.
FLORENCE KING

THE COUNTRY

It is pure unadulterated country life. They get up
early because they have so much to do and go
to bed early because they have so little to think
about. OSCAR WILDE

They can have the good old smell of the earth.
Nine times out of ten it isn't the good old smell
of the earth that they smell so much as the good
old smell of chicken feathers, stagnant pools of
water, outhouse perfumes, cooking odors from
badly designed kitchens and damp wall plaster.
GEORGE JEAN NATHAN

COUPONS

How about all those manufacturers' coupons fea-
turing Exciting Offers wherein it turns out, when
you read the fine print, that you have to send in
the coupon *plus* proof of purchase *plus* your complete dental records by registered mail to Green-
land and allow at least eighteen months for them
to send you *another* coupon that will entitle you
to 29 cents off your next purchase of a product
you don't really want? DAVE BARRY

CRICKET

What is both surprising and delightful is that [baseball] spectators are allowed, and even expected, to join in the vocal part of the game. I do not see why this feature should not be introduced into cricket. There is no reason why the field should not try to put the batsman off his stroke at the critical moment by neatly timed disparagements of his wife's fidelity and his mother's respectability. GEORGE BERNARD SHAW

CRIME

My husband gave me a necklace. It's fake. I requested fake. Maybe I'm paranoid, but in this day and age, I don't want something around my neck that's worth more than my head. RITA RUDNER

CRIMINALS

Criminal: a person with predatory instincts who has not sufficient capital to form a corporation. HOWARD SCOTT

It is a fitting irony that under Richard Nixon, *launder* became a dirty word. WILLIAM ZINSSER

CRITICS

Having the critics praise you is like having the hangman say you've got a pretty neck.

ELI WALLACH

CRUISE SHIPS

If you thought you didn't like people on land . . .

CAROL LEIFER

CYNICISM

Cynicism is the intellectual cripple's substitute for intelligence. It is the dishonest businessman's substitute for conscience. It is the communicator's substitute, whether he is advertising man or editor or writer, for self-respect.   RUSSELL LYNES

QUOTES ON "D"

DARK AGES

Perhaps in time the so-called Dark Ages will be thought of as including our own.

G. C. LICHTENBERG

DARLING

Darling: the popular form of address used in speaking to a person of the opposite sex whose name you cannot at the moment recall.

OLIVER HERFORD

DAY

Day, *n*. A period of twenty-four hours, mostly misspent.

AMBROSE BIERCE

It was such a lovely day I thought it a pity to get up.

W. SOMERSET MAUGHAM

DEATH

Death will be a great relief. No more interviews.

KATHARINE HEPBURN

DECISION

Every decision you make is a mistake.

EDWARD DAHLBERG

DELIBERATION

Deliberation, *n*. The act of examining one's bread to determine which side it is buttered on.

AMBROSE BIERCE

DEMAGOGUE

Demagogue: One who preaches doctrines he knows to be untrue to men he knows to be idiots.

H. L. MENCKEN

DEMOCRACY

The whole dream of democracy is to raise the proletarian to the level of stupidity attained by the bourgeois.

GUSTAVE FLAUBERT

Democracy is a device that ensures we shall be governed no better than we deserve.

GEORGE BERNARD SHAW

Democracy is an abuse of statistics.

JORGE LUIS BORGES

Democracy is the name we give to the people each time we need them.   ROBERT DE FLERS

Giving every man a vote has no more made men wise and free than Christianity has made them good.   H. L. MENCKEN

Democracy means government by discussion, but it is only effective if you can stop people talking.   CLEMENT ATLEE

Democracy consists of choosing your dictators, after they've told you what you think it is you want to hear.   ALAN COREN

Under democracy one party always devotes its chief energies to trying to prove that the other party is unfit to rule—and both commonly succeed, and are right.   H. L. MENCKEN

We must abandon the prevalent belief in the superior wisdom of the ignorant.   DANIEL BOORSTIN

Every government is a parliament of whores. The trouble is, in a democracy, the whores are us.   P. J. O'ROURKE

The crude leading the crud.   FLORENCE KING

DEMOCRATS VS. REPUBLICANS

The Republican and Democratic parties, ancient rivals, do not exist any more as such, there being more fun watching Harvard and Yale. This has brought about a condition where Republican conventions are sometimes attended by Democrats by mistake, and Democratic conventions attended by Republicans on purpose. The only way to tell them apart is by the conditions of the hotel rooms after the convention is over. The Republicans have more gin bottles and the Democrats seem to have gone in more for rye.   ROBERT BENCHLEY

The Democrats seem to be basically nicer people, but they have demonstrated time and again that they have the management skills of celery. They're the kind of people who'd stop to help you change a flat, but would somehow manage to set your car on fire. I would be reluctant to entrust them with a Cuisinart, let alone the economy. The Republicans, on the other hand, would know how to fix your tire, but they wouldn't bother to stop because they'd want to be on time for Ugly Pants Night at the country club.   DAVE BARRY

When you looked at the Republicans you saw the scum off the top of business. When you looked at the Democrats you saw the scum off the top of politics. Personally, I prefer business. A businessman will steal from you directly instead of getting the IRS to do it for him. And when the Republicans ruin the environment, destroy the supply of affordable housing, and wreck the industrial infrastructure, at least they make a buck off it. The Democrats just do these things for fun.

P. J. O'ROURKE

The only difference between the Democrats and the Republicans is that the Democrats allow the poor to be corrupt, too.   OSCAR LEVANT

————DIETS————

My soul is dark with stormy riot,
Directly traceable to diet.

SAMUEL HOFFENSTEIN

I've been on a constant diet for the last two decades. I've lost a total of 789 pounds. By all accounts, I should be hanging from a charm bracelet.   ERMA BOMBECK

————DINNER————

Oh, the pleasure of eating my dinner alone!

CHARLES LAMB

DINNER PARTY

The best number for a dinner party is two—myself
and a damn good head waiter.

NUBAR GULBENKIAN

DIPLOMACY

In archaeology you uncover the unknown. In diplomacy you cover the known.

THOMAS PICKERING

Diplomacy is to do and say
The nastiest thing in the nicest way.

ISAAC GOLDBERG

DISNEYLAND

Disneyland is a white pioneer's idea of what
America is. Wacky American animals. American
conviviality, zappy, zany, congenial and nice, like
a parade of demented, bright Shriners.

JONATHAN MILLER

DOCTORS

Doctors cut, burn, and torture the sick, and then
demand of them an undeserved fee for such
services.   HERACLITUS

They murmured as they took their fees,
"There is no cure for this disease."

HILAIRE BELLOC

DOGS

Dog, *n*. A kind of additional or subsidiary Deity designed to catch the overflow and surplus of the world's worship. The Divine being in some of his smaller and silkier incarnations, takes, in the affection of Woman, the place to which there is no human male aspirant. The Dog is a survival—an anachronism. He toils not, neither does he spin, yet Solomon in all his glory never lay upon a doormat all day long, sun-soaked and fly-fed and fat, while his master worked for the means wherewith to purchase an idle wag of the Solomonic tail, seasoned with a look of tolerant recognition.

AMBROSE BIERCE

Reading about dogs is almost as bad as having them stand on your chest and lick you.

WILFRID SHEED

DRUGS

Half of the modern drugs could well be thrown out of the window, except that the birds might eat them. DR. MARTIN HENRY FISCHER

JOHN WATERS

Things I Hate

WINOKUR: *I'd like to talk about some of the things mentioned in your essay, "101 Things I Hate." Some of your best work, I think.*
WATERS: Thank you, but my specialty is saying nice things about things that most people hate, rather than the other way around. That's why my friends call me "John-dhi"—I never like to be unpleasant. But for this interview I'll try to be as mean as possible.

WINOKUR: *Thanks, I appreciate that. Let's just kind of move from subject to subject, starting with an easy one, just to warm up: mimes.*

WATERS: Well, *everyone* hates mimes. Mother Theresa would punch a mime. I hate Mother Theresa now, too, because she joined the Pro-Lifers. At her age, why can't she just keep on with what she was doing, curing lepers and stuff?

WINOKUR: *You're the only person I know of who has publicly come out against the Amish.*

WATERS: I *hate* the Amish. I hate any religion that forbids you to go to the movies. And I hate them holding up traffic in those carts and talking about "outing the lights" and all that. It's a little too greeting-cardish for me. I feel sorry for the kids.

WINOKUR: *Among the other things you hate are polyester sheets, roll-on deodorants—*

WATERS: I, for one, use spray. It's supposed to be anti-environmental, but I don't believe it. How does spray deodorant make the world end quicker? You could prove it to me and I still wouldn't believe that the world will end one second earlier because I use spray deodorant. As for polyester sheets, I don't even consider them. You sweat and they stick to you. It's like a body bag. If you go to someone's house and they have polyester sheets, you know never to go back.

WINOKUR: *Do you still hate color photos in newspapers?*

WATERS: I'm still not crazy about them. It's the *USA Today* influence. I like *USA Today*, actually, and I get it every day. They started the trend and they seem to be able to do it all right, but it's copied by every local newspaper in the world, and they generally do it very, very badly. If you have an old pair of 3D glasses, just put them on, maybe it will look better.

WINOKUR: *Do you hate computers?*

WATERS: I don't know how to plug the things in. I'm scared of electricity, actually. Every time I plug something in, I think I'm going to die. I'm scared to turn the heat on right now because I'm afraid the house will blow up.

WINOKUR: *Then you're not a home hobbyist?*

WATERS: Are you kidding? My idea of hell would be getting a house you had to fix up.

WINOKUR: *Pets?*

WATERS: I don't mind them if they're *outside.* I like cats because they don't like *you* much. Dogs—I don't need reinforcement ten times a day that I'm an okay person. But I don't wish them evil, you know, I'm not an animal torturer.

WINOKUR: *You're not fond of the U.S. Postal Service.*

WATERS: Well, I love the mail, and my personal mailman is great. But I do get crazed when the mail is late and I have to call the post office. "Are stamps on sale today?" I complain. I also hate those holidays that fall on a Monday where you don't get mail, those fake holidays like Columbus Day. What did Christopher Columbus do, discover America? If he hadn't, somebody else would have and we'd still be here. Big deal.

WINOKUR: *What kind of mail do you get?*

WATERS: It's mostly nice. I've gotten maybe five mean letters in my whole life. A lot of my mail is from kids from small towns who say how great it is to have somebody with their sense of humor. Recently a kid wrote me that Divine was his idol and he wanted to come visit his grave but his mother said, "Oh, no, I'm not taking you to Baltimore to visit the grave of a dead transvestite." I can just hear the mother saying that and the kid saying, "Why not?"

WINOKUR: *You've expressed your distaste for "overweight joggers" and walkathons.*

WATERS: I don't mind exercise, but it's a private activity. Joggers should run in a wheel—like hamsters—because *I* don't want to look at them. And I really hate people who go on an airplane in jogging outfits. That's a major offense today, even bigger than Spandex bicycle pants. You see eighty-year-old women coming on the plane in jogging outfits for comfort. Well, *my* comfort—my mental comfort—is completely ruined when I see them coming. You're on an airplane, not in your bedroom, so please! And I really hate walkathons. Blocking traffic, people patting themselves on the back. The whole attitude offends me. They have this smug look on their faces as they hold you up in traffic so that they can give two cents to some charity.

WINOKUR: *You've said that you don't care much for vegetarian restaurants.*

WATERS: I don't mind vegetables, I just hate people who won't eat meat and pontificate about it all the time. I'll eat meat, vegetables, anything. The most ludicrous thing I've seen in about five years, and I have proof of this—one of the leaders of one of the animal-rights organizations said this in *New York* magazine and I have the clipping—she said, "Yes, six million Jews were killed in the Holocaust, but this year eight million broiler chickens will be put into roasting ovens." I'm not kidding. She said that and she was dead serious. I can only pray she was Jewish.

WINOKUR: *That really is . . . stunning. But getting back to vegetables, do you like sprouts?*

WATERS: In a trough they might be good. On a plate I'm not too fond of them.

WINOKUR: *Iceberg lettuce?*

WATERS: The polyester of green.

WINOKUR: *Brussels sprouts?*

WATERS: I actually had some recently—I've mellowed on Brussels sprouts.

WINOKUR: *Really? You once called them "those little balls of hell."*

WATERS: Well, they were the way my mother made 'em.

WINOKUR: *But you said they're "limp and wilted after a lifetime of being pissed on by birds and other contaminated creatures."*

WATERS: Well, that's true, all vegetables have been pissed on. But I guess as we get older we get less demanding about our food.

WINOKUR: *How about swordfish?*

WATERS: Have you ever been in a restaurant where it isn't on the menu? Yuppies have made swordfish the next endangered species.

WINOKUR: *Do you still hate nude beaches?*

WATERS: I still hate them very much. It's always the worst-looking people who are the most enthusiastic about them. It's always the fattest people with the worst bodies who take their clothes off. I've been to nude beaches and I've never seen the people you *want* to see nude. They're never there.

WINOKUR: *What don't you like about the telephone?*

WATERS: Well, the thing that offends me is a person who gets a weekly paycheck, who is over twenty years old, and you get a busy signal when you dial their number. In this day and age there's no excuse for that. If you have a weekly paycheck, call waiting is a must. And I hate call waiting because it's so rude, but it's still better than a busy signal. If I ever call someone and get a busy signal, I take them less seriously. Although . . . I could imagine someone who is extremely confident and says, "Well, it's *their* problem." I'm not that secure.

WINOKUR: *You've expressed a dislike for dial telephones.*

WATERS: I'm all for keeping up with the times technology-wise, especially if you go to stay at somebody's house. You don't want to put long-distance calls on their phone bill, but what can you do? You *can* dial a credit-card call if you have AT&T, but I try not to give them my money because of how snooty they were twenty years ago. I still remember: You could call up and say, "Fuck you," and they would say, "Thank you, sir." It's like talking to a recording. You could never win. You could say a hundred things and they would only answer you in the six lines they were taught to say. They would never give in. I remember that telephone-company smugness. Don't think they're going to get my business twenty years later. I don't forget.

WINOKUR: *What about outdoor art murals?*

WATERS: Well, I like a few of them. But mostly I hate them, especially the ones funded by government grants. I don't "get" grants anyway. If art is any good, the government wants to stop it, not pay for it. I'm against censorship, but I don't understand all these people who go and try to get a grant. *I* never got a grant. They actually spent money trying to stop my films. Any good art, the government doesn't pay for it. Good art is against the government.

WINOKUR: *How do you feel about New Age?*

WATERS: If I go to a record store or a bookstore and they have a New Age section, I leave immediately. What does New Age mean, anyway? Rotten little crystals? Poor Andy Warhol had a crystal in his pocket when he checked into the hospital—a lot of good it did him.

WINOKUR: *Do you include astrology under the heading of New Age?*

WATERS: New Age is worse than astrology because old hippies are bad enough, but new ones are *really* offensive. People ask me what sign I am and I say, "Feces!" and they change the subject. The only horoscope I've ever liked was one in *Town & Country* that said, "You're going to lose all your money."

WINOKUR: *Do you like science fiction?*

WATERS: No, I've never liked it. But I don't "get" it. I'm not a *buff*. I don't hate it like I hate New Age. I hate Westerns, though. Hate is a word we use quite casually here in Baltimore.

WINOKUR: *And I take it you don't like such American classics as* The African Queen *and* The Philadelphia Story.

WATERS: I don't like Katharine Hepburn. Katharine Hepburn gets on my nerves because she's holier than thou. People in Hollywood can't believe that I hate Katharine Hepburn. It's like you committed blasphemy, like you said the meanest thing about Jesus, that's how they act. Oh, please! She's the kind of person I always fled from, an old preppy with an attitude. She thinks she's creating art every time she steps out of her house. She's humor-impaired about herself. She'll say little things to put herself down, but in the way an old WASP does. That's hardly original. And I find the public's awe of her offensive. Maybe that's why I dislike her, how the public sees her and how she flips out and stops any play she's in if someone takes a picture of her. I always wanted to go to one of her performances with a strobe: "Go, Katy baby! Show it! Go, girl!" Like a stripper, just keep strobing her. What could they do—put you on death row? They'd just throw you out. And she'd have a nervous breakdown.

WINOKUR: *You don't like short subjects.*

WATERS: No! Let's just see the movie! I don't have all day to sit there. Nor do I like computer films, even though I'm not sure what they are. I've seen some, but I left too quickly. I had "contempt before investigation," which I'm big on. A friend of mine who's in AA says that they tell you right in the beginning that you can't have contempt. Well, I have contempt all the time. I actually hate something before I know anything about it.

WINOKUR: *You've criticized the popcorn at movie theaters, too.*

WATERS: The butter in the popcorn—well, it's not butter, is it? It tastes like some horrible grease. And you go to the candy counter and the candy sizes are so huge, you need a shopping cart to lug a box of Jujubes back to your seat. A medium Coke is a *vat*.

WINOKUR: *Do you find the whole experience repugnant?*

WATERS: No, I love to go to the movies during the week. It's the weekends I hate because of "dates." I never go to the movies on a Friday night because those people don't go to see the movie, they go to make out. They're the ones who talk the most, and if the movie is the slightest bit unusual or strange the girl goes, "Ewwwww," or "Gross!" all through the sex scenes so he doesn't think she's a whore. I never go on weekends.

WINOKUR: *Do you watch much TV?*

WATERS: No, whenever it's on it's like having somebody in my house that I want to get rid of and they won't leave. I hate the sound of it. All that noise and light coming from a piece of furniture. And I have a huge TV upstairs; I have the biggest TV you can buy. But I only watch it when I have guests, or if there's a war or a video I want to see.

WINOKUR: *What about the news?*

WATERS: No, I don't watch any of it. I know the local weatherman personally and I don't hate him, but I hate the idea that the people who produce the news feel that for anyone to watch a weatherman he has to be a clown. I hate that. I have always had a mild interest in meteorology, but how can you care if it's going to be sunny tomorrow when Bozo the Clown brings you the weather? I'd prefer a serious meteorologist who would tell you how the weather works, not some imbecile cracking jokes.

And another thing: wind-chill factor. Weathermen made that up in the last ten years to disguise the fact that it's the exact temperature you'd expect it to be. If it's thirty degrees, "the wind-chill factor is ten below." It's *not* ten below, it's *thirty*. If the wind is blowing really hard, if it's a *gale-force* wind, the temperature is still thirty degrees, not ten below zero. The wind-chill factor is hype for the weather.

WINOKUR: *Do you agree with Hunter Thompson that "crack is ruining the drug culture"?*

WATERS: I think it's been ruined for a long time. I don't take drugs anymore, but when they asked me to do antidrug spots I said, "I'm not that much of a hypocrite." I did plenty of drugs when I was young and I'm not sorry about it, but if I had a child I'd be uptight if they took drugs. I had no problems with drugs, but people I took them with are dead from them. The worst drug is the one with smiley face, Ecstasy. Any drug with a smiley face as a symbol has to be bad. It sounds like the most horrible drug I could ever imagine: You wake up and you've invited eight people you hate to dinner. Instead of having a hangover, you have to have eight horrible people sitting in your dining room. I'd rather have a hangover.

WINOKUR: *You've written extensively about Los Angeles, especially its houses.*

WATERS: There's a type of architecture in Los Angeles like nothing I've seen anywhere in the world. The new houses look like modern mausoleums. They fill every inch of the lawn. They look like airports. They're the ultimate in nouveau-riche bad taste. Living in a cold-water flat with dirt floors is classier. I was driving through Trousdale Estates and I actually saw one that had just been knocked down with a wrecker—smoke was coming from where it had just hit the ground. I almost ran off the road from laughing. You see these great Hollywood homes being replaced by things that will end up on postcards as jokes. Which I'm all for—I'll buy the postcard. I see them and I think, "This makes it more fun to take a drive in L.A. Let's ride around and laugh at the excess and the poor taste of these huge joke houses." And they're even better because you know that the people are dead serious about them.

WINOKUR: *At the other extreme, you say that Venice Beach is the only place in L.A. that reminds you of the East Coast.*

WATERS: Well, I don't "get" the charm of Venice Beach. I have many friends who live there—who pay a fortune to live there—but I think it's mostly hideous and dangerous. To me it's a million-dollar slum, and I like a slum that's cheap. Then it's bohemian. It's too expensive to be a real bohemian in Venice, California.

WINOKUR: *But you like Muscle Beach.*

WATERS: Yes, I like it because it's obvious, it's a temple to exhibitionism and voyeurism, so I'm all for that. I go there to watch the voyeurs because they never think you're looking at them.

WINOKUR: *Well, we could go on and on, but I'll let you go. Thanks for the interview.*

WATERS: Was I mean enough?

John Waters' films include Cry-Baby, Polyester, *and* Hairspray.

THE CRITICAL CURMUDGEON
Theater and Film

It is greatly to Mrs. Patrick Campbell's credit that, bad as the play was, her acting was worse. It was a masterpiece of failure.

GEORGE BERNARD SHAW,
reviewing *Fedora*

A great actress, from the waist down.

DAME MARGARET KENDAL
on Sarah Bernhardt

The glass eye in the forehead of English acting.
KENNETH TYNAN on Ralph Richardson

A. E. Matthews ambled through *This Was a Man* like a charming retriever who has buried a bone and can't quite remember where. NOEL COWARD

Queen of the Nil.   GEORGE JEAN NATHAN
on Tallulah Bankhead

Tallulah Bankhead barged down the Nile as Cleopatra and sank.   JOHN MASON BROWN

She has two expressions: joy and indigestion.
DOROTHY PARKER on Marion Davies

There is no sign that her acting would ever have progressed beyond the scope of the restless shoulders and the protuberant breasts; her body technique was the gangster's technique—she toted a breast like a man totes a gun. GRAHAM GREENE on Jean Harlow

Mr. Muni seemed intent on submerging himself so completely in make-up that he disappeared.
BETTE DAVIS on *Juarez*

Her familiar expression of strained intensity would be less quickly relieved by a merciful death than by Ex-Lax. JAMES AGEE on Ida Lupino

One of the most richly syllabled queenly horrors of Hollywood. PAULINE KAEL on Greer Garson

Miss Stapleton played the part as though she had not yet signed the contract with the producer.
GEORGE JEAN NATHAN on Maureen Stapleton

Alan Ladd has only two expressions: hat on and hat off. ANONYMOUS

George Raft and Gary Cooper once played a scene in front of a cigar store, and it looked like the wooden Indian was overacting. GEORGE BURNS

Most of the time Marlon Brando sounds like he has a mouth full of wet toilet paper. REX REED

Miss Moira Lester speaks all her lines as if they are written in very faint ink on a teleprompter slightly too far away to be read with comfort.

BERNARD LEVIN

A pharaonic mummy, moving on tiny casters, like a touring replica of the Queen Mother.

THE SUNDAY TIMES OF LONDON on
Elizabeth Taylor in *The Mirror Crack'd*

Just how garish her commonplace accent, squeakily shrill voice, and the childish petulance with which she delivers her lines are, my pen is neither scratchy nor leaky enough to convey.

JOHN SIMON on Elizabeth Taylor in
The Taming of the Shrew

Olivier's idea of introspection was to hood his eyes, dentalize his consonants and let the camera circle his blondined head like a sparrow looking for a place to deposit its droppings.

ROBERT BRUSTEIN on
Laurence Olivier's *Hamlet*

Another dirty shirt-tail actor from New York.
HEDDA HOPPER on James Dean

Charlton Heston throws all his punches in the first
ten minutes (three grimaces and two intonations)
so that he has nothing left long before he stumbles
to the end, four hours later, and has to react to
the Crucifixion. (He does make it clear, I must
admit, that he quite disapproves of it.)
DWIGHT MACDONALD
on *Ben Hur*

[William Shatner as] Kirk, employing a thespian
technique picked up from someone who once
worked with somebody who knew Lee Strasberg's
sister.
CLIVE JAMES

She's one of the few actresses in Hollywood history who looks more animated in still photographs
than she does on the screen. MICHAEL MEDVED
on Raquel Welch

Mae West, [in *Myra Breckinridge*] playing a ghastly
travesty of womanhood she once played, has a
Mae West face painted on the front of her head
and moves to and fro like the Imperial Hotel during the 1923 Tokyo earthquake.
JOSEPH MORGENSTERN

Ryan O'Neal is so stiff and clumsy that he can't even manage a part requiring him to be stiff and clumsy.   JAY COCKS

When not emitting one of the clever things Frederic Raphael once said (or else *would* have said, but thought of too late, and so is saying now), [Tom] Conti conveyed introspection by encouraging his eyes to glisten wetly, while smiling with secret knowledge.   CLIVE JAMES

[Charles Grodin] keeps threatening to be funny but he rarely makes it.   PAULINE KAEL

His diction (always bad) is now incomprehensible, as if his ego has grown so big that it now fills his mouth like a cup of mashed potatoes.
                          JOHN POWERS on Sylvester Stallone

A testicle with legs.
     PAULINE KAEL on Bob Hoskins

[Judd] Nelson gives a performance with flare: his eyes flare, his nostrils flare, his hair—if such a thing is possible—flares. His tonsils may have been flaring, too, but at least you can't see them.
                          TOM SHALES

Daryl Hannah remains a rotten actress and still
looks like a linebacker in a Lorelei wig.
JOHN SIMON

Five nice things to say about Steven Seagal: (1)
He has very good posture. (2) His ponytail is
neatly trimmed. (3) While his acting repertoire is
limited, he does a brow furrow Jeremy Irons
would kill for. (4) When doing martial-arts ma-
neuvers, he does not emit chickenlike sounds, as
Bruce Lee did. (5) . . . Maybe there are only four.
RALPH NOVAK

Cecil B. De Mille made small-minded pictures on
a big scale. PAULINE KAEL

I learned an awful lot from him by doing the
opposite. HOWARD HAWKES
on Cecil B. De Mille

Cecil B. De Mille returned a script to a screenwriter with the following
note: "What I have crossed out I didn't like. What I haven't crossed out
I am dissatisfied with."

Since [Jean-Luc] Godard's films have nothing to
say, perhaps we should have ninety minutes' si-
lence instead of each of them. JOHN SIMON

Billy Wilder at work is like two people—Mr. Hyde and Mr. Hyde.   HARRY KURNITZ

Wilder is a curdled Lubitsch, romanticism gone sour, 78rpm played at 45, an old-worldling from Vienna perpetually sneering at Hollywood as it engulfs him.   ANDREW SARRIS

A shot that does not call for tracks is agony for dear old Max.   JAMES MASON on Max Ophuls

He perpetually pursues the anticliché only to arrive at anticlimax.   ANDREW SARRIS
on Brian Forbes

Blake Edwards is a man of many talents, all of them minor.   LESLIE HALLIWELL

Several tons of dynamite are set off in this picture—none of it under the right people.
JAMES AGEE on *Tycoon*

During the making of *Pin Up Girl* Betty Grable was in an early stage of pregnancy—and everyone else was evidently in a late stage of paresis.
JAMES AGEE

This film needs a certain something. Possibly
burial.   DAVID LARDNER on *Panama Hattie*

> This film is the Platonic ideal of boredom, roughly
> comparable to reading a three-volume novel in a
> language of which one knows only the alphabet.
> JOHN SIMON
> on *Camelot*

This long but tiny film . . .
       STANLEY KAUFFMANN on *Isadora*

> *My Dinner with Andre* is as boring as being alive.
> QUENTIN CRISP

—————————

The Nazi rocket scientist Wernher von Braun played a key role in the
development of the V2 rocket, which rained terror on the British civilian
population during World War II. After coming to the United States and
joining the U.S. rocket program in 1950, von Braun was the subject of
a Hollywood movie, *I Aim for the Stars*. Mort Sahl suggested that the
title be changed to *I Aim for the Stars, But Sometimes I Hit London*.

—————————

If the writing of *This Was a Man* was slow, the
production by Basil Dean was practically station-
ary. The second act dinner scene between Francine
Larrimore and Nigel Bruce made *Parsifal* in its
entirety seem like a quick-fire vaudeville sketch.
       NOEL COWARD

When Mr. Wilbur calls his play *Halfway to Hell* he underestimates the distance. BROOKS ATKINSON

Good Fielding, no hit. KYLE CRICHTON on a production of *Tom Jones*

[*Last Stop*] is enough to make your flesh crawl—right out of the Ethel Barrymore Theatre.
JOHN CHAPMAN

The play was a great success but the audience was a total failure. OSCAR WILDE

Darling, they've absolutely ruined your perfectly dreadful play.
TALLULAH BANKHEAD to Tennessee
Williams on *Orpheus Descending*

The triumph of sugar over diabetes.
GEORGE JEAN NATHAN on James Barrie

[William Inge] handles symbolism rather like an Olympic weight lifter, raising it with agonizing care, brandishing it with a tiny grunt of triumph, then dropping it with a terrible clang.
BENEDICT NIGHTINGALE
on *Come Back, Little Sheba*

I have nothing against Brecht in his place, which
is East Germany.   CLIVE JAMES

A confusing jamboree of piercing noise, routine
roller-skating, misogyny and Orwellian special effects, *Starlight Express* is the perfect gift for the kid
who has everything except parents. FRANK RICH

The sentimental comedy by the Soviet playwright
Aleksei Arbuzov is said to have had a great success
in its own country. So do fringed lamp shades.
                    RICHARD EDER

With *States of Shock*, Sam Shepard appears to have
finally attained what he was aiming at all along:
total incomprehensibility.   JOHN SIMON

In order to fully realize how bad a popular play
can be, it is necessary to see it twice.
                    GEORGE BERNARD SHAW

It had only one fault. It was kind of lousy.
                    JAMES THURBER

ALEXANDER WOOLLCOTT

The Man Who Came to Dinner

ALEXANDER WOOLLCOTT, wit, raconteur, essayist, critic, lecturer, anthologist, was born in Red Bank, New Jersey, in 1887
and grew up in the Phalanx, an experimental commune based on
the tenets of Fourierism. He hated his absent father ("The son of
a bitch left us dangling from the brink of insecurity over the pit
of poverty. What on God's good earth was there for me to love
about my father? Or even admire?") but was devoted to his

mother. He decided to become a drama critic at the age of ten.

He suffered from a testosterone deficiency, which accounted for his soft skin, round hips, and lack of facial hair. A pudgy, myopic boy, he was teased mercilessly by other children. He immersed himself in books to compensate, and began reviewing them for the Philadelphia *Telegraph* while he was still in high school. After a severe bout of mumps at the age of twenty-two, he spent the rest of his adult life as, in his words, a "semi-eunuch."

Woollcott attended Hamilton College in New York, where his appearance and predilection for dressing in women's clothes made him a social outcast. His response was to exaggerate his differences in the manner of his hero, Oscar Wilde. He was a founding member of the college dramatic club, he played all the female leads, and had calling cards printed with the name "Alexandra Woollcott." He would later describe himself as being "half god, half woman."

He volunteered for service in the Great War and was somehow accepted despite his unusual physique (an officer called him "the pregnant mermaid"). Trained as a medical orderly, he was shipped to France, where he quickly wangled a job on the staff of the enlisted-man's newspaper, *Stars and Stripes*. He was soon the paper's top front-line correspondent, and he became famous both for his impassioned reports and for his uniform, a liberated German officer's coat, a frying pan worn in front for protection, and a shawl across his shoulders.

After the war he realized his childhood ambition and became drama critic for several papers, including the *New York Times*. His critical style was straightforward: if he liked something he would praise it lavishly and eloquently; if he didn't he would go to great lengths to sink it. Thus Mark Connelly said that "rancor was Woollcott's only form of exercise," and George Jean Nathan called his style "lump in the throat reviewing." His fellow critic Wolcott Gibbs wrote, "He wasn't exactly hostile to facts, but he was apathetic about them," and Charles Brackett called him "a competent old horror with a style that combined clear treacle and pure black bile."

During the thirties Woollcott presided over the Algonquin Round Table, a stellar group of wits and raconteurs, of which Edna Ferber wrote:

> Their standards were high, their vocabulary fluent, fresh, astringent, tough. Theirs was a tonic influence, one on the other, and all on the world of American letters. The people they could not and would not stand were the bores, hypocrites, sentimentalists and the socially pretentious. They were ruthless toward charlatans, toward the pompous and mentally dishonest. Casual, incisive, they had a terrible integrity about their work and a boundless ambition.

The Algonquin membership included George S. Kaufman, Marc Connelly, Franklin P. Adams, Heywood Broun, Dorothy Parker, Robert Benchley, and Harold Ross, the founder of the *New Yorker*, for which Woollcott wrote his "Shouts and Murmurs" column, a weekly concoction of theatrical anecdotes, gossip, and true-crime murder stories.

Woollcott's several books were compilations of his articles and reviews. One of them, *While Rome Burns*, sold almost 300,000 copies during the depths of the Depression. He wrote two unsuccessful plays, *The Channel Road* and *The Dark Tower* (both of which he later attempted to disown), he was the host of a popular radio program, and he earned large sums as a peripatetic lecturer. As a critic he had the reputation of being able to make or break a play, and according to *Publishers Weekly*, he had unprecedented power over book sales: a mention of a title on the air could sell thousands of copies.

Radio was his metier. His popular program, "The Town Crier," opened with the announcer calling out, "Hear Ye, Hear Ye, Hear Ye," after which Woollcott would sign on with "This is Woollcott speaking." He knew how to hold an audience; he was a born raconteur, his voice was magnetic, his timing and microphone technique impeccable.

Woollcott was a closet sentimentalist: he valued family ties and remained close to his relatives, giving them unsparing financial and moral support all his life. He quietly supported his alma mater by helping fellow alumni, donating substantial sums of money, paying tuitions of several undergraduates, and waiving his lecture fees for speaking there. Woollcott adopted several charities and publicized them on his radio program and in his columns: he was an early champion of Seeing Eye Dogs for the Blind, and he supported World War I veterans and retired actors.

Although he pretended to hate children, Woollcott was kind and generous to those of his friends, and he took a special interest in his two nieces, though his love for them didn't dull his acerbic wit. When one of the girls visited New York at the age of fifteen, Woollcott introduced her to his friends: "This is my niece Polly, who plans to be a prostitute."

In 1924, Woollcott bought Neshobe Island on Lake Bomoseen, Vermont, and turned it into an exclusive club for his friends. It may have been an attempt to re-create his childhood home, the Phalanx, with its extended family. Neshobe became an expensive summer camp for adults. The initiation fee was a thousand dollars and the annual dues were a hundred dollars per person, with nonstop activities including croquet, badminton, fishing, nude swimming, cribbage, and word games. The members included Alice Duer Miller, Howard Dietz, Ruth Gordon, and Beatrice Kaufman. The guests were a Who's Who of show business, from Noel Coward to Alfred Lunt and Lynn Fontanne, Ethel Barrymore to Harpo Marx, who remarked after seeing Woollcott swimming in the buff: "He looked like something that had gotten loose from Macy's Thanksgiving Day Parade." Woollcott eventually abandoned his riverfront apartment on Fifty-second Street (dubbed "Wit's End" by Dorothy Parker) and moved to Neshobe permanently.

Woollcott's lecture tours put him on the road much of the year, and given his many acquaintances around the country and his aversion to hotels, he was usually a guest in someone's house. According to all accounts he had no compunction about moving in and taking over. He berated servants, changed the dates on his hosts' social calendars to suit his schedule, and even had one hostess's telephone number changed so he could use the phone without interruption from her friends.

Woollcott was often asked by friends to write letters of recommendation, and, always the practical joker, he liked to send them false copies. Thus when S. N. Behrman requested a reference to a prospective landlord, he received a "carbon copy" which read:

> I was astonished to learn that your company was even remotely
> considering accepting as a tenant such a notorious drunkard, bank-
> rupt, and general moral leper as my miserable friend Behrman.

When George and Beatrice Kaufman requested a letter on behalf
of their daughter to the headmistress of an exclusive school,
Woollcott sent them a carbon which alleged that a series of orgies
took place in the Kaufmans' home and which ended, "I implore
you to accept this unfortunate child and remove her from her
shocking environment." And when Dorothy Parker and her husband, Alan Campbell, were foolish enough to give Woollcott as
a credit reference to a department store, he wrote to the store:

> Gentlemen: Mr. Alan Campbell, the present husband of Dorothy
> Parker, has given my name as a reference in an attempt to open
> an account at your store. I hope that you will extend this credit to
> him. Surely Dorothy Parker's position in American letters is such
> as to make shameful the petty refusals which she and Alan have
> encountered at many hotels, restaurants, and department stores.
> What if you never get paid? Why shouldn't you stand your share
> of the expense?

Woollcott bullied Moss Hart and George S. Kaufman into
writing a play in which he could star as himself, and in due course
they came up with *The Man Who Came to Dinner*. The main
character is an imperious houseguest who fractures his leg and
takes over the household, issuing orders, conducting his social
and business affairs—and the affairs of everyone else—from his

wheelchair. Woollcott auditioned and lobbied for the part: "I'm perfect for the part," he told Kaufman, "I'm the only man you know who can strut sitting down." Although he was passed over in favor of Monty Woolley for the Broadway production, he was finally given his chance in a 1940 road company. A friend who had seen the play wrote to Woollcott:

> Dear Alec:
>
> I saw you and your play yesterday and enjoyed both thoroughly except for three unnecessary "God damns" and a half dozen unnecessarily vulgar "wisecracks." If these were deleted, *The Man Who Came to Dinner* would be a rollicking good comedy which I would be glad to recommend to all of my friends without qualification.
>
> T. D. Martin

Woollcott replied:

> My Dear Martin:
>
> This is to acknowledge your letter of March sixth, which really shocked me.
>
> When you speak of "three unnecessary 'God damns'" you imply that there is such a thing as a *necessary* God damn. This, of course, is nonsense. A God damn is never a necessity. It is always a luxury.
>
> Yours very sincerely,
Alexander Woollcott

On January 23, 1943, Woollcott suffered a fatal heart attack while discussing the question "Is Germany Curable?" on the radio show "The People's Platform." He is remembered for his personality, not his literary output. Asked to describe him in one word, George S. Kaufman said, "Improbable." The *New Yorker* noted, "The whole aura of Woollcott was theatrical and delightful, and you approached him as you did the theater—with misgiving but with vast fascination; and you left him as you left a matinee, with dread at emerging from make-believe into a dull side street off Broadway." Walter Winchell said that his reviews were more entertaining than the shows he covered—"even the hits." Walter Lippmann wrote that he had "a piercing eye for sham. He had an acid tongue. But he had gusto, he really liked what he praised, and he cared much more for the men and women he liked than he worried about those he did not like." The actress Margalo Gilmore's assessment of his acting ability could serve as his epitaph: "He wasn't an actor. He was an ego having a lovely time."

WOOLLCOTT SPEAKING

All the things I really like to do are either illegal, immoral, or fattening.

Nothing risqué, nothing gained.

He wrote in reply to a get-well note, "I have no need of your God-damned sympathy. . . . I wish only to be entertained by some of your grosser reminiscences."

To all things clergic
I am allergic.

Accosted on the street by an old acquaintance who said, "You remember me, don't you, Alec?" Woollcott quickly replied, "No, I can't remember your name and please don't tell me."

Apologizing to a friend with whom he had quarreled: "I've tried by tender and conscientious nursing to keep my grudge against you alive, but I find it has died on me."

After a disagreement with Harold Ross, Woollcott sent the message: "I think your slogan 'Liberty or

Death' is splendid and whichever one you decide
on will be all right with me."

Rather than touch any of that slop, I'd just as
soon lie face down in a pail of Italian garbage!

I only posed in public.

A hick town is one in which there is no place to
go where you shouldn't be.

Woollcott seldom took any exercise more strenuous than croquet. While
watching skiers at Sun Valley he took out a memo pad and wrote,
"Remind self never to go skiing."

His review of a volume of poetry written by a woman entitled *And I
Shall Make Music*: "Not on my carpet, lady!"

Prostitution, like acting, is being ruined by
amateurs.

A broker is a man who takes your fortune and
runs it into a shoestring.

When it was suggested he meet the elderly aunt
of an old acquaintance, he replied, "I already know
too many people."

She [Dorothy Parker] is so odd a blend of little Nell and Lady Macbeth. It is not so much the familiar phenomenon of a hand of steel in a velvet glove as a lacy sleeve with a bottle of vitriol concealed in its folds.

On his first visit to Moss Hart's Bucks County estate, Woollcott wrote in the guest book: "This is to certify that on my first visit to Moss Hart's house I had one of the most unpleasant times I ever spent."

[Harold Ross] looks like a dishonest Abe Lincoln.

Michael Arlen, for all his reputation, is not a bounder. He is every other inch a gentleman.

While on a lecture tour Woollcott received a note from a woman who had performed with him in a play when they were four years old. He scribbled a note to her just before assuming the lectern: "Please have your wheelchair brought around to the stage door after my gibberish is completed."

Asked by Helen Hayes and Charles MacArthur to be godfather at the baptism of their daughter Mary, Woollcott sighed, "Always a godfather, never a god."

QUOTES ON "E"

————ECONOMIST————

An economist is a surgeon with an excellent scalpel and a rough-edged lancet, who operates beautifully on the dead and tortures the living.

NICOLAS CHAMFORT

An economist is a man who states the obvious in terms of the incomprehensible.

ALFRED A. KNOPF

In all recorded history there has not been one economist who has had to worry about where the next meal would come from.   PETER F. DRUCKER

An economist is an expert who will know tomorrow why the things he predicted yesterday didn't happen today.   LAURENCE J. PETER

————EDITOR————

Editor: A person employed on a newspaper whose business it is to separate the wheat from the chaff, and to see that the chaff is printed.

ELBERT HUBBARD

EDUCATION

Education is a state-controlled manufactory of echoes. NORMAN DOUGLAS

Education . . . has produced a vast population able to read but unable to distinguish what is worth reading. G. M. TREVELYAN

It has been said that we have not had the three R's in America, we had the six R's: remedial readin', remedial 'ritin' and remedial 'rithmetic.

ROBERT M. HUTCHINS

I went to school so long ago, *Ethics* was a required course. H. MYLES JACOB

EGGS

I'm frightened of eggs, worse than frightened, they revolt me. That white round thing without any holes . . . have you ever seen anything more revolting than an egg yolk breaking and spilling its yellow liquid? Blood is jolly, red. But egg yolk is yellow, revolting. I've never tasted it.

ALFRED HITCHCOCK

EGOTISM

Egotist, *n*. A person of low taste, more interested in himself than in me. AMBROSE BIERCE

Egotism is the anesthetic that dulls the pain of
stupidity.   FRANK LEAHY

ELEVATOR

There's nothing about an elevator I like. It's too
small. It's filled with people I did not invite. And
often these people are wearing conflicting
perfumes.   FRAN LEBOWITZ

ENEMIES

Enemies to me are the *sauce piquante* to my dish
of life.   ELSA MAXWELL

The only thing that will be remembered about my
enemies after they're dead is the nasty things I've
said about them.   CAMILLE PAGLIA

ENGLISH LANGUAGE

To learn English, you must begin by thrusting
the jaw forward, almost clenching the teeth, and
practically immobilizing the lips. In this way the
English produce the series of unpleasant little
mews of which their language consists.
                                        JOSÉ ORTEGA Y GASSET

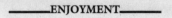
ENJOYMENT

People seem to enjoy things more when they know a lot of other people have been left out of the pleasure.　　　　RUSSELL BAKER

EPCOT CENTER

With Epcot Center the Disney corporation has accomplished something I didn't think possible in today's world. They have created a land of make-believe that's worse than regular life.
　　　　P. J. O'ROURKE

EQUAL OPPORTUNITY

Equal opportunity means everyone will have a fair chance at being incompetent.
　　　　LAURENCE J. PETER

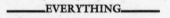
EVERYTHING

Everything is worth precisely as much as a belch, the difference being that a belch is more satisfying.
　　　　INGMAR BERGMAN

Ninety percent of everything is crap.
　　　　THEODORE STURGEON

The only possible form of exercise is to talk, not
to walk.   OSCAR WILDE

I get my exercise acting as a pallbearer to my
friends who exercise.   CHAUNCEY DEPEW

The need of exercise is a modern superstition, invented by people who ate too much and had nothing to think about. Athletics don't make anybody
either long-lived or useful. GEORGE SANTAYANA

The only exercise I get is when I take the studs
out of one shirt and put them in another.
                                 RING LARDNER

When I feel like exercising I just lie down until
the feeling goes away.   ROBERT M. HUTCHINS

I have never taken any exercise except sleeping and
resting.   MARK TWAIN

The word *aerobics* comes from two Greek words:
aero, meaning "ability to," and *bics*, meaning
"withstand tremendous boredom." DAVE BARRY

EXPECTATIONS

Blessed is he who expects nothing, for he shall never be disappointed.   JONATHAN SWIFT

EXPERTS

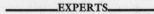

An expert is a person who avoids small error as he sweeps on to the grand fallacy.
BENJAMIN STOLBERG

If you believe the doctors, nothing is wholesome; if you believe the theologians, nothing is innocent; if you believe the military, nothing is safe.
LORD SALISBURY

If the world should blow itself up, the last audible voice would be that of an expert saying it can't be done.   PETER USTINOV

——————FAMILIARITY——————

Familiarity breeds contempt—and children.

MARK TWAIN

Familiarity doesn't breed contempt, it *is* contempt.

FLORENCE KING

——————FAMILY——————

The family is a good institution because it is uncongenial. G. K. CHESTERTON

I have certainly seen more men destroyed by the desire to have a wife and child and to keep them in comfort than I have seen destroyed by drink or harlots. WILLIAM BUTLER YEATS

"Family" this and "family" that. If I had a family I'd be furious that moral busybodies are taking the perfectly good word *family* and using it as a code for censorship the same way "states' rights" was used to disguise racism in the mid-sixties.

JOHN WATERS

FATHERS

Fathers should neither be seen nor heard. That is the only proper basis for family life.

OSCAR WILDE

FBI

The FBI is filled with Fordham graduates keeping tabs on Harvard men in the State Department.

DANIEL PATRICK MOYNIHAN

FEMINISTS

Leaving sex to the feminists is like letting your dog vacation at the taxidermist. CAMILLE PAGLIA

FIDELITY

Fidelity, *n*. A virtue peculiar to those who are about to be betrayed.   AMBROSE BIERCE

FINANCIAL NEWS

You know how on the evening news they always tell you that the stock market is up in active trading, or off in moderate trading, or trading in mixed activity, or whatever? Well, who gives a shit?   DAVE BARRY

FINANCIER

A financier is a pawnbroker with imagination.
ARTHUR WING PINERO

FISHING

There's a fine line between fishing and just standing on the shore like an idiot. STEVEN WRIGHT

FITNESS

The fitness business is about sex and immortality. By toning up the system, you can prolong youth, just about finesse middle age and then, when the time comes, go straight into senility.
WILFRID SHEED

Muscles come and go; flab lasts. BILL VAUGHAN

FLATTERY

It is possible to be below flattery as well as above it.   THOMAS BABINGTON MACAULAY

FLOWER CHILDREN

All the flower children were as alike as a congress of accountants and about as interesting.
JOHN MORTIMER

I don't like food that's too carefully arranged; it makes me think that [the chef is] spending too much time arranging and not enough time cooking. If I wanted a picture I'd buy a painting.

ANDY ROONEY

The game of football is played all over the world. In some countries, such a game may be called a soccer match. In others, a revolution. However, there are several differences between a football game and a revolution. For one thing, a football game usually lasts longer and the participants wear uniforms. Also, there are usually more casualties in a football game. The object of the game is to move the ball past the other team's goal line. This counts as six points. No points are given for lacerations, contusions, or abrasions, but then no points are deducted, either. Kicking is very important in football. In fact, some of the more enthusiastic players even kick the football occasionally.

ALFRED HITCHCOCK

Football combines the two worst features of American life: violence and committee meetings.

GEORGE WILL

If the players were armed with guns, there wouldn't be stadiums large enough to hold the crowds.   IRWIN SHAW

FREEDOM

People demand freedom of speech as a compensation for the freedom of thought which they seldom use.   KIERKEGAARD

When people are free to do as they please, they usually imitate each other.   ERIC HOFFER

FREE SPEECH

I agree with everything you say, but I would attack to the death your right to say it.
                              TOM STOPPARD

THE FRENCH

There's something Vichy about the French.
                              IVOR NOVELLO

If the French were really intelligent, they'd speak English.   WILFRID SHEED

FRIENDSHIP

I like a friend better for having faults that one can
talk about.   WILLIAM HAZLITT

FUN

Most of the time I don't have much fun. The rest
of the time I don't have any fun at all.
                                               WOODY ALLEN

The prospect of a long day at the beach makes me
panic. There is no harder work I can think of than
taking myself off to somewhere pleasant, where I
am forced to stay for hours and "have fun."
                                               PHILLIP LOPATE

FUNDAMENTALISTS

There are scores of thousands of human insects
who are ready at a moment's notice to reveal the
will of God on every possible subject.
                                               GEORGE BERNARD SHAW

FUNERALS

The consumer's side of the coffin lid is never
ostentatious.   STANISLAW J. LEC

FRANK ZAPPA

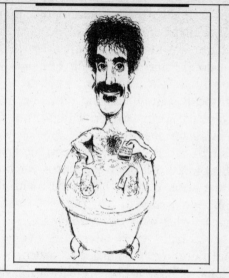

Drowning in the News Bath

JW: *I've read that you're nocturnal.*
FZ: Yes, if left to my own devices I would function exclusively at night and sleep during the day.
JW: *What do you have against sunlight?*
FZ: Aside from the fact that it can be hazardous to your health, which wasn't always the case, I dislike the feeling that you experi-

ence during the daytime, when so many of the world's souls are awake, being industrious. It's a bad feeling and I don't want to participate. But at night it's a whole different thing. The people who are awake at night are my kind of people. The animals that are awake at night are the better animals: owls, raccoons, bats, the insects that don't want to show off. The ones with the bright colors have to go out in the daytime to get their money's worth, but the nighttime is natural for the drab, beetle-like, slug-like, monastic kinds of life forms. Superior life forms, like silverfish.

JW: *You've been quoted as saying that books make you sleepy.*

FZ: Yeah, I don't read. People always send me books, but I can't stand them. People ask me to write intros for books, and even when I know the book is great, I can't deal with it. I read about three paragraphs and I start to pass out.

JW: *Then how do you get your information?*

FZ: I take a "news bath" every afternoon. I've got it down to a science: at four-thirty on Channel 34, which is the Discovery Channel, you tape "Christian Science Monitor"; then you switch over to CNN at five and watch Bernard Shaw make a fool of himself for a little while; then you switch to the local CBS news and hope to see Michael Tuck, who does the most outrageous things on the air. But the fun really starts at six-thirty, when you go to Channel 7 to get the very beginning of Peter Jennings and the ABC News to find out what their lead story is and start taping *that*; while the tape is running, immediately flip over to Channel 2 to see what the lead story is going to be on CBS. The way the commercials are staggered on the six-thirty news, if you start with the ABC News you can get the first big chunk before the commercials start. Then, when Jennings goes to a commercial, you immediately switch over to CBS.

JW: *What about NBC?*

FZ: You skip NBC at this point because Brokaw hardly ever has anything interesting or competitive with the stories on the other networks. You go directly to Channel 2 and pick up another three minutes of news before *they* go to a commercial. At that point you have to decide whether to give Brokaw his riff or go back to Jennings. You ping-pong back and forth like that, ending up on Channel 7 because their news goes longer than the CBS News. When that half-hour block is over you flip it to Channel 6 for the tail end of MacNeil/Lehrer. And when they're done you go back to CNN.

JW: *You once said, "The United States is a nation of laws, badly written and randomly enforced," and within the past few years you've battled censorship and have been active in national politics. How do you assess the health of American democracy in the late twentieth century?*

FZ: Democracy is one of those things that looks good on paper, but we've come to a crossroads in contemporary America where we really ought to decide, Do we *want* it? When you have a preponderance of people in this country who will willingly accept censorship—in fact, *ask* for it, *demand* it in the case of the Gulf War—you've got a problem. Asked random questions about the First Amendment and how they would like to have it applied, if you believe in polls at all, the average American wants no part of it. But if you ask, "What if we threw the Constitution away tomorrow?" the answer is "No, that would be bad!" But living under the Constitution is another story altogether.

I've come to the conclusion that there's only one party in this country and it's divided into two parts: Republicans and Republican wannabes. Republicans stand for evil, corruption, manipulation, greed—everything that Americans think is okay after being conditioned to it during the eighties. Republicans stand for all the values that Americans now hold dear. Plus they have more balloons than God, and for a nation raised on cartoons, that tells you something. Anybody with balloons, they're okay. They don't tell you what kind of crippled people had to blow those suckers up.

The Democrats have no agenda, and when they speak on any topic, they want to sound as Republican as possible while still finding a way to retain the pork. I'll be blunt with you: I'm considering running for president as a nonpartisan candidate because I am sick to death of this stuff. The "news bath" is not a warming experience; it makes me deranged for four or five hours a day.

On a show for Bill Moyers called "The Class of the Twentieth Century" I said that the faces that really belong on Mount Rushmore are J. Edgar Hoover and Joseph McCarthy and Walter Winchell and Hedda Hopper and maybe even Roy Cohn and Michael Milken, because they've had the greatest impact on American society. They have shaped the way things are done in this country. One of the problems with the world in which we live is that people have become accustomed to lies upon lies upon lies.

JW: *Would you call yourself a misanthrope?*

FZ: I have been called a misanthrope, but I prefer curmudgeon;

it's folksier and less threatening. Misanthrope sounds like you'd have to have gone to college to be one.

JW: *Are you an irritable person? Are you tough to get along with?*

FZ: I hardly ever leave the house, and during the day I hardly ever talk to anybody because I work by myself and just type [music] on the computer. So, if I have to have a conversation with somebody, chances are it's either going to be a member of my family or somebody who works here, and I like all of them. The only other people that I'm with are the journalists who come here to do interviews, and most of them are okay.

JW: *Since you don't go out, I don't suppose it bothers you that L.A. has become a zoo.*

FZ: That's one of the reasons why I don't go out. L.A. is like a big cancer cell. You get on the plane and you go away for two weeks and when you come back, another globule of something has been added. It just pops up, and you know it's not going to last more than twenty years, because it's made out of twigs and stucco. Every time I have to leave this house and drive down into Hollywood, which is maybe every two or three weeks, there's incremental growth of ugliness upon ugliness. It never ends.

I used to be the major booster of Southern California, at a time when the world thought San Francisco was the aesthetic center of the universe. I always took great umbrage at that because I thought the whole scene up there was a figment of *Rolling Stone*'s imagination. I used to stick up for L.A., but I don't anymore because there's no longer anything going on here aesthetically that's worth defending.

JW: *What makes you leave the house?*

FZ: There are certain mechanical functions that I can't do in my own studio. I can't do video editing here, so if I have to video edit, I have to leave. If I have an invitation to dinner, I'll go to a restaurant. I've even been to the movies recently. That was a real piece of sociology. I happened to see *Die Hard 2* and it was unbelievable. I was flabbergasted by the audience's response. It made me feel good because the bad guys turn out to be the government and they get their just deserts in the end and the audience loves it. That made me feel good.

JW: *When you are out and around, do you encounter much anti-smoking sentiment?*

FZ: [Lighting a cigarette] Well, I'm not here to impinge on anybody else's lifestyle. If I'm in a place where I know I'm going to harm somebody's health or somebody asks me to please not smoke, I just go outside and smoke. But I do resent the way the nonsmoking mentality has been imposed on the smoking minority. Because, first of all, in a democracy, minorities do have rights. And, second, the whole pitch about smoking has gone from being a health issue to a moral issue, and when they reduce something to a moral issue, it has no place in any kind of legislation, as far as I'm concerned.

JW: *But if you look at the studies, side-stream smoke is harmful.*

FZ: I'm not buying the data. First of all, it comes to you from the United States government. If you thought by stamping out all tobacco smoke in the United States you were going to improve the quality of life for everybody in the country, you'd be a lunatic. The things that will really harm you, the government won't touch.

JW: *For example?*

FZ: Dioxin in toilet paper, dioxin in tampons, dioxin in water filters, dioxin in coffee filters, dioxin in tea bags, dioxin in your vegetables because of the runoff from paper plants. Why do they have to bleach paper to make it white, anyway? It seems paltry, punitive, and insignificant to go after smokers, who are not an insignificant minority but about forty-five percent of the population. The way I would deal with the problem is induce *more* people to smoke, make them the majority and then . . . kick ass!

JW: *Have you ever tried quitting?*

FZ: A couple of times. The one time I really tried the hardest was when I had a chest cold and I was in the middle of a tour. We were in Canada and I had to travel every day and sing every night in these cold, hockey rink-type places. I really didn't feel very well and every time I would smoke with this cold it just made it worse. So I decided to try to quit for a while, and I managed not to smoke for about a week or ten days. Then my sense of smell started coming back and the hotel we were staying at, which *looked* okay, actually smelled very, very bad. Something in the hall—the rugs maybe. In fact, the whole world didn't smell very good, and within a week my cold went away and I was smoking again.

JW: *You haven't toured in a while, but you've recently begun "bootlegging the bootleggers." Can you explain how that works?*

FZ: I think it is conceptually one of my better plans. Through Rhino [Records], we stole the actual records released by the bootleggers, we used digital technology to clean them up, and we're releasing them in very luxurious packages.

JW: *Let me ask you about your tastes as a listener: They've lately been showing the "three tenors" concert on television—Pavarotti, Carreras, and Domingo in Rome. Do you like that kind of music?*

FZ: Guys who sing good with an orchestra in the background? I respect what they do, but that style of music is not something that will retain my interest for any period of time. In fact, I am not particularly amused by any television broadcast of serious music, because usually the pictures detract from the music. When I want to hear that kind of music, I want to listen to it—I don't want to look at it.

JW: *When you say "that kind of music," do you include Mozart?*

FZ: I don't usually listen to Mozart. I like Stravinsky, Varese, Webern, Schoenberg, Bartok, Takemitsu, Messiaen, Penderecky . . .

JW: *How about John Cage?*

FZ: I have many John Cage recordings, but I find his writing more interesting than his music.

JW: *Do you like rap?*

FZ: If it wasn't for rap there would be no poetry in America. I think we went directly from Walt Whitman to Ice-T.

JW: *How do you feel about pop romantic songs, ballads, love lyrics?*

FZ: I think love lyrics have contributed to the general aura of bad mental health in America. Love lyrics create expectations which can never be met in real life, and so the kid who hears these tunes doesn't realize that that kind of love doesn't exist. If he goes out looking for it, he's going to be a kind of love loser all his life. Where do you get your instructions about love? Your mother and father don't say, "Now, son, now, daughter, here's how love works." *They* don't know, so how can they tell their kids? So all your love data comes to you through the lyrics on Top Forty radio, or, in some instances, in movies or novels. The singer–songwriters who write these lyrics earn their living by pretending to reveal their innermost personal turmoil over the way love has hurt them, which creates a false standard that people use as a guideline on how to behave in interpersonal relationships. "Does my heart feel as broken as that guy's heart?" "Am I loving well?" "Is my dick long enough?"

JW: *One of the things that I appreciate about your music is its precision. Are you a taskmaster?*

FZ: Well, I'm not murder on them, but I don't let them mess around. Just because it's a rock 'n' roll band is no reason you shouldn't have the same discipline and precision that you ask for in an orchestra—after all, you're handing a guy a paycheck. You try to hire people who can actually play, but even people who can play get lazy. Musicians are unbelievably lazy. And the discipline that you have to create in order to get them to show up on time, to get from place to place in a group—it's a little bit like running an army. Working with live musicians tends to take some of the fun out of life, I won't make any bones about it. You may like the results when you finally listen to it, but it's just like making sausage: not a pretty process.

JW: *Would you prefer not to have to rely on it?*

FZ: Yes, and that's the way I live now. The things I can do with the synclavier are mind-boggling. It truly does give you the ability, should you choose to do so, to do away with human beings as musical performers. All you've got to do is get a sample of a single note. If you can get a guy to blow one note on the clarinet, he's gone.

JW: *Do you miss performing in front of a live audience?*

FZ: I used to love going on stage and playing the guitar, but now I don't play unless I've got a reason. Why make your fingers wiggle if you already know what the notes are?

JW: *So now you just sit in a room and write music?*

FZ: Right. I'm lucky that I've got a wife who likes that I do that and will take care of the mundane stuff while I'm doing it. Without help, I'd be in deep trouble.

JW: *What do you see for the future of the planet? For example, how are we going to deal with the population explosion?*

FZ: The population has doubled since 1960, it's going to double again before what, 2020? And it's not just that it's doubling, what language is doubling, what skill level, what intelligence level, what education level? And what chemical level? In other words, how many crack babies? They're going to have to be warehoused because they'll have brain damage. They'll be an unemployable work force. And there will be tons of them.

Thank God the yuppies didn't reproduce. Did you ever consider that LSD was really one of the most dangerous drugs ever manufactured because the people who took it turned into yuppies? In the eighties it was not fashionable to stand up for anything. It was a decade where bending over was the thing you did to get ahead. The way up the ladder was with your mouth attached to the anal orifice of the creature—whatever its denomination—in front of you. It was pushing upward and sucking at the same time as you went up the rungs, with junk bonds spilling out of your pockets and your mind reeling from the LSD experience that you had had in the sixties.

The yuppie lived in a special type of aquarium created for him by the Reagan administration. It was an era when there was enough cash and enough movement up and down in the stock market and enough shady deals that these incompetent little shit-heads were able to make vast amounts of money to buy their Ferraris and snort their cocaine and ruin the economy. Now there's nostalgia for the ability to do that. People wish that the good old days of the eighties would come back. When there was still something to steal.

Frank Zappa is a rock 'n' roll legend, a composer of avant garde music, and the CEO of Barking Pumpkin Records. He lives in Los Angeles with his wife and four children.

HAIL TO THE CHIEFS

He was ignorant of the commonest accomplishments of youth. He could not even lie.

> MARK TWAIN on George Washington

The moral character of [Thomas] Jefferson was repulsive. Continually puling about liberty, equality and the degrading curse of slavery, he brought his own children to the hammer, and made money of his debaucheries.

> ALEXANDER HAMILTON

Many persons have difficulty remembering what President Franklin Pierce is best remembered for, and he is therefore probably best forgotten.

> RICHARD ARMOUR

He had about as much backbone as a chocolate eclair.

> THEODORE ROOSEVELT on William McKinley

Theodore Roosevelt thought with his hips.

> LINCOLN STEFFENS

He hated all pretension save his own pretension.

> H. L. MENCKEN on Theodore Roosevelt

When Theodore attends a wedding, he wants to be the bride, and when he attends a funeral, he wants to be the corpse.

ALICE ROOSEVELT LONGWORTH

Taft meant well, but he meant well feebly.

THEODORE ROOSEVELT on
William Howard Taft

The air currents of the world never ventilated his mind.

WALTER PAGE HINES on
Woodrow Wilson

He writes the worst English that I have ever encountered. It reminds me of a string of wet sponges; it reminds me of tattered washing on the line; it reminds me of stale bean soup, of college yells, of dogs barking idiotically through endless nights. It is so bad that a sort of grandeur creeps into it.   H. L. MENCKEN on Warren G. Harding

His speeches leave the impression of an army of pompous phrases moving over the landscape in search of an idea. Sometimes these meandering words would actually capture a straggling thought and bear it triumphantly a prisoner in their midst, until it died of servitude and overwork.

WILLIAM McADOO on Warren G. Harding

President Harding is a good man who ought to be Lieutenant Governor of Rhode Island.

ROBERT BENCHLEY

Harding was not a bad man. He was just a slob.

ALICE ROOSEVELT LONGWORTH

He looked as if he had been weaned on a pickle.

ALICE ROOSEVELT LONGWORTH on
Calvin Coolidge

He slept more than any other president whether by day or night. Nero fiddled, but Coolidge only snored.

H. L. MENCKEN

He's the greatest man who ever came out of Plymouth, Vermont.

CLARENCE DARROW on
Calvin Coolidge

If he became convinced tomorrow that coming out for cannibalism would get him the votes he so sorely needs, he would begin fattening a missionary on the White House backyard come Wednesday.

H. L. MENCKEN on
Franklin D. Roosevelt

A chameleon on plaid.

HERBERT HOOVER on Franklin D. Roosevelt

I'd rather be right than Roosevelt.
HEYWOOD BROUN

Harry Truman proves the old adage that any man
can become president of the United States.
NORMAN THOMAS

Harry S Truman, a feisty, plucky native of Mis-
souri . . . grew up so poor that his family could
not afford to put a period after his middle initial.
DAVE BARRY

I doubt very much if a man whose main literary
interests were in works by Mr. Zane Grey, admira-
ble as they may be, is particularly well equipped
to be chief executive of this country, particularly
where Indian affairs are concerned.
DEAN ACHESON on
Dwight D. Eisenhower

As an intellectual he bestowed upon the games of
golf and bridge all the enthusiasm and persever-
ance that he withheld from books and ideas.
EMMET JOHN HUGHES on
Dwight D. Eisenhower

Eisenhower is the only living Unknown Soldier.
ROBERT S. KERR

Roosevelt proved a man could be president for life; Truman proved anybody could be president; Eisenhower proved you don't need to have a president.   KENNETH B. KEATING

I haven't voted since 1964, when I voted for Lyndon Johnson, the peace candidate.   GORE VIDAL

Richard Nixon is a no-good lying bastard. He can lie out of both sides of his mouth at the same time, and even if he caught himself telling the truth, he'd lie just to keep his hand in.
                    HARRY S TRUMAN

Nixon is the kind of guy who, if you were drowning twenty feet from shore, would throw you a fifteen-foot rope.   EUGENE MCCARTHY
                    (quoted by Mort Sahl)

It is quite extraordinary! He will even tell a lie when it is not convenient to. That is the sign of a great artist.   GORE VIDAL

He is the kind of politician who would cut down a redwood tree and then mount the stump to make a speech for conservation.
                    ADLAI STEVENSON

The integrity of a hyena and the style of a poison toad.   HUNTER S. THOMPSON

The Nixon Political Principle: If two wrongs don't make a right, try three.   LAURENCE J. PETER

Gerry Ford is a nice guy, but he played too much football without a helmet.   LYNDON JOHNSON

[Gerald Ford] looks like the guy in the science fiction movie who's the first to see "The Creature."
DAVID FRYE

Gerry Ford is so dumb that he can't fart and chew gum at the same time.   LYNDON JOHNSON

Jimmy Carter came from a simple, God-fearing homespun southern family that was normal in every respect except that many of its members, upon close inspection, appeared to be crazy. After graduating from the U.S. Naval Academy, he served as an officer aboard a nuclear submarine, where, due to an unfortunate radiation leakage, he developed enormous mutant teeth. DAVE BARRY

Carter is your typical smiling, brilliant, back-stabbing, bullshitting Southern nut-cutter.
LANE KIRKLAND

I would not want Jimmy Carter and his men put
in charge of snake control in Ireland.

EUGENE MCCARTHY

Jimmy Carter: The only American president in
history whose popularity rating dropped below
the Prime Rate.   KEVIN PHILLIPS

I once called Carter a "chicken-fried McGovern,"
and I take that back because I've come to respect
McGovern.   ROBERT DOLE

Sometimes when I look at all my children, I say to
myself, "Lillian, you should have stayed a virgin."

LILLIAN CARTER

[Jimmy Carter] says his lust is in his heart. I hope
it's a little lower.   SHIRLEY MACLAINE

[Jimmy Carter] is the only man since my dear
husband died to have the effrontery to kiss me on
the lips.   THE QUEEN MOTHER

An authentic phony.
                        JAMES RESTON on Ronald Reagan

So shockingly dumb that by his very presence in
the office he numbs an entire country.
> JIMMY BRESLIN on Ronald Reagan

> In the heat of a political lifetime, Ronald Reagan
> innocently squirrels away tidbits of misinforma-
> tion and then, sometimes years later, casually
> drops them into his public discourse, like gum
> balls in a quiche.　LUCY HOWARD

That youthful sparkle in his eye is caused by his
contact lenses, which he keeps highly polished.
> SHEILA GRAHAM on Ronald Reagan

> [George Bush] is the only American statesman
> whose portrait is an authentic classic of Western
> Art, being of course by Paul Klee and entitled *The
> Twittering Machine*.　MURRAY KEMPTON on
> George Bush

A cross between Rambo and Mary Poppins.
> PETER FENN on George Bush

> A toothache of a man.
> JIM HIGHTOWER on George Bush

Every woman's first husband.
> BARBARA EHRENREICH and JANE O'REILLY

The national twit.   MICHAEL KINSLEY

[George Bush] has the look about him of someone
who might sit up and yip for a Dog Yummie.
                                    MIKE ROYKO

                Poor George, he can't help it—he was born with
                a silver foot in his mouth.   ANN RICHARDS

George Bush is Gerald Ford without the pizazz.
                                    PAT PAULSEN

                My theory is that [George Bush] has had to tell so
                many lies—and has such a hard time remembering
                them—that he sounds dyslexic.   GORE VIDAL

Washington couldn't tell a lie, Nixon couldn't tell
the truth, and Reagan couldn't tell the difference.
                                    MORT SAHL

QUOTES ON "G"

GAMBLING

The gambling known as business looks with austere disfavor upon the business known as gambling.
AMBROSE BIERCE

GAY

The love that previously dared not speak its name has now grown hoarse from screaming.
ROBERT BRUSTEIN

GERMAN REUNIFICATION

I view this in much the same way I view a possible Dean Martin–Jerry Lewis reconciliation: I never really enjoyed their work, and I'm not sure I need to see any of their new stuff.
DENNIS MILLER

GIRLS

There are girls who manage to sell themselves, whom no one would take as gifts.
NICOLAS CHAMFORT

Why assume so glibly that the God who presumably created the universe is still running it? It is certainly conceivable that He may have finished it and then turned it over to lesser gods to operate.
H. L. MENCKEN

I respect the idea of God too much to hold it responsible for a world as absurd as this one is.
GEORGES DUHAMEL

You must believe in God in spite of what the clergy say.
BENJAMIN JOWETT

I read the book of Job last night—I don't think God comes well out of it.
VIRGINIA WOOLF

――――――GODS――――――

Men rarely (if ever) manage to dream up a god superior to themselves. Most gods have the manners and morals of a spoiled child.
ROBERT A. HEINLEIN

――――――GOLF――――――

Nobody knows exactly how golf got started. Probably what happened was, thousands of years ago, a couple of primitive guys were standing around, holding some odd-shaped sticks, and they noticed a golf ball lying on the grass, and they said, "Hey! Let's see if we can hit this into a hole!" And then they said, "Nah, let's just tell long, boring anecdotes about it instead."   DAVE BARRY

———GOOD FELLOWSHIP———

What men call good fellowship is commonly but the virtue of pigs in a litter which lie close together to keep each other warm.   THOREAU

———GOOD LISTENER———

A good listener is usually thinking about something else.   KIN HUBBARD

———GOODNESS———

It is better to be beautiful than to be good, but it is better to be good than to be ugly.
                    OSCAR WILDE

———GOVERNMENT———

Government is too big and important to be left to the politicians.   CHESTER BOWLES

Government expands to absorb revenue—and then some. TOM WICKER

In rivers and bad governments, the lightest things swim at the top. BENJAMIN FRANKLIN

Creative semantics is the key to contemporary government; it consists of talking in strange tongues lest the public learn the inevitable inconveniently early. GEORGE WILL

There never has been a good government. EMMA GOLDMAN

QUOTES ON "H"

HAMMER

If I had a hammer I'd use it on Peter, Paul and
Mary.   HOWARD ROSENBERG

HAPPINESS

One of the keys to happiness is a bad memory.
                                          RITA MAE BROWN

Happy is he who causes scandal.
                          SALVADOR DALI

A person is never happy except at the price of
some ignorance.   ANATOLE FRANCE

To be stupid, selfish, and have good health are
three requirements for happiness, though if stupidity is lacking, all is lost. GUSTAVE FLAUBERT

HEALTH FOOD

I refuse to spend my life worrying about what I
eat. There is no pleasure worth forgoing just for
an extra three years in the geriatric ward.
                                          JOHN MORTIMER

What some call health, if purchased by perpetual
anxiety about diet, isn't much better than tedious
disease.   GEORGE DENNISON PRENTICE

Bread made only of the branny part of the meal,
which the poorest sort of people use, especially in
time of dearth and necessity, giveth a very bad and
excremental nourishment to the body: it is well
called *panis canicarius*, because it is more fit for
dogs than for men.   TOBIAS VENNER

————HEALTH NUTS————

Health nuts are going to feel stupid someday,
lying in hospitals dying of nothing. REDD FOXX

————HEAVEN————

It is a curious thing . . . that every creed promises
a paradise which will be absolutely uninhabitable
for anyone of civilized taste.   EVELYN WAUGH

————HISTORY————

We have wasted History like a bunch of drunks
shooting dice back in the men's crapper of the
local bar.   CHARLES BUKOWSKI

The very ink with which history is written is merely fluid prejudice. MARK TWAIN

History teaches us that men and nations behave wisely once they have exhausted all other alternatives. ABBA EBAN

Events in the past may be roughly divided into those which probably never happened and those which do not matter. W. R. INGE

HOLIDAYS

Holidays are often overrated disturbances of routine, costly and uncomfortable, and they usually need another holiday to correct their ravages.
E. V. LUCAS

HOLLYWOOD

Hollywood—that's where they give Academy Awards to Charlton Heston for acting.
SHIRLEY KNIGHT

In Hollywood a marriage is a success if it outlasts milk. RITA RUDNER

Hollywood: They only know one word of more than one syllable there, and that is "fillum."
LOUIS SHERWIN

["Tinseltown" is derived from] the German verb *tinzelle*—literally, "to book a turkey into 1,200 theaters and make one's money before word of mouth hits."
                                                    CHARLIE HAAS

> Ten million dollars worth of intricate and ingenious machinery functioning elaborately to put skin on baloney. GEORGE JEAN NATHAN

The people here seem to live in a little world that shuts out the rest of the universe and everyone appears to be faking life. The actors and writers live in fear, and nothing, including the houses, seems permanent. FRED ALLEN

> The people are unreal. The flowers are unreal, they don't smell. The fruit is unreal, it doesn't taste of anything. The whole place is a glaring, gaudy, nightmarish set, built up in the desert.
>   ETHEL BARRYMORE

Hollywood—an emotional Detroit.
                                                    LILLIAN GISH

> Hollywood is a chain gang and we all lose the will to escape. The links of the chain are forged not with cruelties but with luxuries. CLIVE BROOK

You get called to L.A. by producers. And by the
time you get out there, they sort of forget why
they asked you to come.   MICHAEL HERR

Of all the Christbitten places in the two hemi-
spheres, this is the last curly kink in the pig's tail.
STEPHEN VINCENT BENET

There were times, when I drove along the Sunset
Strip and looked at those buildings or when I
watched the fashionable film colony arriving at
some premiere . . . that I fully expected God in
his wrath to obliterate the whole shebang.
S. J. PERELMAN

You can't find any true closeness in Hollywood,
because everybody does the fake closeness so well.
CARRIE FISHER

——————HONESTY——————

Honesty is a good thing, but it is not profitable
to its possessor unless it is kept under control.
DON MARQUIS

Honesty is the best policy—when there is money
in it.   MARK TWAIN

HOOD ORNAMENTS

Hood ornaments. They were just lovely, and they gave a sense of respect. And they took 'em away because if you can save one human life—that's always the argument—it's worth it, if you can save one human life. Actually, I'd be willing to trade maybe a dozen human lives for a nice hood ornament. I imagine those things really did tend to stick in bicyclists.　MICHAEL O'DONOGHUE

HUMAN NATURE

Everyone would like to behave like a pagan, with everyone else behaving like a Christian.

ALBERT CAMUS

HUMAN RACE

Such is the human race, often it seems a pity that Noah . . . didn't miss the boat.　MARK TWAIN

Most human beings have an almost infinite capacity for taking things for granted.

ALDOUS HUXLEY

The capacity of human beings to bore one another seems to be vastly greater than that of any other animal.　H. L. MENCKEN

Both the cockroach and the bird could get along very well without us, although the cockroach would miss us most.   JOSEPH WOOD KRUTCH

Render unto Caesar the things that are Caesar's, and unto God the things that are God's; and unto human beings, what?   STANISLAW J. LEC

————HUSBAND————

Husband, *n*. One who, having dined, is charged with the care of the plate.   AMBROSE BIERCE

————HYPOCRISY————

I hope you have not been leading a double life, pretending to be wicked and being really good all the time. That would be hypocrisy.

OSCAR WILDE

We are not hypocrites in our sleep.

WILLIAM HAZLITT

LARRY GELBART

Stuck on "Angry"

JW: *Why are movies and television shows so bad?*
LG: Motion picture and television executives tend to clone past successes. They actively discourage originality because of the high financial risks of dream making. And all too many members of the creative community are willing to collaborate with them. American mass entertainment has always been based on the bot-

tom line, but now it's increasingly from the bottom of the barrel. The nation's screens—big and small—are awash with films and programming that are more a reflection of dedicated deal making than they are of meaningful filmmaking. Commissions have replaced commitment. Packaging has replaced passion. Whole forests are being devoured to create the pulp that is transformed into printouts of a never ending flow of mindless screenplays that are replays of former screenplays.

It's hard to believe that in just fifty short years, we've gone from Orson Welles' filmic feast (I have a tough time saying *film*— they used to be *movies* when I was a kid. Film to me is what you have on your teeth) to such standardized, trivialized fare. In half a century we've gone from *Citizen Kane* to candy cane. That's what comes of playing it safe. That's what comes of relying on the kind of market research that asks people whether or not they like a movie that hasn't been made yet, and perhaps never will be if enough of them indicate they won't see it if it ever is. That's what happens when moviemakers take the pulse only of other moviemakers and superimpose the results on an audience they know only as statistics.

JW: *Is that why there are so many sequels?*

LG: A good many of today's studio decision makers began their executive careers in television—some of them while still attending day school. They were quick to learn that in the world of TV, what pays the rent, theirs *and* the networks', are long-running series. And what is a long-running series but a string of sequels that goes on and on? The same title, the same cast, the same basic plot, week after week, year in and year out. By that yardstick, a movie marquee that boasted *Rocky* and *2010* would not necessarily indicate a double feature.

JW: *Haven't there always been movie sequels?*

LG: Of course, but hardly in the numbers we see today. They were, for the most part, B pictures. They had none of the bloated importance of today's sequels, which can often decide the fate of the company that has the nerve-wracking distinction of releasing one.

This cinematic senility has transformed Hollywood into a software factory whose product is designed to make a relatively few wealthy while impoverishing our culture. There were two major turning points in the history of American movies: the first, long ago, was when the movies began to talk. And now, in the last decade of the twentieth century, when it's money that talks. Not that it didn't always, but not in such a loud voice as it does today.

JW: *But aren't today's movie audiences getting the entertainment they demand?*

LG: Well, today's movie audiences are largely television trained, most of them exposed to it almost at birth, learning to watch before they can crawl. And what constitutes their education? What forms their standards? Simple plots, simple problems, everything tied up neatly in twenty-three minutes or forty-eight, or in any case, three minutes before the end of the time slot. Just like real life.

JW: *They aim for mediocrity?*

LG: With tremendous accuracy. Well, I take that back; I don't think they really *aim* for mediocrity. Some things are made deliberately hokey and bad, but most of the time people are not trying to do junk, they are just trying to do safe material and they wind up with mediocrity.

JW: *Why must there always be a happy ending?*

LG: The viewers must be kept happy because unhappy viewers aren't in a mood to go out and buy a car or a beer. Or do both at the same time. No involvement, no emotion. The only way you can get any feeling out of your television set is if you touch it when you're wet.

JW: *Is that why there are so many feel-good movies?*

LG: Feel-good movies, more than anything, mostly make the distributors feel good. They do nothing to reflect or interpret the human condition. And there is, I believe, a group consciousness, some primal need to record our emotions, to remind each other that we *are* each other. That just as we share the same physical fate, so do we share what is in our hearts and our minds. I miss the humanity we once witnessed on the screen.

JW: *Did you have problems with network censors in doing M*A*S*H?*

LG: The one area where I anticipated trouble, but never received any, made me so grateful that I was able to deal with the rest of it quite rationally. The network never asked us to tone down the political content of the show or the humanism we tried to display. For the first three years we had the normal amount of stupidity from Program Practices about language, certain situations—one script they absolutely refused to let us film was about two nurses who pretended Hawkeye had made them pregnant. That was the only show they ever said, "No, not at all, not a page of it, not a minute of it." The rest of it was pretty SOP: "Please delete three 'hells,' two 'damns,' and a partridge in a pear tree." They're always worried about sex and sacrilege; no one says "Goddamn" on television. You can say "God" and you can say "damn," but don't ever try to put them together. But they did let us talk about the futility of war; in some very strong ways, it was a political show. You negotiate with them.

JW: *Have things gotten better since you did* M*A*S*H?

LG: What's gotten a lot better so that it makes things seem a lot worse is communications. We know more about things that used to be kept quiet, we know more about child abuse, we know more about every kind of abuse. Nobody stuck a microphone or a camera in front of Abraham Lincoln's face. Even he probably would have said some foolish things if he had had to provide sound bites for CNN.

I think one of the by-products of the communications explosion is a sort of "corruption fatigue." Someone has called our reaction to all the misery around us "compassion fatigue"—this was when there was all this flooding going on in the U.S. and there was the typhoon in Bangladesh and the Kurds were making their ways—sorry—and all of that. Likewise, I think there's also a corruption fatigue; we've lost our ability to be shocked or enraged by the machinations of politicians. We've been battered with such frequency that we've become indifferent. We're punch drunk with scandal.

JW: *You sound like a thwarted idealist.*

LG: My idealism is not thwarted, my *hopes* have been thwarted, but then I think everybody's have. The conservatives are unhappy because the country isn't Right enough and the liberals are un-happy because it's getting too Right. No one's happy, but I guess some people are able to put it on whatever passes for the back burner, but I don't have a back burner. Everything's in front. That's my problem. My gauge is stuck on "Anger."

JW: *So you see an America in decline?*

LG: Which America? The deprived, denied, absolutely whipped black America? Or the terribly wealthy white America? Which America are we talking about? For some Americans these are the best of times, but not for most. In the past the lower class could in some way visualize themselves as middle or upper, but now the only way these people can rise above their poverty is through drugs and death and crime. Yes, I think we're in decline. I think we're in decline when Japan can take over the dream factory here, when they can take control of our most popular form of mass entertainment. It's one thing to build a better car and have the public prefer that to an Iacocca product, but it's another thing literally to influence the influence makers. Hollywood has always served its masters.

JW: *Hollywood seems all the more important in a world that is spin-ning out of control.*

LG: Yes, because we can't keep up with the backlog, with the inventory of evil. We can't deal with it. The Amazon is still burn-ing, we just don't hear the smoke detectors anymore. No one person is *Time* magazine, with a series of editors handling the various departments of our lives. We're fucking swamped. We turn on the evening news and get the day's toll of child abuse and famine deaths and the murders in the cities and AIDS and crack and . . . fine, let's switch off and go to the movies. Let's go see the latest Arnold Schwarzenegger movie.

JW: *But that's no escape from carnage.*

LG: Actually, it is, because in the movies you can die and still be alive. Thelma and Louise can dive into the canyon, but then you have the closing credits and somehow they're still alive. Speaking of which, *Thelma and Louise* showed me for the first time the vast amount of hatred in women for the way they've been treated. If you're a Jew, you understand what it's like to be thought of as less than equal, and if you're a writer you get it even more. A Jewish woman writer, learn how to work a drill press. And if you're a black Jewish woman writer, forget it.

JW: *Do you vote?*

LG: Yes, I do.

JW: *Then you evidently don't feel that it's a de facto disenfranchisement to be forced to vote for merely the lesser of two evils.*

LG: I just always vote for the Democratic evil, that's all. I can't vote for the party of Thomas E. Dewey and John Mitchell and George Bush and Ronald Reagan and Richard Nixon. I just can't.

JW: *What about Nixon's recent rehabilitation?*

LG: I can never understand why the American people buy such bad performers. It's a good thing they're not producers. I don't think he's capable of being "rehabilitated." He's like the uncle in the room we never opened. He still has to do what he does on the sly. You don't see him in a golf cart with George Bush or any of those people, and he hasn't been invited to address the convention. If anything, he's our Rudolf Hess.

JW: *You travel quite a bit. I think it was Jay Leno who said that most of the people traveling on airplanes today belong on Greyhound buses. Have you noticed a decline in the quality of travel?*

LG: No, because I treat myself very well in the travel department, so I don't really have any complaints. But you know who really hates to fly these days? First-class passengers, because flight attendants assume that everybody in first class is a Frequent Flyer and they don't rush so fast to answer the bell. First class has lost its cachet.

JW: *What about some other modern annoyances? Graffiti, for instance. I've been trying to figure out why the sight of it makes my blood pressure jump.*

LG: It's messy and it's ugly. As ugly as their lives. Every time I drive into Manhattan from JFK I think of visitors coming to America and seeing this stuff on the walls and it makes me sick that it's their first impression of us. Graffiti is preliterate. It all comes from the original hand in the cave, somebody saying, "I was here." We've gone from that simple, wondering eloquence of "I was here" to this excremental scribbling. And you wonder, When do they do it, at four in the morning? When do they *do* it?

Larry Gelbart has written comedy for Jack Paar, Sid Caesar, Bob Hope, and Danny Thomas, among others. He was one of the originators of the television version of M*A*S*H *and served as its principal writer, sometime director, and co-producer during its first four seasons. His screenwriting credits include* Tootsie *and* Oh, God, *and he is the author of two Tony Award-winning Broadway musicals,* A Funny Thing Happened on the Way to the Forum *and* City of Angels.

HOORAY FOR HOLLYWOOD

He was a short man, almost squat, with a vulpine smirk that told you, as soon as his image flashed onto the screen, that no wife or bankroll must be left unguarded.　　　　S. J. PERELMAN on
Erich von Stroheim

The son of a bitch is a ballet dancer.
　　　　　　　W. C. FIELDS on Charlie Chaplin

Making a film with Greta Garbo does not constitute an introduction.　　ROBERT MONTGOMERY

When Jean Harlow was introduced to Margot Asquith, she mistakenly pronounced the "t" in Margot, to which Mrs. Asquith replied, "The 't' is silent, as in Harlow."

A face unclouded by thought.
　　　　　　　LILLIAN HELLMAN on Norma Shearer

She was divinely, hysterically, insanely malevolent.
　　　　BETTE DAVIS on Theda Bara

She has as much sex appeal as Slim Summerville.
CARL LAEMMLE on Bette Davis

The best time I ever had with Joan Crawford was when I pushed her down the stairs in *Whatever Happened to Baby Jane*.
BETTE DAVIS

Toward the end of her life she looked like a hungry insect magnified a million times—a praying mantis that had forgotten how to pray.
QUENTIN CRISP on Joan Crawford

A day away from Tallulah [Bankhead] is like a month in the country.
HOWARD DIETZ

The nicest thing I can say about Frances Farmer is that she is unbearable.
WILLIAM WYLER

A character who, if he did not exist, could not be imagined.
S. N. BEHRMAN on Oscar Levant

Pearl is a disease of oysters. Levant is a disease of Hollywood.
KENNETH TYNAN

There is absolutely nothing wrong with Oscar Levant that a miracle can't fix.
ALEXANDER WOOLLCOTT

George Gershwin played good tennis almost by
ear.   OSCAR LEVANT

> The first time I met and embraced Judy Garland,
> it made pharmaceutical history.   OSCAR LEVANT

Jolson's funeral was widely attended by those who
wanted to make sure.   GEORGE JESSEL

> Larry Parks gives me the creeps.   AL JOLSON

Bogart's a helluva nice guy until 11:30 P.M. After
that he thinks he's Bogart.   DAVE CHASEN

> The great thing about Errol [Flynn] was that you
> knew precisely where you were with him—because
> he *always* let you down.   DAVID NIVEN

When Columbia Pictures boss Harry Cohn died in 1958, Rabbi Magnin
of the Wilshire Boulevard Temple was asked to say one good thing
about the departed movie mogul. The rabbi thought long and hard and
finally said, "He's dead." And Red Skelton explained the large turnout
at Cohn's funeral: "It proves what they always say: Give the public what
they want and they'll come out for it."

You had to stand in line to hate him.
            HEDDA HOPPER on Harry Cohn

Don't worry about Alan . . . Alan will always land on somebody's feet.   DOROTHY PARKER on her ex-husband Alan Campbell

He liked to be the biggest bug in the manure pile.
ELIA KAZAN on Harry Cohn

Gower Street is paved with the bones of my executive producers.   HARRY COHN

When Louis B. Mayer gave his daughter's husband a high-ranking position at MGM, a wag observed: "The son-in-law also rises."

That French broad likes money.
HARRY COHN on Claudette Colbert

I saw an empty cab pull up and out stepped Sam Goldwyn.   SID GRAUMAN

To Raoul Walsh, a tender love scene is burning down a whorehouse.   JACK L. WARNER

The only Greek tragedy I know is Spyros Skouras.
BILLY WILDER

A man whose few successes were even more distasteful than his many failures.
JOHN SIMON on Dore Schary

Ogden Nash on Hollywood moguls' nepotism:
Uncle Carl Laemmle
Has a very large faemmle.

From Poland to Polo in one generation.
ARTHUR MAYER on Darryl F. Zanuck

He's really Martin Bormann in elevator shoes, with a face-lift by a blindfolded plastic surgeon in Luxembourg.   BILLY WILDER on Otto Preminger

Upon my honor
I saw a madonna
Sitting alone in a niche
Above the door
Of the glamorous whore
Of a prominent son-of-a-bitch.
DOROTHY PARKER on Marion Davies'
dressing room

Wet she's a star, dry she ain't.
FANNY BRICE on Esther Williams

During an elegant dinner party given by the producer (and self-styled gourmet) Arthur Hornblow, Jr., the screenwriter Herman Mankiewicz had a bit too much to drink and abruptly excused himself from the table. When he returned, looking greatly relieved, he casually reported to his host, "Don't worry, Arthur, the white wine came up with the fish."

Michael Wilding's in love with himself, but he's not sure if it's reciprocated.   RICHARD BURTON

She looked as if butter wouldn't melt in her mouth—or anywhere else.
    ELSA LANCHESTER on Maureen O'Hara

Clark Gable's ears make him look like a taxicab with both doors open.   HOWARD HUGHES

He's the kind of guy who, if you say, "Hiya, Clark, how are ya?" is stuck for an answer.
    AVA GARDNER on Clark Gable

Lolly was possessed by a fiendish, auntielike excitement when on the trail of a hot "exclusive," and would sit at her telephone all night long if necessary, interpreting the denials of those she was interrogating as the great horned owl interprets the squeaking of distant mice.
    PAUL O'NEIL on Louella Parsons

Her virtue was that she said what she thought, her vice that what she thought didn't amount to much.   PETER USTINOV on Hedda Hopper

I think he'd do well to spend a summer on a ranch.   GARY COOPER on Anthony Perkins

Burt Lancaster! Before he can pick up an ashtray, he discusses his motivation for an hour. Just pick up the ashtray and shut up!   JEANNE MOREAU

Paul Newman has the attention span of a bolt of lightning.   ROBERT REDFORD

Miss Georgia and Mr. Shaker Heights.
      GORE VIDAL on Joanne Woodward
            and Paul Newman

Working with Julie Andrews is like being hit over the head with a Valentine card.
      CHRISTOPHER PLUMMER

A professional amateur.
      LAURENCE OLIVIER on Marilyn Monroe

Working with her is like being bombed by watermelons.   ALAN LADD on Sophia Loren

---

She has no charm, delicacy or taste. She's just an
arrogant little tail-twitcher who's learned to throw
sex in your face.   NUNNALLY JOHNSON on
                               Marilyn Monroe

I've stayed in his house, and he has bored me to
death. He tells the *sa-a-ame* stories he's been telling for years, and all I ever heard were his records,
which he played *over and over* again.
                 PHYLLIS MCGUIRE on Frank Sinatra

I wish Frank Sinatra would just shut up and sing.
                               LAUREN BACALL

A dope with fat ankles.
                         FRANK SINATRA on Nancy Reagan

[Nancy Davis] projects the passion of a Good
Humor ice cream: frozen, on a stick, and all
vanilla.   SPENCER TRACY

Glassy-eyed and overdressed, [she] always looks
as if she has just been struck by lightning in a
limousine.   MARK CRISPIN MILLER
                               on Nancy Reagan

I once shook hands with Pat Boone and my whole
right side sobered up.   DEAN MARTIN

Miss United Dairies herself.
DAVID NIVEN on Jayne Mansfield

Zsa Zsa Gabor is inscrutable, but I can't vouch for the rest of her.
OSCAR LEVANT

He was insatiable. Three, four, five times a day was not unusual for him, and he was able to accept telephone calls at the same time.
JOAN COLLINS on Warren Beatty

He's the type of man who will end up dying in his own arms.
MAMIE VAN DOREN on Warren Beatty

Elizabeth Taylor is so fat, she wears stretch kaftans.
JOAN RIVERS

To the unwashed public, [Joan Collins] is a star. But to those who know her, she's a commodity who would sell her own bowel movement.
ANTHONY NEWLEY

I'd really like to work with [Barbra Streisand] again, in something appropriate. Perhaps *Macbeth*.
WALTER MATTHAU

Jane Fonda . . . is so obsessed with remaining in-humanly taut by working out ninety-two hours a day that it took her more than a decade to notice that she was married to a dweeb.   DAVE BARRY

A bag of tattooed bones in a sequined slingshot.
MR. BLACKWELL on Cher

Cher . . . has had so much cosmetic surgery that, for ease of maintenance, many of her body parts are attached with Velcro.   DAVE BARRY

He has so many muscles that he has to make an appointment to move his fingers.
PHYLLIS DILLER on
Arnold Schwarzenegger

When he's late for dinner, I know he's either hav-ing an affair or is lying dead in the street. I always hope it's the street.   JESSICA TANDY on her
husband, Hume Cronyn

Am I just cynical, or does anyone else think the only reason Warren Beatty decided to have a child is so he can meet babysitters?
DAVID LETTERMAN

OSCAR WILDE

Everything to Declare

OSCAR FINGAL O'FLAHERTIE WILLS WILDE was born in 1854 in Dublin at 21 Westland Row, but, typically, he claimed to have arrived at 1 Merrion Square, a better address. His father was an eminent surgeon and amateur archaeologist, and his flamboyant mother contributed patriotic poems to the nationalist journal *The Nation* under the pen name "Speranza." She once admonished a visitor who described an acquaintance as being "respectable":

"You must never employ that description in this house. It is only tradespeople who are respectable."

Wilde attended Magdalen College, Oxford, where he eliminated his Irish accent and cultivated a penchant for the Pre-Raphaelites, a disdain for conventional morality, and the image of a fop. (He was already a dandy at the age of thirteen: in his first letter to his mother from boarding school he asked for two flannel shirts, one violet and one crimson.) As an undergraduate he gained a reputation for his epigrams and for his outlandish behavior. He briefly considered converting to Catholicism (when asked his religion he would reply, "I don't think I have any—I'm an Irish Protestant"), and he became a disciple of Walter Pater and embraced the doctrine of Aestheticism, the view that aesthetic values take precedence over moral ones. In 1878 he won the Newdigate prize for his poem *Ravenna*, and he published his first collection of poems in 1881.

From Oxford he went down to London and soon acquired a large circle of influential friends, including the actress Lillie Langtry ("I would rather have discovered Lillie Langtry than to have discovered America"). The Prince of Wales asked to meet him, and with the successful opening of his play *Lady Windermere's Fan* (after which he made a curtain speech while scandalously smoking a cigarette), his legend grew. Although he denied the gossip that he walked the streets of London carrying a lily, he boasted that he had made the world *believe* that he did.

Wilde embarked on a lecture tour of the United States in 1882. When he arrived in America aboard the S.S. *Arizona*, a customs officer asked if he had anything to declare, and Wilde replied, "I have nothing to declare but my genius." After his American tour he went to Paris, where he wrote a play, had his hair curled, and met Emile Zola, who in toasting him said, "Mr. Wilde will have to reply in his barbarous tongue." Wilde answered instead in perfect French: "I am Irish by birth, English by race, and as Mr. Zola says, condemned to speak the language of Shakespeare."

He met Constance Lloyd in 1883, they married in 1884, settled in London, and eventually had two sons, Cyril in 1885 and Vivian in 1886, the same year in which Wilde stopped having intercourse with his wife because of a recurrence of the syphilis he had contracted from a prostitute at Oxford. He had his first homosexual encounter soon thereafter, and developed a penchant for young male prostitutes which would continue for the rest of his life. He played the part of a conventional husband, but like the characters in his plays, he was not what he appeared to be.

Wilde published a novel, *The Picture of Dorian Gray*, and a collection of children's stories, *The Happy Prince*, in 1891, and then wrote a series of successful plays, including *Lady Windermere's Fan* (1892), *A Woman of No Importance* (1893), and his masterpiece, *The Importance of Being Earnest* (1895).

A brilliant conversationalist, Wilde coined numerous aphorisms, many of which found their way into his comedies. In fact, the plays were essentially vehicles for his epigrams: "I can't describe action," he said. "My people sit in chairs and chatter." The sheer number and quality of his bon mots prompted Dorothy Parker to lament:

If with the literate I am
Impelled to try an epigram
I never seek to take the credit
We all assume that Oscar said it.

In 1891 Wilde met the young Lord Alfred Douglas, "Bosie," the son of the Marquess of Queensberry, and they began a long and tempestuous affair. After Wilde's refusal to stop seeing his son, Queensberry called at Wilde's London club and left a card addressed to "Oscar Wilde posing Somdomite [sic]." When Wilde sued for libel, Queensberry pleaded and proved justification and thereby won the case. Wilde was then prosecuted under English criminal laws against homosexuality, and was convicted and sentenced to two years at hard labor. He later said, "The two great turning points in my life were when my father sent me to Oxford and when Society sent me to prison." Upon his release in 1897, broken by the harsh prison treatment in body if not in spirit, he exiled himself to France, where he lived in poverty and obscurity under the alias Sebastian Melmoth, after the hero of a Gothic novel who sells his soul for the promise of prolonged life.

He published *The Ballad of Reading Gaol* in 1898, and *De Profundis*, a bitter indictment of Lord Douglas and an apologia for his own conduct, was published posthumously in 1905.

A keen observer of human folly, Wilde skewered the hypocrisy of Victorian society on the sharp point of his elegant wit. He was arrogant, audacious, self-absorbed, but he was also kind and generous and quick to laugh at himself. In the end he was a bona fide tragic figure: noble, heroic, and self-destructive. His biographer Richard Ellmann believed that Wilde struggled to "save what is eccentric and singular from being sanitized and standardized, to replace a morality of severity with one of sympathy." Wilde summed himself up in a remark to André Gide: "Would you like to know the great drama of my life? It is that I've put my genius into my life; I've only put my talent into my works."

He died in Paris in 1900, at the age of forty-six, unrepentant: "A patriot put in prison for loving his country loves his country. A poet put in prison for loving boys loves boys." Unable to pay the medical bills for his last illness, he said, "I am dying as I have lived, beyond my means." And of the shabby wallpaper in his sickroom he remarked: "One of us had to go."

WILDE ON WOMEN

No woman should ever be quite accurate about
her age. It looks so calculating.

> One should never trust a woman who tells one
> her real age; a woman who would tell one that
> would tell one anything.

As long as a woman can look ten years younger
than her own daughter, she is perfectly satisfied.

> Thirty-five is a very attractive age; London society
> is full of women who of their own free choice
> remained thirty-five for years.

No woman should have a memory. Memory in a
woman is the beginning of dowdiness.

> Women have a wonderful instinct about things.
> They can discover everything except the obvious.

A man can be happy with any woman as long as
he does not love her.

Women give men the very gold of their lives. But they invariably want it back in small change.

Between men and women there is no friendship possible. There is passion, enmity, worship, love, but no friendship.

The history of women is the history of the worst form of tyranny the world has ever known. The tyranny of the weak over the strong. It is the only tyranny that lasts.

Women are never disarmed by compliments. Men always are. That is the difference between the sexes.

I am afraid that women appreciate cruelty, downright cruelty, more than anything else. They have wonderfully primitive instincts. We have emancipated them, but they remain slaves looking for their masters all the same.

The only way to behave to a woman is to make love to her, if she is pretty, and to someone else, if she is plain.

Women, as some witty Frenchman once put it, inspire us with the desire to do masterpieces, and always prevent us from carrying them out.

A woman will flirt with anybody in the world as long as other people are looking on.

There is nothing in the world like the devotion of a married woman. It is something no married man knows anything about.

THERE'LL ALWAYS BE AN ENGLAND (ALAS)

A family with the wrong members in control—
that, perhaps, is as near as one can come to de-
scribing England in a phrase. GEORGE ORWELL

There are only two classes in good society in England: the equestrian classes and the neurotic
classes.   GEORGE BERNARD SHAW

English cuisine is generally so threadbare that for
years there has been a gentleman's agreement in
the civilized world to allow the Brits preeminence
in the matter of tea—which, after all, comes down
to little more than the ability to boil water.
                                        WILFRID SHEED

I did a picture in England one winter and it was
so cold I almost got married. SHELLEY WINTERS

A fundamental difference between the U.S. and
Britain is in Britain, no one will talk unless he has
a reason and in America, no one will stop talking
unless he has a reason.   CLIVE JAMES

Trousers—it's such a stumbling word. It epito-
mizes the British bumbling and inability to be
streamlined and coherent. In the States they have
pants and jeans, but in England we still have
trousers.   ROGER RUSKIN SPEAR

The national sport of England is obstacle racing.
People fill their rooms with useless and cumber-
some furniture, and spend the rest of their lives
trying to dodge it. HERBERT BEERBOHM TREE

This is a very horrible country, England. We invented the Macintosh, you know. We invented the
flasher, the voyeur. That's what the press is about.
                                    MALCOLM MCCLAREN

So little, England. Little music. Little art. Timid.
Tasteful. Nice.   ALAN BENNETT

I would like to live in Manchester, England. The
transition between Manchester and death would
be unnoticeable.   MARK TWAIN

In England ... education produces no effect
whatsoever. If it did, it would prove a serious danger to the upper classes, and would probably lead
to acts of violence in Grosvenor Square.
                                    OSCAR WILDE

If England treats her criminals the way she has treated me, she doesn't deserve to have any.

OSCAR WILDE

The Englishman has all the qualities of a poker except its occasional warmth.

DANIEL O'CONNELL

The English are not a very spiritual people, so they invented cricket to give them some idea of eternity.

GEORGE BERNARD SHAW

We English are good at forgiving our enemies; it releases us from the obligation of liking our friends.

P. D. JAMES

You should study the Peerage. . . . It is the best thing in fiction the English have ever done.

OSCAR WILDE

I like the English. They have the most rigid code of immorality in the world.

MALCOLM BRADBURY

One matter Englishmen don't think in the least funny is their happy consciousness of possessing a deep sense of humor.

MARSHALL MCLUHAN

An Englishman does everything on principle: he fights you on patriotic principles; he robs you on business principles; he enslaves you on imperial principles.　GEORGE BERNARD SHAW

> Englishwomen's shoes look as if they had been made by someone who had often heard shoes described but who had never seen any.
> MARGARET HALSEY

I think it is owing to the good sense of the English that they have not painted better.
WILLIAM HOGARTH

> The most dangerous thing in the world is to make a friend of an Englishman, because he'll come sleep in your closet rather than spend ten shillings on a hotel.　TRUMAN CAPOTE

If you eliminate smoking and gambling, you will be amazed to find that almost all an Englishman's pleasures can be, and mostly are, shared by his dog.　GEORGE BERNARD SHAW

> It is quite untrue that English people don't appreciate music. They may not understand it but they absolutely love the noise it makes.
> SIR THOMAS BEECHAM

Even today, well brought-up English girls are taught by their mothers to boil all veggies for at least a month and a half, just in case one of the dinner guests turns up without his teeth.

CALVIN TRILLIN

The English find ill-health not only interesting but respectable and often experience death in the effort to avoid a fuss. PAMELA FRANKAU

There is something remarkably and peculiarly English about the passion for sitting on damp seats watching open-air drama ... only the English have mastered the art of being truly uncomfortable while facing up to culture. SHERIDAN MORLEY

From every Englishman emanates a kind of gas,
The deadly choke-damp of boredom.

HEINRICH HEINE

The English have no respect for their language. It is impossible for an Englishman to open his mouth without making some other Englishman despise him. GEORGE BERNARD SHAW

Americans want to be loved; the English want to be obeyed. QUENTIN CRISP

DAVE BARRY

Passages

JW: *Dave, you're a member of the baby-boom generation, and the things you write about tend to mirror the experiences of your contemporaries.*

DB: Yes, being born in 1947 was the smartest marketing decision I ever made.

JW: *Your work has a "Dave Barry's Passages" aspect, dealing with everything from birth and childhood to middle age and what you call "geezerhood." For example, you've complained that they've changed the rules on having a baby.*

DB: Yes, it's really alarming to me what they've done. The old system of having a baby was much better than the new system, the old system being characterized by the fact that the man didn't have to watch. In the new system you not only have to watch, you have to sit around in a room with people you don't even know and openly discuss things like the uterus. I'm against it. A lot of good people were born under the old system—I was, Dwight Eisenhower was.

JW: *What about the delivery itself?*

DB: When our son was born, I sort of focused on my wife's head. Basically there were two parts of my wife in the delivery room, the head and everything else. The everything else part, there were hundreds of people involved. People we had never seen before. They brought in, like, *tour buses* of people. "Over here, take a look at this." I don't know what was going on in there, but my wife was—my wife's head was—making some pretty awful noises.

And when we brought Robert home from the hospital, I was surprised at his output as opposed to his input. You can put one ounce of beets into the child, and the child will keep putting stuff out for days—from several orifices. It's kind of like the miracle of cold fusion.

JW: *How old is Robert now?*

DB: He's ten. I'm amazed how much little boys are like poltergeists: You don't see them do it, but they'll stand in the middle of a room—one little boy—and there'll be noise from everywhere, things flying off shelves—and you don't know how they do it.

And their attention spans are very limited—comparable to a gnat's. No, gnats are probably a lot better. I'd rather take a group of gnats to a skating rink for a birthday party than a group of ten-year-olds. On Robert's last birthday I took him and a group of his friends to one of those go-cart tracks. Watching them out there I felt like calling the state legislature to warn them not to issue them driver's licenses under any circumstances. For God's sake, keep these people away from vehicles.

JW: *And you've still got the teenage years to look forward to.*

DB: And everybody tells me they're worse. But I've noticed that one thing about parents is that no matter what stage your child is in, the parents who have older children always tell you the next stage is worse. I could picture great-great-grandparents saying, "How old is your child? Eighty-seven? Wait till he's eighty-nine. You wouldn't believe it."

JW: *What about the financial burden of being a parent?*

DB: Every third day you read an article that says by the time *your* kid wants to go to college, it's going to cost you more than the national debt. What do people do, stop eating for four years?

JW: *And you've pointed out that hair gel alone will run you thousands of dollars.*

DB: It's scary when your child stops dressing exactly the way you tell him to and starts developing fashion concepts of his own. They have the same taste in fashion that they have in TV viewing. And of course, underlying all your anguish about this is the knowledge that you did all the same things to your own parents and therefore you have no right to dictate your child's haircut.

So he got one of those haircuts that looks like there's a sea urchin clinging to his head.

JW: *Does he have an earring?*

DB: No, God, please, *sssh, sssh*. And the thing is, if I try to be cool and tell him he can get an earring, he'll get a *nose* ring. Or by the time my son is in high school it will be nose bones, or something like that. It'll be just like when I came home with long hair: we'll have to sit around at Thanksgiving and pretend that my son doesn't have a nose bone.

JW: *In one of your books you confess to being increasingly worried about the condition of your gums. Is that a sign of middle age?*

DB: I would say so, yes. That and the fact that gradually, without noticing it, you turn into a Republican and judge everything on the basis of whether or not it will increase your taxes. And for me another sign is saying things to my son that I thought were hilarious when my father said them to me: "Don't do that, you'll put somebody's eye out!"

But if you put on a scale all the things you cared about when you were twenty-one and all the things you care about now, the two key elements being sex and gums, the scales would slowly tip in the favor of gums, the older you get. I think probably by the time I'm sixty or sixty-five, I'll have joined a religion based on gums, I'll be so concerned about them. See, the dental profession has really let us down. Everything they ever told us was a lie and it—how old are you, Jon?

JW: *I'm your age, Dave.*

DB: Well, then you know. All that time we brushed seventy-three minutes after every meal and thought our teeth would be in great shape, they never told us about flossing. They never even mentioned it. We brushed and brushed with an effective decay-preventive dentifrice, but we never flossed. And now everybody our age has enormous tooth problems. Right?

JW: *Right, and it becomes an obsession. Do you have an Interplak?*

DB: I don't have an Interplak, but I've got a WaterPik.

JW: *I'm afraid you're using outmoded technology.*

DB: What's an Interplak?

JW: *Well, whereas the WaterPik shoots water, apparently—*

DB: Yes, it's a WaterPik. If it shot kerosene, it would be a KerosenePik.

JW: *... the Interplak is actually an electrified toothbrush.*

DB: Oh yes, I've seen ads for that. It looks like an electric toothbrush to me. Big deal.

JW: *Except that thousands of tiny bristles—*

DB: I know, there's a patented action, right?

JW: *Right.*

DB: I bet you also buy the new razor blade with alum on it. Every six months they improve the shaving experience. I've been meaning to do a column about shaving breakthroughs for years. I go way, way back to when they first started doing safety razor commercials. They keep coming up with those incredible shaving breakthroughs, but shaving is still a pain in the butt.

JW: *Do you remember when they introduced the Wilkinson Sword Blade? It was going to revolutionize shaving.*

DB: And now everybody has the one with two blades: The first blade pulls the whiskers up—

JW: *... and the second blade snaps the whiskers off! But to get back* *to aging, you've written that the mid-life crisis is generally triggered when a male realizes one day that he has devoted his entire life to something he hates.*

DB: Which is true of almost every guy I know, though some of them haven't admitted it to themselves yet. Most of them are successful and worked very hard to get there. It's like, when they were twenty-two they said, "What do I really, really hate? I'm going to become *that*." Particularly lawyers. You'd think there would be enough advance warning: No one likes lawyers, so why would you deliberately set out to be one? It's like saying, "I'm going to be a leper when I grow up." And yet all these people go out and pay money to go to law school, and then they become really depressed about it and they have mid-life crises. I'm the only person I know who hasn't had one.

JW: *Why do you think you've been spared?*

DB: I've been really busy. Also, I just tend to be late. I'm just getting to puberty.

JW: *Do you have any advice for women whose husbands are going through mid-life crisis?*

DB: The key here is understanding. If the husband wants to drive a fancy sports car, let him drive a fancy sports car. If he wants to wear gold jewelry, let him wear gold jewelry. If he wants to see other women, shoot him in the head.

Women don't seem to have mid-life crises, and I still don't understand why that is. They just keep battling away. Maybe women are intelligent enough to accept that they're actually getting older, so they try a new makeup—

JW: *While driving.*

DB: Here in Miami, women actually have plastic surgery while driving.

JW: *Another part of growing older is investing your money for retirement, so you've taken it upon yourself to explain various investment vehicles, including the stock market.*

DB: It's a proven Investment Concept, the stock market. Basically you give your money to a stockbroker, who takes some of it right away, so right there we see that your money is going to work. And then he buys stock, which is identified in code in the newspaper. Every day you look it up and you see things like, "The stock market is off today, as many large investors found spots on their underwear." And you watch it some more and it goes down and down and then you call the stockbroker and he sells it and he keeps some more money. And that's your stock market, as far as I can tell. I don't know anybody who has ever made money on the stock market.

JW: *You did a great public service by publishing the self-test questionnaire from the life insurance institute.*

DB: Right. The test consists of three questions: "1. How much insurance do you have? 2. You need more. 3. We'll send somebody over right now." That's always been the way it's been with my life insurance. I've never had my life insurance guy call to say, "Dave, you've got too much life insurance. Let's cut back on it. I'm going to mail *you* some money, Dave."

JW: *And how does Social Security work?*

DB: It's a great idea. Basically the way it works is they take money away from you and they give it to older people, including older people who are so wealthy they use the money to buy sun hats for their racehorses. The idea here is to transfer as much wealth as possible from you to somebody else, which is the idea of, as far as I can tell, the entire government. The theory is that when *you* become an old person, this program will work for you. The problem is that since you didn't have any children—you couldn't afford it because you were giving all your money to old people buying sun hats for their racehorses—there won't *be* any young people to support you, so the entire system will be depending on, like, seventeen kids working at Burger King.

JW: *And then there are the joys of retirement like golf, fishing—*

DB: A great sport, golf. I tried it once, until I ran out of balls, which was somewhere around the first or second tee. I didn't think it was possible for you to swing your club in one direction and have the ball, in defiance of all the laws of physics that I'm familiar with, go in pretty much the opposite direction. The really great thing about golf—and this is the reason why a lot of health experts like me recommend it—you can drink beer and ride in a cart while you play. I just don't get the part about the clubs and the ball. So maybe I'll just do the cart and the beer end of it. Kind of like a specialist.

JW: *You can drink beer while fishing too, can't you?*

DB: Absolutely. And there again, the mistake a lot of people make is they actually put fishing equipment in the boat, which creates the danger that you'll actually wind up with a fish in the boat with you, and some of those things will kill you. I don't want to suggest that fishermen are stupid, but have you ever seen what they put on the hook expecting fish to bite it? It's not food, it's the most digusting thing in the world. I was actually scuba diving once and saw bait. We were in a reef area where people were fishing nearby, and this hook with bait on it drifted down—and the fish were almost laughing! They all probably would have liked to have evolved little hands so they could hold their little bellies.

JW: *What else is there to look forward to upon retirement?*

DB: The joys of geezerhood. Geezer fashion, for example. There's a geezer look that we see a lot down here in Miami. For one thing, you want to show a lot of armpit. I don't think there's anything more visually appealing to other people than an old guy's armpit. Old guys like to wear big, baggy undershirts. And Bermuda shorts that would easily hold not only the guy but seven or eight Labrador retrievers—comfortably—cinched up as high as possible—nice and tight up around the chest area. And of course, a guy's got to have knee socks and a pair of wing tips. And a hat. Your older guy should wear a hat at all times, in the bed, in the shower. The hat identifies him when he's driving, by the way. Whenever you're behind a person going eight miles an hour on an interstate, the guy will always be wearing a hat.

Now, a geezer wants to drive as slow as possible. A true geezer driver will pick a speed ahead of time, say, seventeen miles an hour, and drive that speed under all conceivable conditions, no matter where, no matter what. With the turn signal on. A geezer will put the turn signal on when he buys the car and then just leave it on until he trades it in.

JW: *Is there a standard geezer car?*

DB: The geezer car is actually three to four normal-size cars welded together. It should be much bigger than anything else on the road, or even the road itself. The hood should be so big that it's impossible for the driver to tell what lane he's in, sometimes even what zip code he's in, by merely looking out the window. Planes could take off and land on the hood of the geezer car.

JW: *Among your favorite subjects is Miami, where you've lived with your wife and son for several years. I gather you're still adjusting to life there.*

DB: Well, you're permanently adjusting to Miami because entire new populations wash ashore every day here. It's a challenge for most Americans to visit Miami because it's bilingual. I still don't know what the other language is besides Spanish. To me that's the adventure of it. It's a lot like being in a foreign country in that you're always trying to figure out what exactly is going on. I like it.

JW: *You seem obsessed by the insects there.*

DB: Yeah, well, *you* say I'm obsessed by the insects, but that's because you don't, on your way to work every morning—and I'm only talking about walking across my backyard—confront spiders that in any other area would be registered with the department of motor vehicles. Or I'll just be walking along and reach for the doorknob and there will be a grasshopper the size of a weimaraner sitting on it, just saying, "Yeah, go ahead. Touch me, buddy. Yeah, go ahead, touch me."

JW: *As a successful author, you've had to do those grueling book tours. Do you like to travel?*

DB: Absolutely not. Especially air travel. First, it should be a law that the pilot has to be older than me. Also, why do they go to all that trouble to make sure you don't have a weapon and then give you a dinner roll that you could easily kill a person with?: "Take this plane to Cuba or I'm going to hit you with this roll." And how do they get the crying babies on there? It's got to be an incredible logistical problem to get a crying baby on every plane you ever take. I've been on flights where they've had to hold the plane until the crying baby arrived: "Sorry, we're going to have to wait here ten minutes, the crying baby isn't here yet." There's a crying-baby facility at every airport, and they bring extras in on really busy days. But sometimes you have a breakdown in the system, the baby won't cry, and you have to get another one.

JW: *How do they insure the baby will be seated directly behind you?*

DB: They use the computer to do that.

JW: *And what about the confusing fares?*

DB: You can have 380 people on an aircraft going to the same place and no two of them will have paid the same fare. This is a product of deregulation, under which anybody who can produce two forms of identification is allowed to own an airline. People who used to be in the concrete business are buying airlines: "Do we need all four engines running *all* the time? Can't we cut back on that? And why can't the pilots serve the drinks?"

And under deregulation, they've been obliged to lower the average IQ of the passengers, which is clear from the way they find their seats, or fail to find their seats. Have you ever watched people get on airplanes? They're holding a thing that clearly says "Seat 3A" and they stare at it and stare at it, and some malignant force from another planet tells them, "Go sit in Seat 8F." And then everyone on the plane has to change.

JW: *Do you have a favorite seat on the plane?*

DB: Yes, I like to sit in a seat in first class—without paying for it.

JW: *In your history of the United States,* Dave Barry Slept Here, *you changed the way history will be taught for generations to come. It involves the dates—*

DB: Yes, over the years I got tired of reading story after story about how American students are stupid. Every year they'd say, "We're even stupider than we were last year. Now we're not only behind the Japanese and the Germans and the French, we're actually behind a lot of species of animals." So I asked myself, What can we do? Obviously the kids aren't capable of learning more, and we can't get smarter kids, so let's make history dumber. One of the problems with history when I was a kid was that it was very poorly organized in the sense that you had all these different dates. Whoever thought this system up was just not thinking about the kids. So I developed a system where every date would be October 8th. You can't miss with this system. The children always know it was October 8th. Even July 4th falls on October 8th.

JW: *With the only important date being October 8th, what does that do to your holidays?*

DB: That's a good question! Well, one way to deal with it, we could just have no other holidays at all and then have an enormous party on October 8th, and not go back to work again until, like, May 9th. That would be a good way to handle it.

JW: *Why did you choose October 8th?*

DB: It's my son's birthday. We ought to extend the same principle to math. Think how easy math would be if the answer were always 4. Not to toot my own horn, but I think I ought to get the Nobel Prize for this.

JW: *Speaking of prizes, how did you react to winning a Pulitzer?*

DB: I figured it was just one more indication of the nation's drug problem. When we get to this point, you have to ask yourself, "Shouldn't we all just move to Australia?"

Dave Barry is a nationally syndicated columnist. His books include Dave Barry Talks Back, Dave Barry Turns 40, *and* Dave Barry Slept Here.

QUOTES ON "I"

————IDEAS————

I can't understand why people are frightened of
new ideas. I'm frightened of the old ones.

JOHN CAGE

————IDIOT————

Idiot, *n.* A member of a large and powerful tribe
whose influence in human affairs has always been
dominant and controlling.   AMBROSE BIERCE

————IGNORANCE————

Any frontal attack on ignorance is bound to fail
because the masses are always ready to defend
their most precious possession—their ignorance.

HENDRIK VAN LOON

Ignorance is like a delicate exotic fruit; touch it
and the bloom is gone.   OSCAR WILDE

————IMMORTALITY————

If I have any beliefs about immortality, it is that
certain dogs I have known will go to heaven, and
very, very few persons.   JAMES THURBER

INANIMATE OBJECTS

Inanimate objects are classified scientifically into three major categories—those that don't work, those that break down and those that get lost.

RUSSELL BAKER

INFORMATION

Everybody gets so much information all day long that they lose their common sense.

GERTRUDE STEIN

INSIDER

You can be a rank insider as well as a rank outsider.

ROBERT FROST

INSTANT GRATIFICATION

Instant gratification takes too long.

CARRIE FISHER

INTELLECTUALS

Intellectuals are people who believe that ideas are of more importance than values. That is to say, their own ideas and other people's values.

GERALD BRENAN

INTELLIGENCE

There is no such thing as an underestimate of average intelligence.　　　HENRY ADAMS

INTELLIGENCE SERVICE

An intelligence service is, in fact, a stupidity service.　　　E. B. WHITE

INTELLIGENTSIA

A large section of the intelligentsia seems wholly devoid of intelligence.　　　G. K. CHESTERTON

IRELAND AND THE IRISH

Every St. Patrick's Day every Irishman goes out to find another Irishman to make a speech to.
　　　SHANE LESLIE

Other people have a nationality. The Irish and the Jews have a psychosis.　　　BRENDAN BEHAN

IRONY

Irony is the hygiene of the mind.
　　　ELIZABETH BIBESCO

QUOTES ON "J"

JOIE DE VIVRE

Over the years I have developed a distaste for the spectacle of joie de vivre, the knack of knowing how to live. Not that I disapprove of all hearty enjoyment of life. A flushed sense of happiness can overtake a person anywhere, and one is no more to blame for it than the Asiatic flu or a sudden benevolent change in the weather (which is often joy's immediate cause). No, what rankles me is the stylization of this private condition into a bullying social ritual.

The French, who have elevated the picnic to their highest rite, are probably most responsible for promoting this smugly upbeat, flaunting style. It took the French genius for formalizing the in-formal to bring sticky sacramental sanctity to the baguette, wine, and cheese.   PHILLIP LOPATE

JOURNALISM

The only qualities for real success in journalism are ratlike cunning, a plausible manner and a little literary ability. The capacity to steal other people's ideas and phrases . . . is also invaluable.

NICHOLAS TOMALIN

A professional whose business it is to explain to
others what it personally does not understand.

LORD NORTHCLIFFE

The First Law of Journalism: to confirm existing
prejudice, rather than contradict it.

ALEXANDER COCKBURN

Once a newspaper touches a story, the facts are
lost forever, even to the protagonists.

NORMAN MAILER

The public have an insatiable curiosity to know
everything. Except what is worth knowing. Journalism, conscious of this, and having tradesman-
like habits, supplies their demands.

OSCAR WILDE

Trying to be a first-rate reporter on the average
American newspaper is like trying to play Bach's
St. Matthew Passion on a ukelele: the instrument
is too crude for the work, for the audience and
for the performer.   BEN BAGDIKIAN

————JOURNALISTS————

The lowest depth to which people can sink before
God is defined by the word *journalist*. If I were a
father and had a daughter who was seduced I

should not despair over her; I would hope for her salvation. But if I had a son who became a journalist, and continued to be one for five years, I would give him up. KIERKEGAARD

I believe in equality for everyone, except reporters and photographers. GANDHI

————JUDGES————

Judge: a law student who marks his own papers. H. L. MENCKEN

Appellate Division judges are whores who became madams. MARTIN ERDMANN

————JUNK BONDS————

How does something like this happen? How do people spend ten years buying and selling something with *junk* in the name, and then say, "Oh, my God, you mean those weren't good investments? They sounded so *great*! Junk bonds. We thought we couldn't go wrong with a name like that." JOE BOB BRIGGS

The only time to buy these is on a day with no "y" in it. WARREN BUFFETT

QUOTES ON "L"

LANGUAGE

I personally think we developed language because
of our deep need to complain.   LILY TOMLIN

LAWS

All laws are an attempt to domesticate the natural
ferocity of the species.   JOHN W. GARDNER

LAWYERS

An incompetent attorney can delay a trial for
months or years. A competent attorney can delay
one even longer.   EVELLE J. YOUNGER

Lawyers and tarts are the two oldest professions
in the world. And we always aim to please.
HORACE RUMPOLE (JOHN MORTIMER)

Lawyers as a group are no more dedicated to jus-
tice or public service than a private public utility
is dedicated to giving light.   DAVID MELINKOFF

What's black and white and brown and looks good
on a lawyer? A doberman.   MORDECAI RICHLER

LEGOS

Everyone who ever walked barefoot into his child's room late at night hates Legos. I think Mr. Lego should be strung up from a scaffold made of his horrid little pockmarked arch-puncturing plastic cubes. TONY KORNHEISER

LETTERS TO THE EDITOR

Anyone nit-picking enough to write a letter of correction to an editor doubtless deserves the error that provoked it. ALVIN TOFFLER

LIBERALS

Liberals are very broadminded: they are always willing to give careful consideration to both sides of the same side. ANONYMOUS

LIBRARIANS

On librarians I do speak with prejudice. The profession in general has always seemed to me like the legitimization and financing of an impulse to collect old socks. JOHN CHEEVER

LIFE

You fall out of your mother's womb, you crawl across open country under fire, and drop into your grave. QUENTIN CRISP

When you don't have any money, the problem is food. When you have money, it's sex. When you have both, it's health. If everything is simply jake, then you're frightened of death. J. P. DONLEAVY

For most men life is a search for the proper manila envelope in which to get themselves filed.
CLIFTON FADIMAN

Life is a long lesson in humility.
JAMES M. BARRIE

Life—the way it really is—is a battle not between Bad and Good but between Bad and Worse.
JOSEPH BRODSKY

When we remember we are all mad, the mysteries disappear and life stands explained.
MARK TWAIN

Life would be tolerable but for its amusements.
GEORGE BERNARD SHAW

Not a shred of evidence exists in favor of the idea that life is serious. BRENDAN GILL

LIMOUSINES

Limousines used to be reserved for the ruling class
or, on special occasions, for the working class.
Today, limousines are like taxicabs with the door
handles still intact. ERMA BOMBECK

LIQUID DIETS

The powder is mixed with water and tastes exactly
like powder mixed with water. ART BUCHWALD

LITERATURE

Never judge a book by its movie. J. W. EAGAN

LITIGATION

I have now turned fifty and am going through
menopause and I enjoy a little litigation. It's costly,
perhaps, but salutary, and considerably less expensive than keeping racehorses or getting married.
GORE VIDAL

LOGIC

Logic is like the sword: those who appeal to it shall
perish by it. SAMUEL BUTLER

LONDON

In London they don't like you if you're still alive.
HARVEY FIERSTEIN

It is a geometropolitan predicament rather than a
city. You can no more administer it than you could
administer the solar system.   JONATHAN MILLER

L.A. you pass through and get a hamburger.
                                    JOHN LENNON

Double Dubuque.   H. ALLEN SMITH

The Queen of the Angles.   IAN SHOALES

————LOVE————

Love is like epidemic diseases. The more one fears
it the more likely one is to contract it.
                                    NICOLAS CHAMFORT

Love is more pleasant than marriage for the same
reason that novels are more amusing than history.
                                    NICOLAS CHAMFORT

Ah—love—the walks over soft grass, the smiles over
candlelight, the arguments over just about everything else.   MAX HEADROOM

Love is an exploding cigar we willingly smoke.
                                    LYNDA BARRY

People in love, it is well known, suffer extreme conceptual delusions; the most common of these being that other people find your condition as thrilling and eye-watering as you do yourselves.

JULIAN BARNES

Oh life is a glorious cycle
    of song,
A medley of extemporanea;
And love is a thing that can
    never go wrong;
And I am Marie of Romania.   DOROTHY PARKER

LUCK

I believe in luck: how else can you explain the success of those you dislike?   JEAN COCTEAU

LYING

Lying increases the creative faculties, expands the ego, and lessens the frictions of social contacts.

CLARE BOOTHE LUCE

Carlyle said, "A lie cannot live"; it shows he did not know how to tell them.   MARK TWAIN

QUOTES ON "M"

MAINE

As Maine goes, so goes Vermont.

JAMES A. FARLEY

THE MAJORITY

Whenever you find that you are on the side of the majority, it is time to reform.   MARK TWAIN

MALE BONDING

Can't anything be done about that klunky phrase *male bonding*? What kind of people invent phrases like *male bonding*? Can't anything be done about them, like cutting off their research grants or making them read Keats until they pick up a little respect for the felicitous phrase? RUSSELL BAKER

MAN

A man is the sum of his ancestors; to reform him you must begin with a dead ape and work downward through a million graves.

AMBROSE BIERCE

It is even harder for the average ape to believe
that he has descended from man.

> H. L. MENCKEN

Why did Nature create man? Was it to show that
she is big enough to make mistakes, or was it pure
ignorance? HOLBROOK JACKSON

The proof that man is the noblest of all creatures
is that no other creature has ever denied it.

> G. C. LICHTENBERG

Man is a rational animal who always loses his tem-
per when called upon to act in accordance with
the dictates of reason. ORSON WELLES

Man is an intelligence in servitude to his organs.

> ALDOUS HUXLEY

Man is the only animal that can remain on friendly
terms with the victims he intends to eat until he
eats them. SAMUEL BUTLER

MANKIND

I hate mankind, for I think myself one of the best
of them, and I know how bad I am.

> SAMUEL JOHNSON

If all mankind were to disappear, the world would regenerate back to the rich state of equilibrium that existed ten thousand years ago. If insects were to vanish, the environment would collapse into chaos.　　　　　　　　EDWARD O. WILSON

———MARRIAGE———

Marriage succeeds love as smoke does a flame.
　　　　　　　　NICOLAS CHAMFORT

The conception of two people living together for twenty-five years without having a cross word suggests a lack of spirit only to be admired in sheep.
　　　　　　　　ALAN PATRICK HERBERT

I love being married. It's so great to find that one special person you want to annoy for the rest of your life.　　　　　　　　RITA RUDNER

We were happily married for eight months. Unfortunately, we were married for four and a half years.　　　　　　　　NICK FALDO

If variety is the spice of life, marriage is the big can of leftover Spam.　　　　　JOHNNY CARSON

I don't understand the appeal of Spuds McKenzie. He's always surrounded by beautiful women. Now, I'm single, and I know the pickin's can be mighty slim, but you have to be really desperate to date out of your species. SUSAN NORFLEET

————MEANINGFUL————

The word *meaningful* when used today is nearly always meaningless. PAUL JOHNSON

————THE MEDIA————

The media. It sounds like a convention of spiritualists. TOM STOPPARD

————MEDICINE————

Medicine, *n*. A stone flung down the Bowery to kill a dog in Broadway. AMBROSE BIERCE

————THE MEEK————

Pity the meek, for they shall inherit the earth. DON MARQUIS

The meek shall inherit the earth, but not the mineral rights. J. PAUL GETTY

Meetings are indispensable when you don't want to do anything.   JOHN KENNETH GALBRAITH

Meetings are an addictive, highly self-indulgent activity that corporations and other large organizations habitually engage in only because they cannot actually masturbate.   DAVE BARRY

——————MEMORY——————

Why is it that our memory is good enough to retain the least triviality that happens to us, and yet not good enough to recollect how often we have told it to the same person?
LA ROCHEFOUCAULD

Nothing fixes a thing so intensely in the memory as the wish to forget it.   MONTAIGNE

I can remember when the air was clean and sex was dirty.   GEORGE BURNS

——————MEN——————

All men are frauds. The only difference between them is that some admit it. I myself deny it.
H. L. MENCKEN

The average man does not know what to do with his life, yet wants another one which will last forever. ANATOLE FRANCE

The only thing worse than a man you can't control is a man you can. MARGO KAUFMAN

MIAMI

We had elected to move voluntarily to Miami. We wanted our child to benefit from the experience of growing up in a community that is constantly being enriched by a diverse and ever-changing infusion of tropical diseases. Also they have roaches down there you could play polo with.

DAVE BARRY

MISSIONARIES

When the missionaries came to Africa they had the Bible and we had the land. They said, "Let us pray." We closed our eyes. When we opened them we had the Bible and they had the land.

BISHOP DESMOND TUTU

MISUNDERSTANDING

It is by universal misunderstanding that all agree. For if, by ill luck, people understood each other, they would never agree. CHARLES BAUDELAIRE

MODERATION

Moderation is a fatal thing: nothing succeeds like
excess.   OSCAR WILDE

MODERN ARCHITECTURE

The [Birmingham, England] Central Library looks
like a place where books are incinerated, not kept.
                                        PRINCE OF WALES

MODERN ART

Skill without imagination is craftsmanship and
gives us many useful objects such as wickerwork
picnic baskets. Imagination without skill gives us
modern art.   TOM STOPPARD

MONEY

Money, to be worth striving for, must have blood
and perspiration on it—preferably that of someone
else.   WILSON MIZNER

I'm tired of love, I'm still more tired of rhyme,
but money gives me pleasure all the time.
                                          HILAIRE BELLOC

MORALITY

There is no moral precept that does not have something inconvenient about it.

DENIS DIDEROT

MORNING

The average, healthy, well-adjusted adult gets up at seven-thirty in the morning feeling just plain terrible.

JEAN KERR

MOTHER

Why do grandparents and grandchildren get along so well? They have the same enemy—the mother.

CLAUDETTE COLBERT

MOVIES

Movies are one of the bad habits that have corrupted our century. They have slipped into the American mind more misinformation in one evening than the Dark Ages could muster in a decade.

BEN HECHT

The movies are the only business where you can go out front and applaud yourself.

WILL ROGERS

There's only one thing that can kill the movies, and that's education. WILL ROGERS

It is my indignant opinion that ninety percent of the moving pictures exhibited in America are so vulgar, witless and dull that it is preposterous to write about them in any publication not intended to be read while chewing gum. WOLCOTT GIBBS

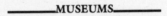

MUSEUMS

Visiting museums bastardizes the personality just as hobnobbing with priests makes you lose your faith. MAURICE VLAMINCK

MUSIC

Classical music is the kind we keep thinking will turn into a tune. KIN HUBBARD

There are two kinds of music—good music and bad music. Good music is music that I want to hear. Bad music is music that I don't want to hear. FRAN LEBOWITZ

Extraordinary how potent cheap music is. NOEL COWARD

Music makes one feel so romantic—at least it always got on one's nerves—which is the same thing nowadays.
OSCAR WILDE

I hate music, especially when it's played.
JIMMY DURANTE

The public doesn't want new music; the main thing it demands of a composer is that he be dead.
ARTHUR HONEGGER

———MUSICOLOGIST———

A musicologist is a man who can read music but can't hear it.
SIR THOMAS BEECHAM

FLORENCE KING

Go Away

JW: *Do you consider yourself a curmudgeon? A misanthrope? A reactionary?*

FK: I have been a misanthrope for as long as I can remember, but I didn't know it because I never heard the word until I read Moliere's *Le Misanthrope* in college. As a child I simply thought of myself as "different." As an adolescent I preferred "aloof" and as a young adult going through my Ayn Rand stage I called myself "objective." When the Randian heat wore off I settled for "loner."

The beginning of self-knowledge came when I discovered Shakespeare's *Timon of Athens*, who won my heart because he had "Go Away" carved on his tombstone—just the sort of thing I would do. I looked Timon up in Plutarch's *Lives* and found that *misanthrope* was also an English word—up till then I thought it was French.

All misanthropes are curmudgeons, but all curmudgeons are not misanthropes. I'm the real McCoy. I agree with Sartre that "hell is other people," but I also agree with Jonathan Swift, who said, "I hate and despise the animal called Mankind, but I like the occasional Tom, Dick, and Harry."

A reactionary? Of course; misanthropy is by definition an illiberal stance. It's the only means left to be against everything Martin Sheen is for.

JW: *You've written a book about misanthropy.*

FK: Firsthand, behind-the-scenes information is the kind America likes. Not unmindful of other portions of the equine anatomy, we are the land of the horse's mouth. Alcoholics write books about alcoholism, drug addicts write books about drug addiction, madams write books about madaming, so I wrote a book about misanthropy.

JW: *You've been called "the thinking man's redneck"*—

FK: The thinking man desperately needs a redneck, so it might as well be me.

JW: *You appear on the cover of one of your books brandishing a semi-automatic pistol. What are you, some kind of gun nut?*

FK: Not really. I'm not the hobby type, and God knows I'm not the outdoors type. I simply like guns because you can't shoot people without them. Criminals have declared war on America and I have declared war on criminals. Anybody who messes with me had better be prepared to carry his ass home in a bucket.

JW: *On the back cover of the same book, it says that you don't suffer fools gladly. What are the consequences of that attitude, to both you and the fools?*

FK: The consequences to the fools? I don't suffer fools and I like to see fools suffer. The consequences to me? "He who tells the truth must have one foot in the stirrup." Old Armenian proverb.

JW: *Do you regret not having married and had children?*

FK: At this point in my life I would rather be dead than married. Occasionally in my naive youth, I thought it would be nice to be married so I could have regular sex without a lot of distraction and bother, but as time went on, it began to dawn on me that marriage was the least efficient source of what I wanted. As for not having had children, let's put it this way: My hero is Good King Herod. I have never understood child molestation because in order to molest a child, you have to be in the same room with a child, and I don't know how perverts stand it.

JW: *You've referred to radical left-wing female gay rights activists as a "gang of muff-diving Druids." What do you have against them?*

FK: They have so politicized sex that it's gone from raucous to caucus.

JW: *You've been critical of yuppies in a variety of ways. For example, you've likened yuppie nutrition to a mortification of the flesh. What are they trying to atone for?*

FK: Those who have lost their characters have nothing left but their bodies to make them feel like good people. Intense, obsessive interest in health, nutrition, and exercise arouses my suspicions. I distrust anybody who worries too much about such things. I take my leaf from Seneca: "Scorn pain. Either it will go away or you will."

JW: *Has the American male changed since 1978, when you published*
He: An Irreverent Look at the American Male?

FK: He's no longer a wimp, he's a state-of-the-art pussy. Molly Yard should be declared a common scold and subjected to the ducking stool. That woman looks like a stubbed toe and behaves like a little old tennis shoe among ladies.

JW: *What else is wrong with America today?*

FK: We worship education but hate learning. We worship success but hate the successful. We worship fame but hate the famous. We are a nation of closet misanthropes, which is why I decided to "come out," so to speak. There's no national glue holding us together because somebody put too much pluribus in the unum. Our fabled Great Diversity is so divisive that every president is forced to be a fence-straddling "moderate"—we literally make a strong man weak.

JW: *What can we do about it?*

FK: Nothing. We'll have to wait until it collapses and then start all over again. It won't be long now.

JW: *You've defined democracy as "the crude leading the crud." What form of government would you prefer?*

FK: I believe in absolute monarchy and the divine right of kings. One thing I like about Bloody Mary: She never nagged her sub-

---

jects about lung cancer. I would much rather be at the mercy of someone with the power to say, "Off with her head!" than be nibbled to death by a bureaucratic duck.

JW: *If called upon, would you "support, protect, and defend" the Constitution of the United States?*

FK: The Constitution as written and intended no longer exists, so I can't very well support it. I would fight to restore it, to wrest it from the clutches of ACLU types who are using it as a cover for their collectivist-egalitarian agenda.

JW: *Where do you stand on prayer and sex education in the schools?*

FK: I'm for prayer in the schools because ritual and ceremony are calming and civilizing, and the little fartlings should be tamped down whenever possible.

I am against sex ed in schools because sex is more fun when it's dirty and sinful.

JW: *You've been variously critical of agents, publishers, and editors, from which I gather that you're not enamored of the publishing business.*

FK: I'm enamored of my agent, Mel Berger, who is one of the few people in the world for whom I feel warm affection—he's Tom, Dick, and Harry rolled into one. I also like my publisher and my editor. It's copy editors I hate because I've been burned by them too often, like the one who thought the Cavaliers and Roundheads were football teams, or the one who found my opinions too strong and softened them by adding "alas and alack." The bitch *rewrote* me.

Most copy editors are free-lancers and female, which is a large part of the problem. More and more women want a flexible work-at-home arrangement so they can take care of their kids, but if they expect me to feel compassion for them, they have their Florences mixed up: I'm King, not Nightingale, and I don't want my manuscript competing with a screaming brat because I know which gets priority.

Ideally, copy editors should fit the description in Mary McCarthy's *The Group*: "Old maids mostly, with a pencil behind their ear and dyspepsia. We've got a crackerjack here, Miss Chambers. Vinegary type."

Obviously a job for me, which is why I do my own.

JW: *How do you feel about doing author tours to promote your books?*
FK: Being a citizen of the Republic of Nice, the person I most admire and wish to emulate is the man who died on the "Dick Cavett Show." I forget his name but it doesn't matter; to a veteran of book-promotion tours who has walked through the valley of the shadow of Happy Talk, he will go down in history as the Man Who Got Even.

I will never go on the "Today Show." I'd rather corner them in a dungeon and pull the caps off their teeth. The only thing I have in common with those people is a sofa.

JW: *You review books for a number of publications, including the* American Spectator. *What are your critical ground rules?*
FK: I believe books should be reviewed for their literary, not political, content. I am proud of my own adherence to this rule. I have raved three liberal feminists—Susan Brownmiller, Andrea Dworkin, and Kate Millett—and panned a fellow conservative: Ben Stein. Felix Unger thinks it's fun to be neat; I think it's fun to be fair. The simplest rule of reviewing is the one most often

ignored: A review must say (1) what the book is about, and (2) what the reviewer thinks of it.

The writer I hate most is Robert Fulghum, author of *All I Really Need to Know I Learned in Kindergarten* and *It Was on Fire When I Lay Down on It*. Titles like these are immensely popular with people-lovers, so if I ever write *As Soon As I Figure Out How to Make a Sword Out of This Friggin' Plowshare* you will know I have gone soft.

JW: *What do you find offensive in reviews of your own books?*

FK: I can't stand confused, inarticulate people who have trouble getting to the point, especially when they're reviewing a book of mine. Nothing irritates me more than a reviewer who uses my navel for his navel-gazing.

JW: *Why have you given up writing for women's magazines?*

FK: I discovered I'm not really a woman; there's just an "F" on my driver's license. These things happen.

JW: *Do you have any advice to young writers?*

FK: Reject the bohemian image of the writer; there is nothing creative about decadence and squalor. Be neat and organized in your workroom and your materials; outward disorder leads to inner chaos. Beware of writer groupies; the writer's self-sufficiency and bent for solitude attract insecure types whom I call the Love people. Their unconscious motivation is the destruction of the Work people. Either kick them out of your life or don't admit them in the first place, because they will become jealous of your work. These are the individuals who phone you every day to make sure you still love them, so you are always being forced into the position of telling them that you never did.

JW: *You've written about the beneficial effects of going through meno-pause. Do you have any advice for other women regarding "the change"?*

FK: You will lose your sex drive, but every magazine article, talk show, and self-help book will assure you that you're as horny as ever. Pay no attention to them, it's just another American conspiracy.

JW: *What are some other "American conspiracies"?*

FK: There is an American conspiracy that says everyone is highly sexed, but everyone is not. It takes a certain bandit persona to go at everything with real elan, and most people simply aren't like that. Speaking in another context, George Orwell said: "The great mass of human beings are not acutely selfish. After the age of about thirty they abandon individual ambition—in many cases, indeed, they almost abandon the sense of being individuals at all—and live chiefly for others, or are simply smothered under drudgery."

Another American conspiracy of more recent vintage holds that women are as highly sexed as men. This is the insane side of equality: everybody's got a right to climb the walls and live in torment. Women have a cyclical sex drive that leaves us quiescent for most of the month. Moreover, the female sex drive is sixty percent vanity, thirty percent curiosity, and ten percent physical. I didn't masturbate until I was seventeen—find me the man who can make that statement. My chief sexual fantasy involved show-ering together, and I was compelled to visualize it so that no water splashed on the floor and messed up my nice clean bath-room. Find me the man who would give a damn about the mess even in real life, never mind fantasy.

JW: *Are you a good housekeeper?*

FK: You could eat off my floor, but I can't guarantee the table: I write on it.

JW: *When you receive a letter from a stranger, what form of salutation do you prefer: Dear Miss King; Dear Ms. King; Dear Florence King; Dear Florence?*

FK: Dear Miss King.

JW: *Why?*

FK: Because I'm a spinster. My whole life has been a feminist statement, so I don't need Ms. to prove who I am. As for Dear Florence King, it makes me feel as if they want all of me, and nobody ever gets that.

JW: *Do you watch television?*

FK: I watch old movies—it's interesting to gauge my present reactions and compare them to my original reactions when I saw the movies for the first time as a child or a young woman. And of course I watch baseball, the Orioles mostly. I don't watch any sitcoms; judging from the previews I see while I'm watching something else, they are all sit and no com. I never laugh at sight gags; my idea of wit is a verbal thrust or an oblique understatement such as Noel Coward's definition of a gentleman: "A man who can play the bagpipes, but doesn't." I loved "Upstairs, Downstairs," but I am not an unquestioning devotee of Masterpiece Theatre: some of them are terribly boring. "Fall of Eagles" because it was about the history of the belle epoque, which I wish I'd lived in. And anything about FDR, because the socialist sonofabitch was the personification of my childhood.

JW: *Are you religious?*

FK: I believe in reincarnation and can't wait to see who I'm going to be next. I hope I'll be male and a major-league baseball player. I'm not religious in the conventional sense; as an Episcopalian child I thought *trinity* meant going to church three times a year, but I approve of religion and think society needs it. As Napoleon said: "Religion is necessary because it keeps the poor people from killing the rich people." A certain opulence of imagination draws me to the old Latin-and-incense Roman Catholicism, and the doctrine of papal infallibility appeals to the exhausted American in me: Debate must stop somewhere if the mind and society are to have peace.

JW: *Do you sleep well?*

FK: Like a goddam baby.

Florence King's books include the autobiographical Confessions of a Failed Southern Lady, *two collections of essays*, Lump It or Leave It *and* Reflections in a Jaundiced Eye, *and* With Charity Toward None: A Fond Look at Misanthropy. *She lives in Virginia.*

QUOTES ON "N"

———NARCISSIST———

A narcissist is someone better-looking than you
are.   GORE VIDAL

———NASA———

Some agencies have a public affairs office. NASA
is a public affairs office that has an agency.

JOHN PIKE

———NATION———

A nation is a society united by delusions about its
ancestry and by common hatred of its neighbors.

W. R. INGE

———NATIONALISM———

Every nation ridicules other nations, and all are
right.   SCHOPENHAUER

Every nation thinks its own madness normal and
requisite; more passion and more fancy it calls
folly, less it calls imbecility.   SANTAYANA

NATURE

Now, nature, as I am only too well aware, has her enthusiasts, but on the whole, I am not to be counted among them. To put it rather bluntly, I am not the type who wants to go back to the land; I am the type who wants to go back to the hotel. FRAN LEBOWITZ

Nature: that lovely lady to whom we owe polio, leprosy, smallpox, syphilis, tuberculosis, cancer. STANLEY N. COHEN

NEIGHBORS

I was much distressed by next-door people who had twin babies and played the violin; but one of the twins died, and the other has eaten the fiddle—so all is peace. EDWARD LEAR

NETWORK EXECUTIVES

Dealing with network executives is like being nibbled to death by ducks. ERIC SEVAREID

NEWSPAPERS

Trying to determine what is going on in the world by reading newspapers is like trying to tell the time by watching the second hand of a clock. BEN HECHT

Newspapers have degenerated. They may now be
absolutely relied upon.   OSCAR WILDE

> A newspaper consists of just the same number of
> words, whether there be any news in it or not.
>   HENRY FIELDING

The average newspaper, especially of the better
sort, has the intelligence of a hillbilly evangelist,
the courage of a rat, the fairness of a prohibitionist
boob–jumper, the information of a high school
janitor, the taste of a designer of celluloid valen-
tines, and the honor of a police-station lawyer.
                                    H. L. MENCKEN

————NEW YEAR'S————

> The proper behavior all through the holiday sea-
> son is to be drunk. This drunkenness culminates
> on New Year's Eve, when you get so drunk you
> kiss the person you're married to.
>   P. J. O'ROURKE

————NEW YORK————

If a day goes by and I haven't been slain, I'm
happy.   CAROL LEIFER

It is one of the prime provincialities of New York that its inhabitants lap up trivial gossip about essential nobodies they've never set eyes on, while continuing to boast that they could live somewhere for twenty years without so much as exchanging pleasantries with their neighbors across the hall.   LOUIS KRONENBERGER

New York Taxi Rules:
1. Driver speaks no English.
2. Driver just got here two days ago
from someplace like Senegal.
3. Driver hates you.   DAVE BARRY

A marriage, to be happy, needs an exterior threat. New York provides that threat.

GARRISON KEILLOR

New York: the only city where people make radio requests like "This is for Tina—I'm sorry I stabbed you."   CAROL LEIFER

New York has more commissioners than Des Moines, Iowa, has residents, including the Commissioner for Making Sure the Sidewalks Are Always Blocked by Steaming Fetid Mounds of

Garbage the Size of Appalachian Foothills, and, of course, the Commissioner for Bicycle Messengers Bearing Down on You at Warp Speed with Mohawk Haircuts and Pupils Smaller Than Purely Theoretical Particles.   DAVE BARRY

When we moved to New York we had to get rid of the children. Landlords didn't like them and, in any case, rents were so high. Who could afford an apartment big enough to contain children?
                                    RUSSELL BAKER

_____NOBEL PRIZE_____

Nobel Prize money is a lifebelt thrown to a swimmer who has already reached the shore in safety.
                            GEORGE BERNARD SHAW

_____NOVEMBER_____

November, *n*. The eleventh twelfth of a weariness.
                                    AMBROSE BIERCE

_____NUCLEAR WAR_____

There will be no nuclear war. There's too much real estate involved.   FRANK ZAPPA

OPERA

Going to the opera, like getting drunk, is a sin
that carries its own punishment with it, and that
a very severe one.   HANNAH MOORE

If a thing isn't worth saying, you sing it.
PIERRE BEAUMARCHAIS

No opera plot can be sensible, for people do not
sing when they are feeling sensible.
W. H. AUDEN

Opera is when a guy gets stabbed in the back and
instead of bleeding, he sings.   ED GARDNER

One goes to see a tragedy to be moved; to the
opera one goes either for want of any other interest or to facilitate digestion.   VOLTAIRE

An unalterable and unquestioned law of the musical world required that the German text of French
operas sung by Swedish artists should be trans-
lated into Italian for the clearer understanding of
English-speaking audiences.   EDITH WHARTON

I do not mind what language an opera is sung in so long as it is a language I don't understand.

SIR EDWARD APPLETON

OPTIMISM

I find nothing more depressing than optimism.

PAUL FUSSELL

ORCHESTRA

Orchestras only need to be sworn at, and a German is consequently at an advantage with them, as English profanity, except in America, has not gone beyond a limited technology of perdition.

GEORGE BERNARD SHAW

OXFORD

Oxford: a sanctuary in which exploded systems and obsolete prejudices find shelter and protection after they have been hunted out of every corner of the world.

ADAM SMITH

I was a modest, good-humored boy; it is Oxford that has made me insufferable.

MAX BEERBOHM

OYSTERS

I will not eat oysters. I want my food dead. Not sick, not wounded, dead.

WOODY ALLEN

JOHN LEO

Wanted by the Niceness Police

JW: *I'd like to talk about what you've called "hypersensitive minorities"*—

JL: I think this is the age of great touchiness. Everybody is in the business of burnishing their image and hammering anybody who gets in the way. A couple of guys complained that one of my columns was antigay, and I pointed out that the same column had a crack about Catholics, Arabs, fat people, thin people, and

Native Americans. Only they didn't notice that. They were a perfect illustration of how incredibly touchy everybody is these days. You can't attack anybody. We have "niceness police" all around us.

JW: *Is* everything *sacred*?

JL: What isn't? WASPS? Are they the only fair game left? I used to think that middle-aged white businessmen were the only ones left, but then someone complained that there were too many middle-aged-white-businessman villains on TV. So there's nobody to pick on anymore. We'll have to have villains with Martian last names, because obviously you can't use an *ethnic* last name, and everybody can't be called "Green" and "Smith."

And while we're on the subject, I should tell you that every time a street gang is portrayed it has to be perfectly integrated; it's got to have blacks, Puerto Ricans, and whites, because otherwise someone might get the idea that people hang around in ethnic groups of their own. We can't have that! The best example of this was *The Long Hot Summer* with Don Johnson. The mob calling for his lynching was the only totally integrated lynch mob ever seen in America. Now, why blacks would be in a lynch mob in the South is obscure, except that the producers felt uncomfortable having an all-white mob. What it comes down to is you're never going to see a black shoeshine guy or a homosexual villain. We're going for mainstream, white-bread, middle-aged, middle-sized villains.

JW: *Is this new touchiness confined to Hollywood?*

JL: Not at all: In a campaign against political incorrectness, Smith College recently warned its freshpersons about ten dangerous "isms." In that spirit I would propose my own list of political taboos. To the big three of *racism, sexism,* and *heterosexism*, I would add *ageism*, bias against seniors by the temporarily young, and *ableism*, bias against the "physically challenged" and "differently abled" (formerly the "disabled" or "handicapped") by the "temporarily abled." "Blind to the truth" would be an example of ableist language; stairs would be an example of ableist architecture. And there's *speciesism*, the doctrine that people are somehow more valuable than mice or insects. A philosopher of animal rights named Peter Singer writes that "speciesists allow the interests of their own species to override the greater interests of members of other species." A person swatting a mosquito would thus be a speciesist. So would a bird eating an insect, a snake eating a bird, a jackal eating a snake, or a lion eating Peter Singer.

JW: *Was it an example of some sort of "ism" when the Federal Aviation Administration banned blind persons from sitting next to the exits on airliners?*

JL: Yes, it was a blatant case of "sightism," the belief that visually impaired people cannot do as well as sighted people at all tasks.

JW: *And there must be "isms" based on appearance.*

JL: Lots of them: *Lookism* is the belief that some people are easier on the eyes than others, which creates an unacceptable hierarchy based on mere appearance. There's *sizeism*, the prejudice against the differently sized. Thus articles on dieting and overeating are biased. And there's *birthmarkism*, the refusal to see that it is not birthmarks that are unsightly but rather the society that frowns upon them. Ted Kennedy, Jr., wrote to the *Boston Globe* to complain about an article on birthmark treatment techniques when actually, he pointed out, "our attitude is the problem, and that can never be corrected surgically."

It goes beyond appearance: "Inappropriately directed laughter" has been banned at the University of Connecticut, hence *laughism*. Micky Kaus of the *New Republic* wrote that while growing a beard, he was disinvited by a cable TV show out of *blatant shavism*. And a Boston-based group of militant lesbians, pointing out that some women are especially sensitive to odors, argued that social events "should be advertised as scent-free, and sniffers posted at the entrance to ensure that all who enter are in compliance." This is nothing short of *scentism*. I suppose splashing on some Old Spice would combine scentism and shavism into *aftershavism*. You've got to be careful out there.

JW: *Is this all part of what you've called the "relentless manufacture of new rights"?*

JL: Absolutely. As a cursory reading of almost any newspaper will show, American politics is awash in rights talk. We have criminal rights, computer rights, animal rights, children's rights, victim's rights, abortion rights, privacy rights, housing rights, the right to know the sex of a fetus, the right to own AK-47s for hunting purposes, the right not to be tested for AIDS, and the right not to inform anyone that we may be infected. Recently we have acquired the right to die, and according to some rather imaginative theorists, a damaged fetus has "a right not to be born." Mental patients used to have a right to treatment, but now that they have been dumped on the streets, they have an ACLU–protected right to no treatment and, therefore, the right to die unhelped in alleys. According to the ACLU, airline pilots have a right not to be randomly tested for alcohol, leaving passengers with an implied right to crash every now and then.

And speaking of alcohol, have you noticed that whereas you used to be just a drunk, now you are "alcohol disabled"? Almost everybody is clamoring to *become* handicapped. A woman in Virginia was arrested for trying to poison her two-year-old son by mixing mouse poison with breakfast cereal and ice cream, and the defense was that she is suffering from "Munchausen's syndrome by proxy." Now, Munchausen's syndrome is a mental disorder in which people mutilate themselves to elicit attention. So to get this woman into the Munchausen's syndrome, it had to be by "proxy" since she had attempted to harm not herself but her child. The devil made her put the mouse poison in the ice cream. That's the "manufacture of disability." We do that more and more.

JW: *Are things any better at the university level?*

JL: I think the universities are suffering from a breakdown that goes back to the sixties, when they gave up the in loco parentis approach and allowed the kids to start running the university. Now they're regretting it because a lot of the kids are anti-female, anti-black, and so forth, so you have friction all the time. Instead of trying to build a community, they're trying to become niceness police. For example, they want to bar certain words. So now if a male student has an argument with a female student and it gets heated and he calls her a bitch, he can be taken up on charges or expelled, which is an absolutely preposterous suspension of free speech.

JW: *Another disturbing trend in American society is the shrinking of attention spans. Life grows increasingly less linear, sequences and story lines are disappearing from newspaper and magazine stories and even comic strips, political discourse degenerates further into sound bites. There's even a radio psychiatrist in L.A. who takes you through five years of therapy in five minutes—*

JL: And the price is right, too. It's all true about attention spans. And it's beginning to affect our politics because the easily understood things are becoming our major issues. Everybody goes nuts over animal rights because the issue can be explained to a three-year-old in eight seconds, but no one gives a damn about the S&Ls—it's five hundred billion dollars lost, but no one can understand it. We talk about the instantly graspable, emotional issues that a moron can understand. Things that make good "visuals." A tormented animal or a burnt flag is terrific—it gets you emotionally.

JW: *Some of the "visuals" employed by the animal-rights movement are indeed compelling, but where do you come down on the issue itself?*

JL: I'm of two minds about it. First of all, I think the anticruelty people are absolutely right: There's a lot of pointless cruelty to animals, particularly to develop perfumes and powders, and that seems unconscionable. The part I don't like is the emotional "feel-good" aspect of it, the implication that you can feel morally superior and wonderful and engaged worrying about the torment of a dog, the way you would never be engaged about the much more vivid torment of actual human beings that goes on without anyone picketing against it. There's a kind of moral one-upmanship about it. You get to feel superior to the woman who wears dead minks.

JW: *You've also complained about the spread of advertising. In one*

*column you described taking the world's shortest cab ride because when
you got in the taxi there was a ticker tape showing a commercial.*

JL: The only response you can have when you're being sold something nine inches from your face inside the cab is: "Let me out of here!" The only other thing you could do is destroy it, but I didn't have a crowbar with me.

It's getting worse and worse. The ad slogan has to cut through the clutter, which means that plain English creates more clutter for people like you and me. They have ads now on hot dogs. You buy a hot dog and there will be a commercial for some other product on the hot dog.

JW: *On the wrapper?*

JL: On the *skin*. Edible. You're eating the commercial. Someone wrote and told me they have them on the inside of men's room doors—talk about captive audiences. They're putting ads everywhere they can think of: life guard platforms, golf carts, tee markers, golfer's cards, parking meters, bus shelters. They'll put them on anything they can.

JW: *Even the names of sporting events: There's the "Sunkist Fiesta Bowl," the "John Hancock Sun Bowl"—what's next?*

JL: The Preparation-H Bowl.

JW: *But are there any encouraging signs? Disney recently announced that they wouldn't allow commercials in theaters where their movies are shown.*

JL: But Disney plants the ads in their own movies: *Roger Rabbit* had an ad for Lucky Strikes embedded in it. Why get pious and say you're going to protect your viewers from having to watch ads when the ads are already in your movies? What they mean is, *we'll* handle the ads inside our product, thank you very much, and we don't want anybody putting ads around us because we don't get paid for them.

JW: *How about perfumed perfume ads?*

JL: You open a magazine and an incredible stench comes floating out. There are five or six naked narcissists posing languidly and this yellow *gas* comes up toward your nostrils. You need a gas mask.

JW: *All aimed at the baby boomers, the most affluent segment of society, fewer than half of whom follow public affairs or read a daily newspaper.*

JL: It seems to me that the whole electorate is in the business of going to sleep as rapidly as possible. Look at the whole census thing: No one returned his form. But that may be a protest against junk mail. There are so many stupid things in the mail, saying "Important Thing About the Environment," while it's really a pitch for some club or something. People just heave that stuff out. If you look at the dismal census response and the small voter turnout and nobody reading anything important, you find a somnolent public. I think people are just in shock about change, and the easiest way to resist that shock is to insert your head in the sand and keep it there until you grow old.

JW: *And we seem to be getting increasingly jaded when it comes to entertainment.*

JL: That's certainly true when it comes to rock bands, whose sacred mission is to offend as many parents as possible. Which is an increasingly arduous assignment in a culture growing cruder by the day. Ozzy Osbourne had to bite the head off a living bat, thus risking the wrath of animal-rights people *and* rabies at the same time. God knows what the next generation will have to do. Autopsies on TV? It's getting harder and harder to gross us out.

JW: *Standards are eroding all over the place. You did a piece about increasing use of the "F-word." Who are the worst offenders?*

JL: I don't know if [Los Angeles Dodger Manager] Tom Lasorda is the all-time champion, but he's certainly in the finals. He once used the word forty-four times in a minute and a half during a visit to the mound. Now, I figure that if you use it forty-four times every time you change pitchers, with an average of three pitching changes a game, you would use it a million times in a year—just while standing on the mound. I think that whoever has the patent on the F-word sure owes most of their livelihood to Tom Lasorda's use of it.

JW: *You're an avid baseball fan, and you've compiled a list of favorite baseball clichés, and I'd like you to translate a few of them. "He came to play," for instance.*

JL: A guy with no talent at all, you can always say he "came to play" or he "gives 110 percent," or you can call him a "scrappy player." A "scrappy player" is a player with no known skills at all who is not legally dead. If he moves at all, he's "scrappy." "Scrappy" people tend to leave the big leagues after one year because it takes more than "scrappiness" now. What else? A "great natural athlete." Darryl Strawberry is "a great natural athlete." "A great natural athlete" is someone with wonderful talent and ability who doesn't use them at all. If he has a great arm and great hitting ability but hits .220, strikes out, and can't catch a fly ball, you say he has "great natural ability." "We can hold our own with any team in this league" means we will be lucky to have a .500 season; if we win as many as we lose, it will be a truimph of the human spirit because we have no ability whatsoever. "This year we will be working on fundamentals" means there's no hope. We can't do anything right. "We're rebuilding" means we need eight, maybe nine more players in the starting lineup. "This is a rebuilding year" translates to "we're going to try to teach them which base to run to if they get a hit."

JW: *How about "This is a team to watch"?*

JL: Only if you've already seen everything else on TV and every movie ever made.

JW: *You've written about your passion for another "sport," bird-watching. How did you get involved?*

JL: One day you just look up and you say, "Holy smoke, I never noticed *that* thing before." And then you discover it's a mourning dove, a really beautiful bird. Then you start *chasing* them, and before you know it you're *collecting* them. It's the grown-up version of a little boy's attempt to collect every baseball card. It becomes a kind of hunting game in which you begin to notice the beautiful things around you. And it gets you away from the humdrum of daily life. It's an obsession: I know a lot of birders who divorced non-birders and then married birders. You have to organize your life around birding, including your wife, or otherwise your new wife will think you're as nuts as your old one did. You have to make sure that you have matched obsessions in the family.

JW: *How obsessive are you?*

JL: A couple of years ago I went to Attu. Attu is the last Aleutian

Island, closer to Tokyo than it is to Anchorage. It's way out in the middle of nowhere. They drop you there, and if you get sick, hard luck. There's nothing on the island. You get stuck there for three weeks in the most primitive conditions. There's nothing to do. You sleep in a room with nineteen of your closest friends, all of whom are either coughing or snoring or both. You put up with this because of the chance that you might see five or six "Asian specialties." The big-time birders go there—sometimes every year, sometimes twice a year—with the hope of seeing maybe one bird that they haven't seen before to add to their lifetime list. That is truly obsessive.

JW: *"Lifetime list"*?

JL: Lifetime *North American* list. Attu is really an Asiatic island, but technically it's part of Alaska, so any Asian bird that flies over it can be counted on your North American list. So you spend five thousand dollars and three unbearable weeks to see a bird you could see two minutes outside Paris, just so you can get it on your North American list.

My idea of a great birding chase is one where you can drive right to the top of the mountain, hop out, see the bird, and jump right back into air-conditioned comfort. But every once in a while some idiotic bird will position itself at the bottom of some enormous canyon so that you have to go down to get it. It's a four-hour descent and then you have to climb back up with the sun in your face and there's no water and you're climbing and—you just want a helicopter at that point.

I once tried to drive down into something called California Gulch in an '87 Buick. No one had ever tried that before, because

California Gulch is a sheer rock face. We're sitting there, maybe a foot and a half from the edge, and this fellow says, "John, maybe we should get out now." I said, "Perhaps you're right." So we went out and got the bird.

JW: *Are there differences between women birders and men birders?*

JL: There are a lot of very successful and competitive female birders, but I think by and large the sexual differences do assert themselves. I noticed that of the people who send in their life list to the American Birding Association, about ninety percent are male. I guess it's because the collecting, the drivenness, the hunting instinct, tends to be male, whereas women are more automatically drawn to the beauty and flight and freedom of birds and then only secondarily do they amass their list. Whereas the male will drive five hundred miles, look up at the bird, say, "That's it," write it down on his list, and completely miss the beauty of it.

JW: *With men it's a form of acquisitiveness?*

JL: Yes, it's nonfinancial avarice. You want every bird, to have and to hold.

John Leo is a journalist.

QUOTES ON "P"

PAINTING

Painting, *n*. The art of protecting flat surfaces from the weather and exposing them to the critic.
AMBROSE BIERCE

PANAMA

It's not like they make or grow anything. The whole country is based on international banking and a canal the United States can take back any time it wants with one troop of Boy Scouts.
P. J. O'ROURKE

PARENTS

Parents were invented to make children happy by giving them something to ignore. OGDEN NASH

They fuck you up, your mum and dad . . .
PHILIP LARKIN

PÂTÉ

It scored right away with me by being the smooth, fine-grained sort, not the coarse, flaky, dry-on-the-

outside rubbish full of chunks of gut and gristle
to testify to its authenticity.   KINGSLEY AMIS

PATIENCE

You must first have a lot of patience to learn to
have patience.   STANISLAW J. LEC

PATRIOTISM

Patriotism is your conviction that this country is
superior to all other countries because you were
born in it.   GEORGE BERNARD SHAW

Love makes fools, marriage cuckolds, and patriotism malevolent imbeciles.   PAUL LEAUTAUD

A patriot must always be ready to defend his country against his government.   EDWARD ABBEY

PEOPLE

How I hate the attitude of ordinary people to life.
How I loathe ordinariness! How from my soul I
abhor nice simple people, with their eternal price-
list. It makes my blood boil.   D. H. LAWRENCE

People could make the world a nice place to live
. . . if there weren't so goddamn many of them.
CLAYTON HEAFNER

People will buy anything that is one to a customer. SINCLAIR LEWIS

People (a group that in my opinion has always attracted an undue amount of attention) have often been likened to snowflakes. This analogy is meant to suggest that each is unique—no two alike. This is quite patently not the case. People . . . are quite simply a dime a dozen. And, I hasten to add, their only similarity to snowflakes resides in their invariable and lamentable tendency to turn, in a few warm days, to slush.

FRAN LEBOWITZ

There are more fools in the world than there are people. HEINRICH HEINE

—PERSONAL QUESTIONS—

Once upon a time a chap in Virginia, I believe it was, pressed me publicly on the recurrence of adulterous triangles in my earlier novels. Had I myself been a vertex in such a triangle? "Only once," I told him: "with your mother."

JOHN BARTH

————PESSIMIST————

A pessimist is a man who has been compelled to live with an optimist. ELBERT HUBBARD

Where there are two Ph.Ds in a developing country, one is head of state and the other is in exile.
EDWIN HERBERT SAMUEL

The average Ph.D thesis is nothing but the transference of bones from one graveyard to another.
J. FRANK DOBIE

———PHILADELPHIA———

They have Easter egg hunts in Philadelphia, and if the kids don't find the eggs, they get booed.
BOB UECKER

———PHILANTHROPY———

Giving away a fortune is taking Christianity too far.
CHARLOTTE BINGHAM

———PHILOSOPHER———

There is only one thing a philosopher can be relied upon to do, and that is to contradict other philosophers.
WILLIAM JAMES

———PLASTIC SURGERY———

One popular new plastic surgery technique is called lipgrafting, or "fat recycling," wherein fat cells are removed from one part of your body that is too large, such as your buttocks, and injected into your lips; people will then be literally kissing your ass.   DAVE BARRY

―――――PLATITUDE―――――

Platitude: an idea (a) that is admitted to be true by everyone, and (b) that is not true.
                              H. L. MENCKEN

―――――PLEASANTRIES―――――

Nothing is as irritating as the fellow who chats pleasantly while he's overcharging you.
                              KIN HUBBARD

―――――PLEASURE―――――

Illusion is the first of all pleasures.
                              OSCAR WILDE

I despise the pleasure of pleasing people that I despise.   MARY WORTLEY MONTAGU

One of the simple but genuine pleasures in life is getting up in the morning and hurrying to a mousetrap you set the night before.
                              KIN HUBBARD

Poetry is nobody's business except the poet's, and everybody else can fuck off. PHILIP LARKIN

POLITICAL CONVENTION

The dirty work at political conventions is almost always done in the grim hours between midnight and dawn. Hangmen and politicians work best when the human spirit is at its lowest ebb.
RUSSELL BAKER

_____POLITICIANS_____

If a politician found he had cannibals among his constituents, he would promise them missionaries for dinner. H. L. MENCKEN

If you want to find a politician free of any influence, you can find Adolf Hitler, who made up his own mind. EUGENE MCCARTHY

A candidate for office can have no greater advantage than muddled syntax; no greater liability than a command of the language. MARYA MANNES

The saddest life is that of a political aspirant under democracy. His failure is ignominious and his success is disgraceful. H. L. MENCKEN

My choice early in life was either to be a piano player in a whorehouse or a politician. And to tell the truth, there's hardly any difference.

HARRY S TRUMAN

The volume of political comment substantially exceeds the available truth, so columnists run out of truth, and then must resort to imagination. Washington politicians, after talking things over with each other, relay misinformation to Washington journalists, who, after intramural discussion, print it where it is thoughtfully read by the same politicians, who generally believe it. It is the only successful closed system for the recycling of garbage that has ever been devised.

JOHN KENNETH GALBRAITH

Nine politicians out of ten are knaves who maintain themselves by preying on the idiotic vanities and pathetic hopes of half-wits.

H. L. MENCKEN

Here richly, with ridiculous display,
The politician's corpse was laid away.
While all of his acquaintance sneered and slanged,
I wept; for I had longed to see him hanged.

HILAIRE BELLOC

Unfortunately, politicians have the Paul Masson theory of government—"We will deal with no problem before its time." MERVIN FIELD

Ninety percent of the politicians give the other ten percent a bad name. HENRY KISSINGER

Politicians are interested in people. Not that this is always a virtue. Fleas are interested in dogs.
P. J. O'ROURKE

————POLITICS————

Politics is the art of looking for trouble, finding it whether it exists or not, diagnosing it incorrectly, and applying the wrong remedy.
ERNEST BENN

Politics is the skilled use of blunt objects.
LESTER B. PEARSON

Nothing can so alienate a voter from the political system as backing a winning candidate.
MARK B. COHEN

Politics is perhaps the only profession for which no preparation is thought necessary.
ROBERT LOUIS STEVENSON

Politics makes estranged bedfellows.

GOODMAN ACE

The more you observe politics, the more you've
got to admit that each party is worse than the
other.   WILL ROGERS

I have never found in a long experience of politics
that criticism is ever inhibited by ignorance.

HAROLD MACMILLAN

————POSTERITY————

Leaving behind books is even more beautiful—
there are far too many children.

MARGUERITE YOURCENAR

————POWER————

If absolute power corrupts absolutely, does absolute powerlessness make you pure?

HARRY SHEARER

————PRAYER————

I squirm when I see athletes praying before a
game. Don't they realize that if God took sports
seriously He never would have created George
Steinbrenner?   MARK RUSSELL

Forgive, O Lord, my little jokes on Thee, and I'll forgive Thy great big joke on me. . . . Forgive me my nonsense as I also forgive the nonsense of those who think they talk sense.
ROBERT FROST

Please, O ye Lord, keep Jim Bakker behind bars.
DANA CARVEY

PRESIDENTS

The best reason I can think of for not running for president of the United States is that you have to shave twice a day.
ADLAI STEVENSON

If I were the president, I'd bring some *life* to the White House. The theme of my administration would be summarized by the catchy and inspirational phrase: "Hey, the Government Is Beyond Human Control, So Let's at Least Have Some Fun with It."
DAVE BARRY

We need a president who's fluent in at least one language.
BUCK HENRY

If presidents don't do it to their wives, they do it to the country.
MEL BROOKS

Any American who is prepared to run for president should automatically, by definition, be disqualified from ever doing so. GORE VIDAL

PRINCIPLE

When a man says he approves of something in principle, it means he hasn't the slightest intention of putting it into practice. BISMARCK

PRIVACY

Privacy—you can't find it anywhere, not even if you want to hang yourself. MENANDER

PRIZES

The Pulitzer Prize was awarded to Saul Bellow for fiction only after Bellow had won the Nobel Prize, which must have seemed like being given a cup of warmed-over instant coffee twenty minutes after having drunk the world's most expensive cognac. JOSEPH EPSTEIN

PROCREATION

Any man who, having a child or children he can't support, proceeds to have another should be sterilized at once. H. L. MENCKEN

PRODUCERS

"Nervous producer" is a redundancy. So is "complaining producer."
MORLEY SAFER

PROFANITY

Under certain circumstances, profanity provides a relief denied even to prayer.
MARK TWAIN

There ought to be a room in every house to swear in.
MARK TWAIN

PROGRESS

Progress was all right. Only it went on too long.
JAMES THURBER

Usually, terrible things that are done with the excuse that progress requires them are not really progress at all, but just terrible things.
RUSSELL BAKER

PROSPERITY

Everything in the world may be endured except continued prosperity.
GOETHE

PSYCHIATRY

If the Prince of Peace should come to earth, one of the first things he would do would be to put psychiatrists in their place.   ALDOUS HUXLEY

PSYCHOBABBLE

To err is dysfunctional, to forgive co-dependent.
BERTON AVERRE

THE PUBLIC

The public is wonderfully tolerant. It forgives everything except genius.   OSCAR WILDE

The public will believe anything, so long as it is not founded on truth.   EDITH SITWELL

PUBLIC FIGURES

Today's public figures can no longer write their own speeches or books, and there is some evidence that they can't read them either.   GORE VIDAL

PUBLISHERS

One of the signs of Napoleon's greatness is the fact that he once had a publisher shot.
SIEGFRIED UNSELD

QUOTES ON "R"

RADIO

I don't hold with furniture that talks.
FRED ALLEN

Radio news is bearable. This is due to the fact that while the news is being broadcast, the disc jockey is not allowed to talk.   FRAN LEBOWITZ

REACTIONARY

A reactionary is someone with a clear and comprehensive vision of an ideal world we have lost.
KENNETH MINOGUE

READING

No place affords a more striking conviction of the vanity of human hopes than a public library.
SAMUEL JOHNSON

REAGAN LIBRARY

Prepare yourself for some bad news: Ronald Reagan's library just burned down. *Both* books were destroyed. But the real horror: he hadn't finished coloring either one of them.   GORE VIDAL

REALITY

Reality is nothing but a collective hunch.

LILY TOMLIN

REFORM

The only way to reform some people is to chloro-
form them. THOMAS C. HALIBURTON

REFORMERS

Those who are fond of setting things right have
no great objection to seeing them wrong. There
is often a great deal of spleen at the bottom of
benevolence. WILLIAM HAZLITT

REPORTER

Reporter, *n*. A writer who guesses his way to the
truth and dispels it with a tempest of words.

AMBROSE BIERCE

REPUBLICANS

In this world of sin and sorrow there is always
something to be thankful for; as for me, I rejoice
that I am not a Republican. H. L. MENCKEN

Republicans are the party that says government
doesn't work, and then they get elected and prove
it. P. J. O'ROURKE

REPUTATION

One can survive everything, nowadays, except death, and live down everything except a good reputation. OSCAR WILDE

THE RICH

Prior to the Reagan era, the newly rich aped the old rich. But that isn't true any longer. Donald Trump is making no effort to behave like Eleanor Roosevelt as far as I can see. FRAN LEBOWITZ

Someday I want to be rich. Some people get so rich they lose all respect for humanity. That's how rich I want to be. RITA RUDNER

ROCK 'N' ROLL

Monotony tinged with hysteria.
VANCE PACKARD

No amount of electronic amplification can turn a belch into an aria. - ALAN JAY LERNER

I May Be Wrong ...

ROBERT BENCHLEY once proposed his own autobiographical sketch to *Current Biography*: "Born on the Isle of Wight, September 15, 1807, shipped as cabin boy on the *Florence J. Marble* in 1815, wrote *A Tale of Two Cities* in 1820, married Princess Anastasie of Portugal in 1831 (children: Prince Rupprecht and several little girls), buried in Westminster Abbey in 1871."

Robert Charles Benchley was actually born in Worcester,

Massachusetts, in 1889 to Maria Jane Moran Benchley and Charles Benchley. He showed early comedic tendencies when he recited these lines during his first year at Phillips Exeter Academy:

> My mother-in-law has lately died;
> For her my heart doth yearn.
> I know she's with the angels now
> 'Cause she's too tough to burn.

He attended Harvard College, where he was a member of Hasty Pudding and where as editor of the *Lampoon* he published a parody of *Life*, the first in what would be a long series of *Lampoon* magazine parodies. Two years after graduating from Harvard in 1912 he married his childhood sweetheart, Gertrude Darling. The Benchleys eventually had two sons, Nathaniel and Robert, Jr., prompting Benchley to remark of sex, "We tried it twice and it worked both times."

By 1915 he was a city reporter for the New York *Tribune*, where Franklin P. Adams was his sponsor and his co-workers included George S. Kaufman and Heywood Broun. By his own admission, Benchley was "the worst reporter, even for his age, in New York City." His problem was the inability to ask questions he considered indelicate. He thus welcomed an invitation to join the staff of the *Tribune Magazine*, where he wrote book reviews and features on New York life. In 1919 he was hired as managing editor of *Vanity Fair*, where he met the diminutive Dorothy Parker and the six-foot, seven-inch Robert E. Sherwood. Benchley said that when the three of them walked down the street together they looked like a "walking pipe organ." When they resigned en masse from *Vanity Fair* in 1920, Sherwood embarked on his career as a playwright and Benchley and Mrs. Parker shared a freelance office. (Parker: "If the office were any smaller it would have been adultery.")

Benchley was the theater critic for *Life* from 1920 to 1929 and wrote a column in the *New Yorker* under the pseudonym "Guy Fawkes" from 1929 to 1940. His theater criticism was exacting but not cruel. He had rigorous standards, but he often inserted the disclaimer "I may be wrong."

He was a charter member of the Algonquin Round Table along with Alexander Woollcott, Marc Connelly, and Edna Ferber. In 1922 he wrote and performed a satirical monologue entitled "The Treasurer's Report" in a revue put on by members of the Round Table. Irving Berlin and Sam Harris were in the audience and signed Benchley to perform it in their Broadway production, *The Music Box Review*. The show ran for nine months, and in 1928 "The Treasurer's Report" was made into the first all-talking motion picture, establishing Benchley as a national celebrity. He went on to write, produce, and star in some forty movie "shorts," including *The Courtship of the Newt*, *How to Figure the Income Tax*, and *How to Sleep*, which won an Oscar in 1935. He also had many small movie parts in which he played a character much like himself, and he once advertised in *Variety* for "society drunk" roles.

He was an expert procrastinator ("Anybody can do any amount of work, so long as it isn't the work he is supposed to be doing"), and whenever a writing assignment was overdue he displayed a positive genius for finding something else to do instead. Thus he once labeled all the spice jars in the pantry rather than complete an important piece. And according to his son, Nathaniel, his ability to evade the task at hand could go to even greater extremes:

Once, he had been trying to start a piece but couldn't get it under way, so he went down the corridor to where a poker game was in progress, just to jolt his mind into starting up. Some time later, he returned to his room, sat down to the clean sheet of paper in the typewriter, and pecked out the word "The." This, he reasoned, was as safe a start as any, and might possibly break the block. But nothing else came, so he went downstairs and ran into a group of Round Table people, with whom he passed a cheerful hour or so. Then, protesting that he had to work, he went back upstairs, where the small, bleak "The" was looking at him out of the expanse of yellow paper. He sat down and stared at it for several minutes, then a sudden idea came to him, and he finished the sentence, making it read "The hell with it," and got up and went happily out for the evening.

Though he published fifteen books of humorous essays, including the best-selling *Of All Things*, he was plagued by professional self-doubt. He desperately wanted to be a serious writer, but his sense of humor kept getting in the way. He feared he was wasting his time in frivolity, and he regarded whatever he was working on a temporary detour from the *real* work, which he could never manage to do. "It took me fifteen years to discover that I had no talent for writing," he said, "but I couldn't give it up because by that time I was too famous."

Benchley had a puritanical streak. During Prohibition he

would accompany his friends to speakeasies and lecture them on the evils of drink. But he eventually succumbed to the spirit of the times (perhaps reasoning that if the government was so opposed to drinking, it must have some redeeming value), and he began to drink with the zeal of a convert. When a friend warned him that alcohol was "slow poison," Benchley replied, "So who's in a hurry?" His drinking got progressively worse through the twenties and thirties, and he died in 1945, at the age of fifty-six, of a cerebral hemorrhage.

Both James Thurber and E. B. White considered Benchley the finest American humorist since Mark Twain, and Stephen Leacock judged him "the most finished master of the technique of literary fun in America." His gentle humor came from his sense of outraged decency, but he was generous to others and he stood up for causes he considered worthy. Dorothy Parker called him "a kind of saint."

QUINTESSENTIAL BENCHLEY

Why don't you get out of that wet coat and into
a dry martini?

> Drinking makes such fools of people, and people
> are such fools to begin with, that it's compound-
> ing a felony.

A man showed a supposedly unbreakable watch to Benchley and Dorothy Parker in a speakeasy. They promptly shook it, slammed it on the
bar, and stamped on it. The dismayed owner picked it up, put it to his
ear and exclaimed, "It stopped." "Maybe you wound it too tight," said
Benchley.

Asked whether he knew the six-foot-seven Robert E. Sherwood, Benchley climbed on a table, reached to the ceiling with one hand, and said,
"Why, I've known Bob Sherwood since he was this high."

A great many people have come up to me and
asked how I manage to get so much work done
and still keep looking so dissipated.

I do most of my work sitting down; that's where I shine.

Tell us your phobias, and we will tell you what you are afraid of.

I haven't been abroad in so long that I almost speak English without an accent now.

Six days after Charles Lindbergh's triumphant landing at Le Bourget, Benchley sent a cable to a friend in Paris: ANY TIDINGS OF LINDBERGH? LEFT HERE WEEK AGO. AM WORRIED.

Benchley came out of a Manhattan restaurant and said to a uniformed man at the door, "Would you get me a taxi, please?" "I'm sorry," replied the man, "I'm an admiral in the United States Navy." "All right," said Benchley, "then get me a battleship."

An ardent supporter of the hometown team should go to a game prepared to take offense, no matter what happens.

In America there are two classes of travel—first class, and with children.

Drawing on my fine command of the language, I said nothing.

The surest way to make a monkey of a man is to quote him.

THE CRITICAL CURMUDGEON
Music

There are more bad musicians than there is bad music.   ISAAC STERN

A vile, beastly, rottenheaded, foolbegotten, brazenthroated, pernicious, priggish, screaming, tearing, roaring, perplexing, splitmecrackle, crashmecriggle, insane, ass of a woman is practicing howling below-stairs with a brute of a singing master so horribly that my head is nearly off.
                                                        EDWARD LEAR

After playing the violin for the cellist Gregor Piatigorsky, Albert Einstein asked, "Did I play well?" "You played *relatively* well," replied Piatigorsky.

The chromatic scale is what you use to give the effect of drinking a quinine martini and having an enema simultaneously.   PHILIP LARKIN

The sound of a harpsichord—two skeletons copulating on a thin roof in a thunderstorm.
                                                SIR THOMAS BEECHAM

Harpists spend ninety percent of their lives tuning
their harps and ten percent playing out of tune.
IGOR STRAVINSKY

I could eat alphabet soup and *shit* better lyrics.
JOHNNY MERCER on a British musical

Mozart died too late rather than too soon.
GLENN GOULD

Beethoven always sounds to me like the upsetting
of a bag of nails, with here and there an also
dropped hammer.   JOHN RUSKIN

Art is long and life is short: here is evidently the
explanation of a Brahms symphony.
EDWARD LORNE

I love Wagner, but the music I prefer is that of a
cat hung up by its tail outside a window and trying to stick to the panes of glass with its claws.
CHARLES BAUDELAIRE

If the reader were so rash as to purchase any of
Béla Bartók's compositions, he would find that
they each and all consist of unmeaning bunches of
notes, apparently representing the composer
promenading the keyboard in his boots. Some can

---

be played better with the elbows, others with the flat of the hand. None require fingers to perform or ears to listen to.   FREDERICK CORDER

Dvorak's *Requiem* bored Birmingham so desperately that it was unanimously voted a work of extraordinary depth and impressiveness, which verdict I record with a hollow laugh, and allow the subject to drop by its own portentous weight.
GEORGE BERNARD SHAW

In the first movement alone, I took note of six pregnancies and at least four miscarriages.
SIR THOMAS BEECHAM on
Bruckner's Seventh Symphony

What can you do with it? It's like a lot of yaks jumping about.   SIR THOMAS BEECHAM on
Beethoven's Seventh Symphony

Sir Thomas Beecham was once asked if he had played any Stockhausen. "No," he replied, "but I have trodden in some."

Rossini would have been a great composer if his teacher had spanked him enough on his backside.
LUDWIG VAN BEETHOVEN

Anton Bruckner wrote the same symphony nine times (ten, actually), trying to get it just right. He failed.   EDWARD ABBEY

Schoenberg is too melodious for me, too sweet.
                              BERTOLT BRECHT

He'd be better off shovelling snow.
            RICHARD STRAUSS on Arnold Schoenberg

When told that a soloist would need six fingers to perform his concerto, Arnold Schoenberg replied, "I can wait."

I would like to hear Elliott Carter's *Fourth String Quartet*, if only to discover what a cranky prostate does to one's polyphony.   JAMES SELLARS

Exit in case of Brahms.
            PHILIP HALE's proposed inscription over
                the doors of Boston Symphony Hall

Why is it that whenever I hear a piece of music I don't like, it's always by Villa-Lobos?
                              IGOR STRAVINSKY

His music used to be original. Now it is aboriginal. SIR ERNEST NEWMAN on Igor Stravinsky

Claude Debussy played the piano with the lid down. ROBERT BRESSON

If he'd been making shell-cases during the war it might have been better for music. MAURICE RAVEL on Camille Saint-Saëns

He has an enormously wide repertory. He can conduct anything, provided it's by Beethoven, Brahms or Wagner. He tried Debussy's *La mer* once. It came out as *Das Merde*. ANONYMOUS ORCHESTRA MEMBER on Georg Szell

———

Someone commented to Rudolph Bing, manager of the Metropolitan Opera, that "Georg Szell is his own worst enemy." "Not while I'm alive, he isn't!" said Bing.

———

There was one respect in which Landon Ronald outshone all other conductors. This was in the gleam of his shirtfront and the gloss of his enormous cuffs, out of which peeped tiny, fastidious fingers. He made music sound as if it, too, had been laundered. JAMES AGATE

Madam, you have between your legs an instrument capable of giving pleasure to thousands—and all you can do is scratch it.
SIR THOMAS BEECHAM to a lady cellist

After I die, I shall return to earth as a gatekeeper of a bordello and I won't let any of you enter.
ARTURO TOSCANINI to the NBC Orchestra

Already too loud! BRUNO WALTER, on seeing the orchestra reach for their instruments at the beginning of a rehearsal

We cannot expect you to be with us all the time, but perhaps you could be good enough to keep in touch now and again.
SIR THOMAS BEECHAM to a musician during a rehearsal

Jack Benny played Mendelssohn last night. Mendelssohn lost. ANONYMOUS

The great German conductor Hans von Bülow detested two members of an orchestra named Schultz and Schmidt. Upon being told that Schmidt had died, von Bülow immediately asked, "Und Schultz?"

Her voice sounded like an eagle being goosed.
RALPH NOVAK on Yoko Ono

If a horse could sing in a monotone, the horse would sound like Carly Simon, only a horse wouldn't rhyme "yacht," "apricot" and "gavotte."
ROBERT CHRISTGAU

Not content to have the audience in the palm of his hand, he goes one further and clenches his fist.
KENNETH TYNAN on Frankie Laine

When she started to play, Steinway came down personally and rubbed his name off the piano.
BOB HOPE on Phyllis Diller

Yesterday the performance of *Rheingold* took place. From the scenic point of view it interested me greatly, and I was also much impressed by the marvellous staging of the work. Musically it is inconceivable nonsense.
PYOTR ILICH TCHAIKOVSKY

Parsifal is a work of perfidy, of vindictiveness, of a secret attempt to poison the presuppositions of life—a *bad* work. . . . I despise anyone who does not experience *Parsifal* as an attempted assassination of basic ethics. NIETZSCHE

I was not able to detect in the vocal parts of *Parsifal* anything that might with confidence be called rhythm or tune or melody; one person performed at a time—and a long time, too—often in a noble, and always in a high-toned, voice; but he only pulled out long notes, then some short ones, then another long one, then a sharp, quick, peremptory bark or two—and so on and so on; and when he was done you saw that the information which he had conveyed had not compensated for the disturbance. MARK TWAIN

Parsifal—the kind of opera that starts at six o'clock and after it has been going three hours, you look at your watch and it says 6:20. DAVID RANDOLPH

One can't judge Wagner's opera *Lohengrin* after a first hearing, and I certainly don't intend hearing it a second time. GIOACCHINO ROSSINI

I liked the opera very much. Everything but the music. BENJAMIN BRITTEN on Stravinsky's *The Rake's Progress*

Her singing reminds me of a cart coming downhill with the brake on. SIR THOMAS BEECHAM on an unidentified soprano in *Die Walküre*

How nice the human voice is when it isn't singing. RUDOLPH BING

MARGO KAUFMAN

Redhead

JW: *You've done magazine and newspaper columns on a variety of issues. For example, you recently tackled the recession from an unusual perspective.*

MK: This is going to sound awful, but the worse the economy, the harder it gets for pets. Because a pet is a high-expense item. It's not so bad for the first six to eight years, when the pet is still cute; but when the pet gets older, then the pet becomes an economic factor. Every time you take an old pet to the vet, you're looking at a minimum of $100. Vets are like cab drivers—you're at their mercy. You can't budget, say, $50 for the pet this month because if the pet should suddenly get an itch, you're looking at $300 in an instant. You're struggling to pay your MasterCard and your mortgage and you're not buying new clothes—you're not doing anything for yourself, and suddenly your pet gets an eye infection and it's $40 a month for the drops. [My Pug] Stella's drops are $40 a month, but can she see me? Nooooo. She can't see anything that isn't edible, but just to keep her little eyes clear and mucus-free, forty bucks a month.

JW: *Have you considered—*

MK: The vet absolutely refuses to put the dog to sleep. I have two Pugs and I love them and I've been a very good mother and they've had a glorious life, but they're both thirteen years old and it's rough. Stella has bad arthritis and she can't walk much farther than the mailbox, which is right outside the door. She basically sleeps all day, except the twenty minutes when she's eating. But the vet refuses to put her to sleep as long as she's "still interested in her dish." This dog would come up from the grave to eat. My vet says there are "still things we could try." He doesn't want to try anything under $200.

JW: *Have you thought of changing vets?*

MK: What am I going to do? Pick up the phone, call around, and go, "Hi. Will you kill my dog?"

JW: *What exactly is it about Pugs that appeals to you?*

MK: They're living proof that God has a sense of humor.

JW: *Some people find them a bit unattractive.*

MK: *I* think they're cute. They look like little gargoyles or gremlins. I think the Pug's charm is its aesthetic quality. Anywhere a Pug is, a Pug makes you smile. If a Pug's on a sofa, it looks ornamental. When you take them outside, they're like lawn art. You take the Pug to the country, you put the Pug in the desert, you walk it on the beach, it's money in the bank of good cheer.

JW: *But how are they as pets?*

MK: They have a Jewish princess personality, squared. My Pugs have the greatest sense of entitlement of anything I've ever known. I wish I were a Pug. I wish I had their personality. They don't have any idea that they should do anything in exchange for what they get. I always try to be a good sport, and it's my worst quality. The Pug is never a good sport.

JW: *You wrote a piece recently in which you said that there are certain things you don't want to hear about—*

MK: I don't want to know if people are bulimic, I really don't. I went out to lunch with a friend and she told me she was bulimic. What was I supposed to say, "Let's go in the ladies' room and throw up together"? I've always had a weak stomach, and if somebody gets sick, I get sick, too. So when she got up in the middle of lunch and went to the bathroom, what was I supposed to think? I'll never invite her to dinner again.

A friend of mine is seeing a guy who goes to a different "anonymous" group every day, and she says it's a wonder he still knows his last name. I think it's wonderful that all these people are getting help, but do I need to know about it? I never drank, so why do I have to sober up vicariously? I realize it's fashionable to be a drug addict or a drunk or a sexaholic, but I'd rather be out of that loop.

Sensitive men are also a problem. My nightmare is that my husband will want to go to a Robert Bly seminar. The day he starts telling me how he feels . . .

JW: *You don't want him to share his feelings? I thought that was what women want.*

MK: Women only want men to share certain feelings, like how they feel about us if it's positive: "Honey, you're the most wonderful person in the world and I couldn't live without you." Women analyze everything to death—every emotional nuance. If men did that it would be a nightmare. Think about when a guy has a cold: a woman's cold and a man's cold are not the same thing. A woman's cold is a minor complaint. A woman's cold is a cheap excuse to get out of sex. But a man's cold is pneumonia. A man's cold requires major intervention. A woman gets a cold, the flu, the guy goes out and works on the car. A man gets a cold and it's the end of the world. Now imagine that attitude, only with feelings. It's asking for trouble. I also think it's a mistake to expect a man to understand your feelings or give you any kind of emotional support.

JW: *Are there any instances in which men are good at expressing their feelings?*

MK: Yes, when they get "head-pop." Men go through cycles where their head gets larger and larger. When a man is involved in an exciting project, his head becomes larger and larger and he gets very full of himself. Then, one day someone says something

---

negative to him—it can be really minor, like "I don't like that report," or "I don't like the way you put the commas in that sentence," and the guy's head pops. You can chart your relationship with a man by how big his head is on a given day. Like the phases of the moon. In the early stages, when the head is just beginning to puff up, you can really make progress, but when the head gets big again, you have to wait until it pops and then start over. Unfortunately, the head always re-inflates.

I think the best way to communicate with a man is just to tell him what you want. Women expect guys to be mind readers, but they don't run on the same program. For example, women all know what to say to each other: you call any woman and you say, "I'm not feeling very cute now, I'm bloated and I have cramps," the woman will say exactly the right thing. *Any* woman—pick one off the street. Say this to a man and he will always say the wrong thing. If you say, "I'm bloated and I have cramps," he'll say, "Yeah, you do look a little puffy." Men never know what to say. They don't know their own feelings, so how could they know yours?

JW: *Is that because of the male ego?*

MK: The male ego knows no bounds and I want one desperately. I would give anything for one. Anything that happens to a man is the most important thing in the world. It doesn't matter what you do, it doesn't matter what happens to you—it's not as important as what happens to him. You cannot win. You can never be more *x*—fill it in—than a guy. You can't be happier, sadder, more depressed, more successful, busier, sicker. It seems to be a survival mechanism, and I don't mean it as a criticism, I mean it almost in admiration.

JW: *Do you like sports?*

MK: Mostly as a male soporific. I was trained by my mother to be a good date, which meant I learned the basics of all the popular sports. I think women make a big mistake complaining about sports, because with sports you always know exactly where your husband/boyfriend/lover is: in front of the TV. They're not doing anything harmful, they're sitting there peacefully for an hour, hour and a half.

I'm sort of fascinated by trash sports, like tractor pulling or dwarf tossing. Are people really that bored? There's cat chasing, where sky divers throw the cat out of the plane and try to catch it. And hacky sack, where the brain-dead kick around a beanbag. Or mountain biking: you go out on a trail for a nice hike and there they are, huffing and puffing. They completely ruin it for hikers. On the way up they look like little rats on a treadmill, and then they come speeding down at you at about ninety miles an hour. They wear those stupid pants that no one in America looks good in. To be a mountain biker you have to have serious Spandex. It's amazing: women who rejected the panty girdle are now happily encasing themselves like sausage.

JW: *Why do they wear them?*

MK: Just to show they can. It's like wearing a hat. If you put a hat on, you get a certain number of points for just having the guts to wear it.

JW: *Do you like to shop?*

MK: For me, shopping is a transcendental experience. It can cure anything, as long as you shop for the right reasons. Like, you're depressed, you're happy, you're sad, you're uncomfortable, you're afraid, you're a success, you're a failure. See, the only thing in life you can control is your wardrobe. You can't control your friends and you can't control your house and you can't control your career—but as long as the cleaner returns it, you have complete control over what you put on your back in the morning.

JW: *What about shopping for things other than clothes?*

MK: I think it's strange how expensive and ugly things are. It's not so much sticker shock, it's aesthetic shock. I mean, who decided that appliances in America should be wood grain? *Simulated* wood grain. Who wants an oak toaster? Do they have wood grain Xerox machines? Of course not. Then why are all kitchen appliances wood grain? Is it supposed to conjure up the hearth?

I think bad taste should be a felony. They should arrest whoever invented "decorator colors." A decorator color is a color that is not found in nature. Like avocado, there's nothing that's avocado, not even an avocado.

JW: *And food shopping?*

MK: I hate markets, except for Gelson's [an upscale supermarket chain in Southern California]. That's God's market. I like to go, get the few items I need, and leave. My premarriage refrigerator was just fruit, bagels, frozen yogurt, and Diet Coke. But my husband is a maniac. When we were first married, he would go to four different markets to find the cheapest peach. It made me insane. And when I put the toilet paper in the cart, he would multiply the squares times the price times the *ply* and put it back on the shelf. Life is too short to count the squares on the toilet paper. Now we've been together long enough that if I go to the market with him, I only buy the sanctified brands—the ones he has preordained the cheapest.

And he has another interesting habit: whenever we're about to get in the checkout line he disappears in search of the elusive whatever, which means that I have to unload all the groceries and check them through. Invariably all the items are rung up, he's still not back, the person behind me is hitting my shins with their cart, it's freezing in the market, they're playing the instrumental version of "Yellow Submarine," and he's nowhere to be found. So I have him paged. I do it all the time now. It's great. He just slinks right over. He's much better about sticking with me since I started the paging system.

JW: *Is he any better in restaurants?*

MK: Well, I'm a boring eater, I always order the same thing, and he's really adventurous. Whenever he's mad at me—you know how there's one accusation in every marriage that gets pulled out when everything else fails?—the charge he throws at me is "You don't like Mexican food." The ultimate indictment. I'm sorry, honey, but I just don't wake up in the middle of the night with a hankering for flautas.

Everybody is so damned sophisticated about food these days. The other night we went to a *Yucatán* Mexican restaurant! Is this necessary? Suddenly people who can't find Mexico on a map know the difference between chorizos and chimichanga. And people judge you by what you order for lunch. You might as well shoot yourself if you order a chef's salad, and if you order meat in some circles, you're doomed. It's best to order something you can't pronounce, or something raw. Raw always scores big points. For lunch it used to be either a hamburger, the deli, or Chinese. Now it's Ethiopian food.

JW: *Overnight houseguests are another problem. How do you handle them?*

MK: I won't have them. My sister spent the night recently and she had the audacity to take a shower in my bathroom. I'm not good in the morning—nothing positive has ever happened to me before noon. So when I woke up and I went to the bathroom and saw that she was there, I wanted to cut her heart out. Houseguests are just too much trouble. Does anybody really want somebody staying in their house? If you live in a big house and have servants, okay, I can understand it. But if you live in a single-family dwelling, a houseguest is a problem. The only exception is if you're in some kind of dysfunctional relationship where you need a buffer. Those people *like* houseguests. Ever notice that when the marriage is breaking up they invite you to stay with them for weeks? "We don't care, you can have our bed."

JW: *And then there's the ultimate domestic inconvenience, remodeling.*

MK: A nightmare. It's like houseguests to the twenty-eighth power. Strangers come into your house with saws. There you are, in *your* territory, and strangers are there with all these destructive instruments and you have no idea whether they know what they're doing. They come and they demolish and they track dirt and they make a lot of noise and, in the end, it's never quite right. But you don't care anymore because you're beaten down and broke.

And I work at home, so I'm all alone. My husband always says, "Honey, I'm going to the office. They're going to raze the house today, but don't worry, it won't be intrusive." That's what my husband always says, "It won't be intrusive." Which means I won't be able to do anything remotely normal for a year.

Home remodeling is the epitome of a lose-lose situation. Oh, you *might* get one of those *Architectural Digest* results—maybe. But it still won't be exactly what you wanted. It will look good in the magazine because they'll come and put flowers everywhere and arrange the ashtrays at ninety-degree angles, but if you really think about it, when you see those houses that have been redone, you don't know what the people thought they were going to get. And you don't know the miserable life they led while they were doing it. You don't know whether they're in debt for the rest of their lives, or whether they're still speaking to each other. The problem with home remodeling is one word: dream. When you get your car fixed, you don't expect your dream car. When you get your teeth fixed, you don't expect your dream teeth. But when you remodel, you expect your dream house.

JW: *And you've written about your neighbors in Venice [California].*
MK: My neighbors are very strange. I remarked to one of them the other day that I hadn't seen him for a while, and he said, "Me and Sally and the baby have moved down the street." I said, "Oh, is Sally your wife?" (I didn't know him that well.) And he said, "No, she's sort of my friend." "And the baby, is it yours?" "Well, I'm not sure, it could be." Then I asked him why he was wearing a wedding ring, and he replied that he had married this Viet-

namese girl so she could get her green card but now she's in New Zealand. The scariest part about it is, that was a normal conversation in my neighborhood.

My husband has lived in Venice for a long time, and he doesn't think anybody is strange. We had this woman next door—a nutcase—who had a cat named Spot. Every day she would put Spot in a little basket and lower him into our yard, which he was using as a litter box. She would stand on her balcony watching him dig up our flowers crooning, "Spot, Spot." It drove me nuts. My husband, of course, thought she was just lonely—the male rationale for all weird female behavior—and told me I should be nicer to her. I actually felt guilty.

Then one day I heard the shot. There was a woman all dressed for success—with the unmistakable carmine talons of a real estate agent—bleeding in our driveway. Our neighbor, Lonely Girl, had shot her in the leg because she was seeing her ex-husband. I know that doesn't make sense, but nothing about the neighbor ever did. The paramedics were working on the victim and her purse started ringing. She said, "Get it, get the phone." The paramedic said, "Lie down, you're in shock." She said, "I'm in escrow."

The neighbor stood on the balcony and called to my husband. She said, "I shot her." He said, "Don't tell me." The police took her away. I got stuck feeding the cat.

JW: *Aside from neighbor problems, do you like working at home?*
MK: Yes, but it has its drawbacks. For one, nobody believes you're ever doing anything. They think you just sit around all day and eat bonbons. They call you at any time and expect you to

talk, expect you to take them to the airport, pick up the cleaning, do the laundry. If you work in an office, you have a secretary and office workers and a Xerox machine, all these ego props to enhance your sense that you're really working, that what you do is absolutely vital. So, when the person who works in an office says, "I had a terrible day, the copier didn't work, Sylvia broke up with her boyfriend, the phones went down," these are perceived to be terrible tragedies. But if you say, "I've had nine rejections in the last twenty-five minutes," the reply is "Did you get to the cleaners?"

I once had a job in an office where I did absolutely nothing. I went there every day but there was nothing for me to do. I would just sit there. I finally had to quit because it was making me homicidal. Then I began to work at home again, where I was doing much more work, but it was perceived that I had left my "real" job. That's how it is: if you say you work at home, people think you're a failed real estate agent. Not that I think being a writer is a career people respect. Almost everyone thinks they could write if only they had the time. People think they can do it, so they don't really think what you do is anything special. They think you're getting away with something.

JW: *You do a lot of travel writing, most recently about something you call "vacation bravado."*

MK: When people go on vacation, they do things they would never do at home. If somebody were to say to you, "Hey, let's climb a volcano!" at home, you would look at them like they were crazy. But if you're in another country, up you go! And when you get there, there's a crowd of people all dressed alike: the women in cute little shorts, the guys with cameras. Have you seen that Reebok commercial where they climb the pyramid in Guatemala? This gorgeous woman going *boing, boing, boing*, right up to the top? Well, I was *at* that pyramid, and women aren't going *boing*, they're clinging to the sides and begging their husbands not to take their picture till they get to the bottom.

So far I have been convinced on vacation to climb a volcano and a pyramid and to ride a donkey down a canyon. The only thing in my defense, I haven't para-sailed. Can you imagine being a human kite in your own neighborhood? You'd never do it. People will do anything for the pictures. They risk their lives for the Fotomat.

JW: *What about the perils of getting there in the first place?*

MK: I don't like buses. To ride a bus is to wonder how you're going to die. Is the bus going to break down? Is the driver going to run it off a cliff? Is the guy in the next seat going to stab you? Are you going to get off the bus somewhere you shouldn't and never be heard from again? Think about it. Think of the form of transportation where there's the most mass death. Bus.

JW: *But you do like to travel, and you like to get off the beaten track, judging by your recent travel pieces about Thailand and Indonesia.*

MK: There's no such thing as off the beaten track anymore. Anywhere you go, they have it marketed. Thailand is more marketed than most places. Thailand is Disneyland. Go to any part of Thailand and they have *rides*: a ride on a raft, a ride on an elephant, a trip to a butterfly farm. And when you land in Bali, after being on the plane for twenty-four hours, the first thing you see is a Colonel Sanders. There's no place in the world where you can't get Coca-Cola. They may not have indoor plumbing, but all the shops have stacks of beer and cigarettes.

JW: *What's your policy on hotel rooms?*

MK: I love luxury hotels, but I'm married to someone who would stay in a youth hostel. We've gradually reached a compromise: I don't pick where we go and I don't pick how we get there, but I've retained veto power on the accommodations. Call me fussy, but I demand clean sheets and a private bathroom.

JW: *Do you travel light?*

MK: Not really, but my husband does. But a funny thing about people who travel light: they invariably travel with someone like me who's lugging around a set of Vuitton luggage. My husband leaves with one little bag, but he puts anything he might need in my suitcase. And he's always buying things—stone carvings, jackets, rugs—and putting them in my suitcase. People who travel light make me nervous. People who travel light are the same people who will say to you with a straight face, "Honey, do you have an inflatable pillow? Do you have a book light?"

JW: *Does he at least give you credit for carrying all the stuff?*

MK: No. When I'm going to, let's say, a malaria kingdom, I first go to the doctor and get every medication I might possibly need, and my doctor sends me away with prescriptions for anything that could possibly happen in the jungle. And my husband accuses me of carrying around a small pharmacy. But in Thailand he got dysentery—for a man it's dysentery, for a woman it's diarrhea—and I suddenly realized I had the medicine for it. What a wonderful moment when he crawled over and begged for it.

JW: *One last question: how do you feel about bottle redheads?*

MK: I wish they would round up all these fake redheads. They're everywhere. I used to be the only redhead in my dance class, but now there are all these women with hair the color of Ethan Allen furniture. Cherry wood. Mahogany. These fake redheads did not pay their dues. They never got called "Freckles" or "Carrot Top." They never had to swim with a T-shirt to avoid getting sunburned. They weren't constantly asked by sleazy men on the street, "Where did you get that red hair from?" "Is it real?" And now they all walk around with this hot-shit attitude, which no real redhead has. Real redheads are incredibly direct and usually very nice. These fake redheads are everywhere. Yesterday my sister called to say she was thinking of dyeing her hair red. I warned her that it would seriously affect our relationship. Am I done?

Margo Kaufman is the Hollywood correspondent for Pug Talk, *a contributing editor of the* Los Angeles Times Magazine, *and a born redhead. She is the author of a collection of columns,* 1 800 Am I Nuts?

QUOTES ON "S"

SATIRE

You can't make up anything anymore. The world itself is a satire. All you're doing is recording it.
ART BUCHWALD

SCOUT TROOP

A scout troop consists of twelve little kids dressed like schmucks following a big schmuck dressed like a kid.
JACK BENNY

SENATORS

There ought to be one day—just one—when there is open season on senators.
WILL ROGERS

SENILITY

I am in the prime of senility.
JOEL CHANDLER HARRIS

SEX

The big difference between sex for money and sex for free is that sex for money usually costs a lot less.
BRENDAN BEHAN

A woman in a hotel bar told the sportswriter Woody Paige that she would do anything he wanted for a hundred dollars. "I'm in Room 125," he replied. "Go up and write a column and a sidebar."

As I grow older and older
And totter towards the tomb,
I find that I care less and less
Who goes to bed with whom.

DOROTHY L. SAYERS

Sex hasn't been the same since women started enjoying it.

LEWIS GRIZZARD

SHOPPING

I like to walk down Bond Street, thinking of all the things I don't want.

LOGAN PEARSALL SMITH

SIN

Sin is a dangerous toy in the hands of the virtuous. It should be left to the congenitally sinful, who know when to play with it and when to let it alone.

H. L. MENCKEN

SKIING

I do not participate in any sport with ambulances at the bottom of a hill.

ERMA BOMBECK

The sport of skiing consists of wearing three thousand dollars' worth of clothes and equipment and driving two hundred miles in the snow in order to stand around at a bar and get drunk.

P. J. O'ROURKE

———SOCIALISM———

Can you imagine lying in bed on a Sunday morning with the love of your life, a cup of tea and a bacon sandwich, and all you had to read was the *Socialist Worker*?   DEREK JAMESON

———SPORTS———

It is a noteworthy fact that kicking and beating have played so considerable a part in the habits which necessity has imposed on mankind in past ages that the only way of preventing civilized men from beating and kicking their wives is to organize games in which they can kick and beat balls.

GEORGE BERNARD SHAW

Baseball is what we were, football is what we have become.   MARY MCGRORY

Serious sport has nothing to do with fair play. It is bound up with hatred, jealousy, boastfulness, disregard of all rules and sadistic pleasure in witnessing violence. In other words, it is war minus the shooting.   GEORGE ORWELL

Rugby is a beastly game played by gentlemen; soccer is a gentleman's game played by beasts; football is a beastly game played by beasts.

HENRY BLAHA

———SPRING———

Every year, back spring comes, with nasty little birds, yapping their fool heads off, and the ground all mucked up with arbutus. DOROTHY PARKER

Spring makes everything look filthy.

KATHERINE WHITEHORN

———STOCKHOLDER———

An excellent monument might be erected to the unknown stockholder. It might take the form of a solid stone arc of faith apparently floating in a pool of water. FELIX RIESENBERG

———STUDENT ATHLETES———

Can't anything be done about calling these guys "student athletes"? That's like referring to Attila the Hun's cavalry as "weekend warriors."

RUSSELL BAKER

———STUPIDITY———

Some scientists claim that *hydrogen*, because it is so plentiful, is the *basic building block of the universe*. I dispute that. I say there is more *stupidity* than *hy-drogen*, and *that* is the *basic building block of the universe*. FRANK ZAPPA

———STYLING MOUSSE———

Styling mousse, which is gunk that looks like shaving cream . . . was invented by a French hair professional whom, if you met him, you would want to punch directly in the mouth. DAVE BARRY

——SUBSCRIPTION CARDS——

I have . . . had a disturbing dream in which I break through a cave wall near Nag Hammadi and discover urns full of ancient Coptic scrolls. As I unfurl the first scroll, a subscription card to some Gnostic exercise magazine flutters out.

COLIN MCENROE

————SUCCESS————

The penalty for success is to be bored by the people who used to snub you. NANCY ASTOR

Success is a great deodorant.

ELIZABETH TAYLOR

Nothing fails like success: LESLIE FIEDLER

Sunday: a day given over by Americans to wishing they were dead and in heaven, and that their neighbors were dead and in hell.

H. L. MENCKEN

SUPERMARKET TOMATOES

You've probably noticed that modern supermarket tomatoes are inedible. This is because they're not bred for human consumption. They're bred to be shipped long distances via truck, which requires that they have the same juicy tenderness as croquet balls. Even as you read these words, top vegetable scientists are field-testing the Tomato of Tomorrow, which can withstand direct mortar fire and cannot be penetrated by any known kitchen implement except the Veg-o-Matic Home Laser Slicer (Not Sold in Stores). DAVE BARRY

————SWITZERLAND————

In Italy, for thirty years under the Borgias, they had warfare, terror, murder and bloodshed, but they produced Michelangelo, Leonardo da Vinci, and the Renaissance. In Switzerland they had brotherly love, they had five hundred years of democracy and peace, and what did they produce? The cuckoo clock.

ORSON WELLES in *The Third Man*
(Screenplay by Graham Greene)

QUOTES ON "T"

TAXES

The avoidance of taxes is the only intellectual pursuit that carries any reward.

JOHN MAYNARD KEYNES

I wish the government would put a tax on pianos for the incompetent. EDITH SITWELL

TECHNOLOGY

For a list of all the ways technology has failed to improve the quality of life, please press three.

ALICE KAHN

TELEPHONE

Telephone, *n*. An invention of the devil which abrogates some of the advantages of making a disagreeable person keep his distance.

AMBROSE BIERCE

Today the ringing of the telephone takes precedence over everything. It reaches a point of terrorism, particularly at dinnertime.

NIELS DIFFRIENT

Refried Jesus-wheezing TV preachers.

P. J. O'ROURKE

————TELEVISION————

Television has done much for psychiatry by spreading information about it, as well as contributing to the need for it.   ALFRED HITCHCOCK

Television is the first truly democratic culture—the first culture available to everybody and entirely governed by what the people want. The most terrifying thing is what the people do want.

CLIVE BARNES

I have had my television aerials removed. It's the moral equivalent of a prostate operation.

MALCOLM MUGGERIDGE

You have to work years in hit shows to make people sick and tired of you, but you can accomplish this in a few weeks on television.

WALTER SLEZAK

Seeing a murder on television . . . can help work off one's antagonisms. And if you haven't any antagonisms, the commercials will give you some.

ALFRED HITCHCOCK

All television is children's television.

RICHARD P. ADLER

The one function that TV news performs very well is that when there is no news we give it to you with the same emphasis as if there were.

DAVID BRINKLEY

Television has raised writing to a new low.

SAM GOLDWYN

Art is moral passion married to entertainment. Moral passion without entertainment is propaganda, and entertainment without moral passion is television.

RITA MAE BROWN

If vaudeville had died, television was the box they put it in.

LARRY GELBART

___TEN COMMANDMENTS___

Say what you will about the Ten Commandments, you must always come back to the pleasant fact that there are only ten of them.

H. L. MENCKEN

_____THANKSGIVING_____

Most turkeys taste better the day after; my mother's tasted better the day before.

RITA RUDNER

We're doing something a little different this year for Thanksgiving. Instead of a turkey, we're having a swan. You get more stuffing.

GEORGE CARLIN

Thanksgiving is so called because we are all so thankful that it comes only once a year.

P. J. O'ROURKE

Thanksgiving dinners take eighteen hours to prepare. They are consumed in twelve minutes. Halftimes take twelve minutes. This is not coincidence.

ERMA BOMBECK

THEATER DIRECTOR

Theater Director: a person engaged by the management to conceal the fact that the players cannot act.

JAMES AGATE

THINKING

There is no expedient to which a man will not go to avoid the labor of thinking.

THOMAS EDISON

TRUTH

Ye shall know the truth, and the truth shall make you mad.

ALDOUS HUXLEY

The second half of the twentieth century is a complete flop. ISAAC BASHEVIS SINGER

The horror of the twentieth century was the size of each event, and the paucity of its reverberation. NORMAN MAILER

ABSENT FRIENDS

Her features did not seem to know the value of teamwork. GEORGE ADE

She was a professional athlete—of the tongue. ALDOUS HUXLEY

She's descended from a long line her mother listened to. GYPSY ROSE LEE

Nature played a cruel trick on her by giving her a waxed moustache. ALAN BENNETT

She looked as if she had been poured into her clothes and had forgotten to say "when." P. G. WODEHOUSE

The finest woman that ever walked the streets. MAE WEST

She's been on more laps than a napkin. WALTER WINCHELL

When he dances he's all feet and when he stops he's all hands. ARTHUR SHEEKMAN

Although he is a very poor fielder, he is a very
poor hitter.   RING LARDNER

If not actually disgruntled, he was far from being
gruntled.   P. G. WODEHOUSE

He can compress the most words into the smallest
ideas of any man I ever met.
                                ABRAHAM LINCOLN

He continued to be an infant long after he ceased
to be a prodigy.   ROBERT MOSES

I've just learned about his illness. Let's hope it's
nothing trivial.   IRVIN S. COBB

He was like a cock who thought the sun had risen
to hear him crow.   GEORGE ELIOT

He doesn't know the meaning of the word fear,
but then again he doesn't know the meaning of
most words.   ANONYMOUS

He was *audibly* tan.   FRAN LEBOWITZ

He knew the precise psychological moment when
to say nothing.   OSCAR WILDE

He fell in love with himself at first sight and it is a passion to which he has always been faithful.

ANTHONY POWELL

His words leap across rivers and mountains, but his thoughts are still only six inches long.

E. B. WHITE

No one can have a higher opinion of him than I have, and I think he's a dirty little beast.

W. S. GILBERT

Some cause happiness wherever they go; others whenever they go.

OSCAR WILDE

She always tells stories in the present vindictive.

TOM PEACE

Remember, men, we're fighting for this woman's honor, which is more than she ever did.

GROUCHO MARX in *Duck Soup*

You could throw her in the river and skim ugly for three days.

ANONYMOUS

You may have genius. The contrary is, of course, probable.

OLIVER WENDELL HOLMES

Called upon to eulogize an acquaintance he detested, Voltaire at first refused but was finally persuaded to say a few words: "I have just been informed that   is dead. He was a hardy patriot, a gifted writer, a faithful friend and an affectionate husband and father—provided he is really dead."

His imagination resembled the wings of an ostrich. It enabled him to run, though not to soar.
THOMAS BABINGTON MACAULAY

She's afraid that if she leaves, she'll become the life of the party.
GROUCHO MARX

She was a singer who had to take any note above A with her eyebrows.
MONTAGUE GLASS

He was a gentleman who was generally spoken of as having nothing a year, paid quarterly.
ROBERT SMITH SURTEES

His mind is so open that the wind whistles through it.
HEYWOOD BROUN

He hasn't an enemy in the world—but all his friends hate him.
EDDIE CANTOR

Dear boy, it isn't that your manners are bad—it's
simply that you have no manners at all.

MARGOT ASQUITH

If brains was lard, he couldn't grease a pan.

BUDDY EBSEN in "The Beverly Hillbillies"

He's a fine friend. He stabs you in the front.

LEONARD LOUIS LEVINSON

The louder he talked of his honor, the faster we
counted our spoons.   EMERSON

I don't like her. But don't misunderstand me: my
dislike is purely platonic.

HERBERT BEERBOHM TREE

Their insatiable lust for power is only equalled by
their incurable impotence in exercising it.

WINSTON CHURCHILL

He's the only man I ever knew who had rubber
pockets so he could steal soup. WILSON MIZNER

His lack of education is more than compensated
for by his keenly developed moral bankruptcy.

WOODY ALLEN

CARRIE FISHER

Aghast in Her Own House

CF: [Entering the room] So I had a dream last night in which someone spoke the words "Aghast in her own house," and then I dreamed I was on the bottom of the pool, drowning, and I didn't have any toes! You need those toes to spring up to the surface, you know.

JW: *Do you put your dreams into your novels?*

CF: I usually can't remember them; what's left I certainly *plumb*,

I suppose is the word, but I really have trouble remembering them.

JW: *Because of the drugs?*

CF: I couldn't say. I actually remember things much more vividly that happened when I was *on* drugs than anything when I was off them. I always made it a point to remember, in case someone asked, "Are you on acid?" "I am *not* on acid and to prove it I will tell you what you're wearing and what you're thinking and how you feel."

JW: *I get the impression that you don't entirely regret your experience with what, acid and Percodan?*

CF: I had a good time.

JW: *Why such a strange combination?*

CF: Percodan I needed, acid I liked. First everything hurts and then nothing makes sense. I wanted it either melted down or blown away. Medicine: "Take two of these and you'll feel better." Well, if two make me feel better, eight will make me feel fantastic, and sixteen will make me feel nothing at all. There's a great line of Jerry Garcia's: "It cuts away care." I mean, could any of us care less? Yes, if properly medicated, you could care far less. And then it comes crashing back.

JW: *No free lunch?*

CF: No, and quite a piper to have to pay.

JW: *And you did and—*

CF: Here I am in the House That Acid Decorated.

JW: *Did you rely exclusively on your own drug experiences in writing* Postcards from the Edge?

CF: Not entirely. People told me stuff. I was Joan of Narc, the patron saint of the addict. Just after I got divorced I went on a wine date with this very funny writer who said that he'd read my book and felt that we'd gone out before and had split up because of something *I* did, but that he had forgiven me and so now we could go out again. People think that everything I write is hyper-autobiographical, which is so and not so. I have friends who still think I shot heroin because Alex [a character in *Postcards from the Edge*] did. I guess it's inevitable, so you might as well have fun with it. I once facetiously said I was going to write about a lesbian grandmother who seduces her whole family, and the press took me seriously. They thought I was talking about my Grandma Red! Fortunately, she thought it was funny, so I'm relieved. I "outed" her at the age of eighty.

JW: *You've been outed yourself.*

CF: Yes, they outed Penny Marshall and me! Both of us talk so much, I can just imagine the moment it happened: "Will you shut up already about scouting locations? I'll go down on you if you just—where's your vibrator? What, we're going to have to hear about the casting thing again? Just lay down!" I've always thought that sex is about *contact*, and that I could achieve conversationally what most people achieve carnally, so why go through all that messiness? Why put myself, at five-one and a half, up against somebody who's going to be taller than I am? I mean, let's face it, I'm going to be at a disadvantage. *They* fuck and *you* get fucked. It's psychologically and philosophically incorrect for me. But then I come from a long line of short, frigid women.

But if I were a lesbian, maybe I could find a girl my height. I've always said that I wanted to find myself before somebody bigger did. Which isn't hard at five-one and a half. Before I left for India, Treat Williams said to me, "I hope you find what you're looking for." And I hope I don't have to take it back and get it in my size.

JW: *Didn't you sort of find yourself when you got off drugs? In fact, don't you credit rehab with saving your life?*

CF: I credit overdose. I credit dramatic incident that very graphically tells you, "This isn't working." I credit that with *getting* to rehab, and rehab was unfortunately one of the most interesting things that ever happened to me. Which says something about my life. I would never have met people like that. And I was humiliated. It really tears you down. Which is good. I'd spent a good five years telling you I wasn't a drug addict, that I was tired, that I was on antihistamines, that I was anything but an addict. In rehab I began to watch that denial process. It's the same mechanism that functions when you're in a destructive relationship. You just watch while your brain vomits up the piece of news of why you're not really doing what you are in fact doing.

JW: *What about the "higher power" aspect?*

CF: I believe in God and strong turbulence. I also call my mother, who says, "Well, you've had a good life." Thanks, Mom. I love the idea of God, but it's not stylistically in keeping with the way I function. I would describe myself as an enthusiastic agnostic who would be happy to be shown that there is a God. I can see that people who believe in God are happier. My brother is. My dad is, too. But I *doubt*. I mean, come on, we're really going to go to Heaven? Even if we are, I don't have anything to wear. So I don't completely get the higher-power thing, but I know it's helped friends of mine enormously, so I would never try to tear it down.

JW: *What did you think of the Just Say No campaign?*

CF: If I hadn't been taking drugs already, it would have made me start immediately. You can't say to teenagers, "It's bad. We only did it because we were stupid and it wasn't fun." It *was* fun, and they know we're lying.

JW: *Didn't you once say that humor is your armor because you actually take things very seriously?*

CF: That's my most hilarious gag. I think everything is very, very heavy, so I joke about everything. The worse the situation, the better the gag. I had a friend staying with me who had AIDS, and we had lots of laughs.

JW: *Is nothing sacred?*

CF: No. Are you kidding? Death? You drag out the big artillery for death. The worst thing that could happen to me would be to lose my sense of humor.

JW: *Have you ever lost it?*

CF: Yes, when I broke up with my ex-husband. I didn't make a joke for a couple of days. People were waiting around on the outskirts of my personality for the superstructure to re-occasion itself. But you can observe your own lack of humor and eventually *that* becomes funny. You feel sorry for yourself, and *that's* funny. You can't stay there anymore.

JW: *Are you a moody person?*

CF: I'm annoyed most of the time.

JW: *Are you athletic?*

CF: No. I make myself exercise, but I don't like much movement

---

at all. If talking were aerobic, I'd be the thinnest person in the world.

JW: *You've been quoted as saying that you feel particularly qualified on two subjects, drugs and relationships, and since you've already demonstrated your expertise on the subject of drugs, I'll ask you to pontificate a little about relationships. First of all, do you think they're easier for men?*

CF: Yes, of course. Men get their identity from their work, women get their identity from their men. If a woman gets a good job, it's great, but better still because she might meet a great guy—fight her way to the top and then meet a richer guy who will take care of her while she has babies.

Whenever you hear of two people breaking up, the man has usually instigated it—there are of course exceptions to this rule—but the man has generally scouted another sexual location prior to the split-up, and if he's a powerful man, in five seconds he can be in a relationship with any one of a vast array of women.

JW: *Is life easier for men?*

CF: Well, it's longer for women, but only at the bad end. I wish we got our seven extra years up front, or in the middle somewhere. We look worse faster. Wrinkles on men is character; on women, it's "Oh, *shit!*" And men are fertile forever. You can be Hugh Hefner at sixty and have a baby with a twenty-one-year-old and it's not seen as vampiric. But if a woman does it, it's pathetic.

JW: *Is sex better for women?*

CF: I don't know about that. There are some women who have something, I've heard, like a "multiple orgasm," like firecrackers going off all throughout their system, and they can have a series of orgasms if they are set up right. I can't confess to this tendency myself. In general, I think it's true that women fuck to love and men love to fuck. When *we* do it, we're hoping he'll call us and love us. When they do it, they're just doing it. It's biological for them and it's emotional for us.

JW: *What about romance?*

CF: I heard a great definition of it: "Not founded in reality." Romance is based on uncertainty, so when you don't know where you stand and you're waiting for somebody to sort of define the direction, which is usually the male, that's romance. Romance is searing uncertainty, which creates sexual excitement, which is only there for as long as you're not settled in. When certainty kicks in, sex fades out. If marriage is based on romance, it's over. That tends to shock people. A girlfriend of mine left her boyfriend because he didn't ask her to waltz or something, or he didn't hold her chair out, and I thought, *You'll* have a great life.

JW: *Do you think people expect too much from their relationships?*

CF: I don't know, but I don't see the point of constantly having your relationship in a line through every situation. What are you going to bring to it if you're always in it? I once said to Paul at a party, "Please don't stand next to me, people will think we're salt and pepper shakers." But that's the bad part of me; I didn't grow up with a family that was ever around me, so I got very invested in entertaining myself. I used to make up stories about furniture. Telling myself little jokes, making the best of not too bad of a time. I was alone.

JW: *And you read a lot.*

CF: The first drug. It blocks out the world. They could tear the house down and I would be playing with my hair, my tongue out, reading. To this day I read like a horse. I bring the book up to my face like a feedbag. My family used to call me a book-worm—and they meant it in a derogatory way—they said it like "Jew"—like that *Jew* part of the family that we never see. So, I don't rely on other people for my experience, but I'm sensitive, and if you start criticizing my behavior, judging me, then I have to get your approval back, because I have a problem with people being mad at me. The one thing I've figured out from twenty years of therapy is that I must have decided that [my father] Eddie Fisher was very mad at me, personally.

JW: *You once said that you were "born of a golden womb," and you've talked about being photographed by* Modern Screen *when you were three days old. So, my question is—*

CF: Do I have a soul left?

JW: *No, my question is, What do you think of when you pass the guy on Sunset who sells the Maps to the Stars Homes?*

CF: I wonder how they get the addresses. We were on it when I was little and when the tourists came, if they had a movie camera we would stand still, and if they had a still camera, we'd move.

JW: *Do you observe any sort of celebrity code of conduct?*

CF: Yes, absolutely. It's funny because you don't know there is one till you see someone breaking it. If I'm out with Meryl [Streep], *I'm* the moat. If people come up to her, I must deflect them; if they come up to both of us, I must deflect them. I still get treated as Princess Leia, or lately it's "You're my favorite writer," or even "I loved your Madonna interview."

JW: *Do you have a preference as to how you'd like to be recognized?*

CF: As a writer. I loved doing those movies, but if you liked them, tell George [Lucas]. That's not my accomplishment. I was there. It was a great party, but it wasn't my house. The book thing is my party.

JW: *I'd like to mention a few names and just get some quick reactions: Julia Phillips.*

CF: I heard that she said my book is like me: "Tiny, witty and eager to be loved." You want to say, "What, we should *all* try to get everyone to hate us?"

JW: *Ron Reagan.*

CF: I still want to do more on Julia Phillips.

JW: *Go ahead.*

CF: That's okay. Who *is* Ron Reagan? Is he a ballet dancer? A talk-show host? I do respect the fact that it's hard to be somebody's kid. Patti Davis called me to get some advice about *Mother*. She was going to go after *Mother*. I said, well, do it, but be a little bit funny. It's not like it's going to be a shock. "Really? Nancy's not nice? Oh, my God, that's so weird! I thought she was just adorable with those tiny shoulders and that big helmet hair."

JW: *Mr. Blackwell.*

CF: I made his Worst Dressed list, which I think is hilarious. But is that a career? You set yourself up as the discerning measure of all fashion based on what? What does *he* wear? Where does he come from? Who the fuck is he? I know there are answers to these questions, but I don't want them.

JW: *Arnold Schwarzenegger.*

CF: Oh, the name alone. What does that name mean? I saw him at this [George] Bush dinner (*I* wasn't invited, I went with [David] Geffen). Arnold's a Republican. A Republican bodybuilder. For the same reasons that Reagan was president, Schwarzenegger is our biggest star.

JW: *Bret Easton Ellis.*

CF: Sweet guy. Adorable. So what if he's written a book about headless women being fucked in the neck: "Honey, don't interrupt me right now, I'm reading about someone being sodomized while their brains are lying on the floor. Just one sec, okay? It's poetry."

JW: *Jerry Lewis.*

CF: Terrible hair.

JW: *Oprah Winfrey.*

CF: I saw the Oprah Winfrey show only once, on a trip to Omaha, and I've never watched it again. The theme was abused children who finally couldn't take it anymore and murdered their parents. She's talking to this young woman whose father had raped her every day for her whole life and she finally got a gun. Then he came to rape her again. Oprah Winfrey says, "What happened the day you murdered your father?" And the woman says, "I said that I didn't want to talk about the particulars of that." Oprah looks at the camera and the audience and goes, "You're on a show about children who murdered their parents and you don't want to talk about that?" Oprah does a look like, "Hey, you're here to sell beef and you don't want to talk about the burger you had?" Talk about cold. Talk about not having a soul.

JW: *David Letterman.*

CF: He has no life, from what I understand. I said to him on the air, "My sense of this is, I get nervous coming on the show, you get nervous when the show ends." He said, "You're not far off from the truth," and then he changed the subject. He will not talk to you in the halls because if you say, "Hello," you're wasting it. He wants it all saved up. The only thing that's important is when the camera's on. The guy isn't interested in people, he's interested in the show.

JW: *Cher*.

CF: She's a little long in the tubes to be prancing around naked in public. I'm sorry, but that's the way it is. I don't make up the facts, I just report them.

JW: *Gore Vidal*.

CF: There are certain people who are elder statesmen in the community of letters, and I occasionally meet these people and I just try not to fawn. Actually, the best person for that is [William] Styron, who I gave that little toy that says, "Fuck you, Eat shit, You're an asshole." He loved it. He'd never seen it and he was so thrilled he sent me a book with the inscription "Fuck you, fuck you, fuck you. Eat shit, eat shit, eat shit. You're an asshole. Love and Kisses." Hilarious. He's a genius. He once said, "I'd call her a cunt, but she lacks the depth and the charm." Genius. Maybe you should interview him.

JW: *Ali MacGraw?*

CF: Well, she's does this makeup commercial I watch all the time. They do it like it's a talk show. My fantasy is that I'm watching the show and people come in and I go, "Shhh, shhh, wait, I love this part about highlighting."

JW: *Sam Donaldson.*

CF: He doesn't move his face when he talks. His eyes are like shark eyes. Dead.

JW: *Jesse Jackson.*

CF: Fun to watch being interviewed. He'll answer any question because he's genuinely interested in himself. He loves himself, and I love to watch people who love themselves. It's like watching a great bath. But I don't care for all that weeping. I don't believe anybody should weep in public. And people should weep in private only if they have a note from their doctor saying they have some kind of fever or are vomiting uncontrollably. It's wrong to weep in public. There's no justification for it unless your husband has been murdered in a motorcade. There are only a very few extenuating circumstances in which there should be any lachrymal license whatsoever.

JW: *Norman Mailer.*

CF: Well, he asked for $50,000 to do the Madonna interview [for *Rolling Stone*] and they wouldn't go for it. $50,000! I did it for $3,500 and they printed it twice.

JW: *Prince.*

CF: I like Prince. I think he's really good. He's sleeping with all these gorgeous white women and never talking about it himself but getting *them* to talk about it and ruin their careers in the South.

JW: *Jack Nicholson.*

CF: He's fun because he doesn't make sense. I told him recently at a party that he should sleep with me so that I could write about it. I got him to think about it for a couple of minutes.

JW: *Warren Beatty*.

CF: He claims that I came on to him in London. Now, I've never come on to anyone. I'm sure I said to him, "Come on, Warren, I didn't give my virginity to you, so let's do it now." And he took it seriously, because humor is not Warren's strongest suit. He must think of me as a failure. His one failure.

JW: *You've said that you declined his offer to relieve you of your virginity when you made* Shampoo *together*.

CF: Right, I chose reality over anecdote. I didn't want to be at the receiving end of his technique.

JW: *Spike Lee*.

CF: Get a sense of humor! It makes total sense that the first hot black director we have is angry and racist, because there have been so many racist white directors, and we never talk about that. And I can see that it would be difficult to be both funny and that angry. But his interviews are so heavy. Lighten up, Spike, you got the job. He's a powerful guy. In fact, he would be a great boyfriend for me. Torture, black eyes. Can you imagine? I'm the wife Spike Lee deserves. A white woman, which he says he would never be with, so let's get someone really white. I am Spike Lee's Wife from Hell. I'm white and weird and I won't pay enough attention to him. If he does any more of those angry interviews, I'm going to write him and see if he wants the wife he deserves.

Carrie Fisher is the author of Postcards from the Edge *and* Surrender the Pink, *as well as several short stories and screenplays. She is also known for her portrayal of Princess Leia in the* Star Wars *pictures.*

QUOTES ON "V"

VCR

I suppose I should get a VCR, but the only thing
I like about television is its ephemerality.

P. J. O'Rourke

VEGETARIANS

Most vegetarians look so much like the food they
eat that they can be classified as cannibals.

Finley Peter Dunne

VIOLIN VS. VIOLA

The difference between a violin and a viola is that
a viola burns longer. Victor Borge

VIRGIN MARY

If I had been the Virgin Mary, I would have said
"No." Stevie Smith

VIRTUE

The love of money is the root of all virtue.

George Bernard Shaw

Virtue is its own punishment. ANEURIN BEVAN

———VOX POPULI———

Vox Populi, vox humbug.
WILLIAM TECUMSEH SHERMAN

QUOTES ON "W"

———WAITERS———

When those waiters ask me if I want some fresh
ground pepper, I ask if they have any aged pepper.
ANDY ROONEY

———WAR———

I have given two cousins to war and I stand ready
to sacrifice my wife's brother.   ARTEMUS WARD

Wars teach us not to love our enemies, but to hate
our allies.   W. L. GEORGE

———WASHINGTON, D.C.———

People come to Washington believing it's the center of power. I know I did. It was only much later
that I learned that Washington is a steering wheel
that's not connected to the engine.
RICHARD GOODWIN

Washington is . . . a city of cocker spaniels. It's a
city of people who are more interested in being
petted and admired, loved, than rendering the exercise of power.   ELLIOT RICHARDSON

Washington is a city of Southern efficiency and
Northern charm.   JOHN F. KENNEDY

Washington is an endless series of mock palaces
clearly built for clerks.   ADA LOUISE HUXTABLE

Washington is the only place where sound travels
faster than light.   C.V.R. THOMPSON

Standing, standing, standing—why do I have to
stand all the time? That is the main characteristic
of social Washington.   DANIEL BOORSTIN

————WEDDING————

A wedding is just like a funeral except that you
get to smell your own flowers. GRACE HANSEN

————WHITE BARBECUE————

Going to a white-run barbecue is, I think, like
going to a gentile internist: it might turn out all
right, but you haven't made any attempt to take
advantage of the percentages. CALVIN TRILLIN

————WIFE————

The only time some fellows are ever seen with
their wives is after they've been indicted.
                              KIN HUBBARD

WINNING

Anybody can win, unless there happens to be a second entry.
GEORGE ADE

WOMEN

After years of effort, women have won the right to be taken more seriously than they deserve.
STANLEY BING

It's not the frivolity of women that makes them so intolerable. It's their ghastly enthusiasm.
HORACE RUMPOLE (JOHN MORTIMER)

WOMEN'S STUDIES

Women's studies is a jumble of vulgarians, bunglers, whiners, French faddicts, apparatchiks, doughface party-liners, pie-in-the-sky utopianists, and bullying, sanctimonious sermonizers.
CAMILLE PAGLIA

WORK

Anyone who works is a fool. I don't work—I merely inflict myself on the public.
ROBERT MORLEY

Hard work is damn near as overrated as monogamy.
HUEY P. LONG

It is not a fragrant world.

RAYMOND CHANDLER

The world is so dreadfully managed, one hardly
knows to whom to complain. RONALD FIRBANK

We do not have to visit a madhouse to find disor-
dered minds; our planet is the mental institution
of the universe. GOETHE

The world is divided into people who do things—
and people who get the credit.

DWIGHT MORROW

The world is made up for the most part of morons
and natural tyrants, sure of themselves, strong in
their own opinions, never doubting anything.

CLARENCE DARROW

The trouble with the world is that the stupid are
cocksure and the intelligent are full of doubt.

BERTRAND RUSSELL

Everyone thinks of changing the world, but no
one thinks of changing himself. TOLSTOY

QUOTES ON "Y"

YEAR

Year, *n.* A period of three hundred and sixty-five
disappointments. AMBROSE BIERCE

YOUTH

I am not young enough to know everything.
JAMES M. BARRIE

YUPPIES

In college, they major in Business Administration.
If, to meet certain academic requirements, they
have to take a liberal-arts course, they take Business Poetry. DAVE BARRY

BEDFELLOWS

EARL OF SANDWICH: Sir, I do not know whether you will die on the gallows or of the pox.

JOHN WILKES: That will depend, my lord, on whether I embrace your principles or your mistress.

> He is a man of splendid abilities, but utterly corrupt. Like rotten mackerel by moonlight, he shines and stinks.
> JOHN RANDOLPH on
> Edward Livingston

He is a self-made man who worships his creator.
JOHN BRIGHT on Benjamin Disraeli

> If Gladstone fell in the Thames, that would be a misfortune. But if someone fished him out again, that would be a calamity.   BENJAMIN DISRAELI

Lord Birkenhead is very clever, but sometimes his brains go to his head.   MARGOT ASQUITH

> He could not see a belt without hitting below it.
> MARGOT ASQUITH on David Lloyd George

Mr. Lloyd George . . . spoke for a hundred seventeen minutes, in which period he was detected
only once in the use of an argument.

ARNOLD BENNETT

David Lloyd George did not care in which direction the car was travelling, so long as he remained
in the driver's seat.   LORD BEAVERBROOK

When they circumcised Herbert Samuel they
threw away the wrong bit.

DAVID LLOYD GEORGE

Neither of his colleagues can compare with him
in that acuteness and energy of mind with which
he devotes himself to so many topics injurious to
the strength and welfare of the state.

WINSTON CHURCHILL on
Stafford Cripps

Decided only to be undecided, resolved to be ir-
resolute, adamant for drift, solid for fluidity, all-
powerful to be impotent. WINSTON CHURCHILL
on Stanley Baldwin

One could not even dignify him with the name of
stuffed shirt. He was simply a hole in the air.

GEORGE ORWELL on Stanley Baldwin

Neville Chamberlain looked at foreign affairs through the wrong end of a municipal drainpipe.

WINSTON CHURCHILL

Listening to a speech by Chamberlain is like paying a visit to Woolworth's. Everything is in its place and nothing above sixpence.

ANEURIN BEVAN

[Chamberlain has] the mind and manner of a clothesbrush.

HAROLD NICOLSON

I thought he was a young man of promise, but it appears he was a young man of promises.

A. J. BALFOUR on Winston Churchill

He mistakes verbal felicities for mental inspiration.

ANEURIN BEVAN on Winston Churchill

When I am right, I get angry. Churchill gets angry when he is wrong. We are angry at each other much of the time.

CHARLES DE GAULLE

In defeat unbeatable; in victory unbearable.

WINSTON CHURCHILL on
Field Marshal Montgomery

[Clement Atlee] reminds me of nothing so much as a dead fish before it has had time to stiffen.

GEORGE ORWELL

He is forever poised between a cliché and an indiscretion.

HAROLD MACMILLAN on
Anthony Eden

He was not only a bore, he bored for England.

MALCOLM MUGGERIDGE on
Anthony Eden

No one who knows Mr. Randolph Churchill and wishes to express distaste for him should ever be at a loss for words which would be both opprobrious and apt.

EVELYN WAUGH

He immatures with age.

HAROLD WILSON on Tony Benn

La Pasionaria of middle-class privilege.

DENIS HEALEY on Margaret Thatcher

She sounded like the Book of Revelations read out over a railway station address system by a headmistress of a certain age wearing calico knickers.

CLIVE JAMES on Margaret Thatcher's
television technique

She is democratic enough to talk down to anyone.
AUSTIN MITCHELL on Margaret Thatcher

An artlessly sincere megalomaniac.
H. G. WELLS on Charles De Gaulle

In Pierre Elliott Trudeau, Canada has at last produced a political leader worthy of assassination.
IRVING LAYTON

His mind was like a soup dish, wide and shallow; it could hold a small amount of nearly everything, but the slightest jarring spilt the soup into somebody's lap.
IRVING STONE on William Jennings Bryan

You really have to get to know Dewey to dislike him.
ROBERT A. TAFT on Thomas E. Dewey

Dewey looks like the bridegroom on the wedding cake.
ALICE ROOSEVELT LONGWORTH

I fired MacArthur because he wouldn't respect the authority of the president. I didn't fire him because he was a dumb son of a bitch, although he was.
HARRY S TRUMAN

I studied dramatics under him for twelve years.
                              DWIGHT D. EISENHOWER
                              on Douglas MacArthur

Mr. John Foster Dulles—the world's longest-range misguided missile.   WALTER REUTHER

Smooth is an inadequate word for Dulles. His prevarications are so highly polished as to be aesthetically pleasurable.   I. F. STONE

He gave a fireside speech and the fire went out.
      MARK RUSSELL on Henry "Scoop" Jackson

He would have made a very good bartender.
                    GORE VIDAL on Teddy Kennedy

John Connally's conversion to the GOP raised the intellectual level of both parties.
                              FRANK MANKIEWICZ

His campaign sounded a note of the bogusly grand. [Gary] Hart is [John F.] Kennedy typed on the eighth carbon.   LANCE MORROW

Dukakis is Greek for *Mondale*.   JAY LENO

Susan Estrich, the left-leaning tower of pissantry who served as Michael Dukakis's campaign manager in the 1988 presidential race.

FLORENCE KING

Henry Kissinger . . . became the nation's top foreign-policy strategist despite being born with the handicaps of a laughable accent and no morals or neck.   DAVE BARRY

Compared to Imelda Marcos, Marie Antoinette was a bag lady.   STEPHEN SOLARZ

Jesse Jackson is a man of the cloth. Cashmere.

MORT SAHL

If a tree fell in a forest and no one was there to hear it, it might sound like Dan Quayle looks.

TOM SHALES

Dan Quayle deserves to be Vice President like Elvis deserved his black belt in karate.

DENNIS MILLER

Barbara Bush reads *House and Garden* for fashion
tips.   JUDY TENUTA

The Billy Carter of the British monarchy . . .
                        ROBERT LACY on Princess Margaret

Such an active lass. So outdoorsy. She loves nature
in spite of what it did to her.
                        BETTE MIDLER on Princess Anne

She walks like a duck with a bad leg.
                              RICHARD BLACKWELL on
                                 the Duchess of York

He is neither a strategist, nor is he schooled in
the operational art, nor is he a tactician, nor is he
a general, nor is he a soldier. Other than that, he's
a great military man.
                     GENERAL NORMAN SCHWARTZKOPF
                              on Saddam Hussein

Saddam Hussein is the father of the mother of all
clichés.   CHARLES OSGOOD

P. J. O'ROURKE

Why I Am a Republican

JW: *You've characterized the S&L scandal, agricultural subsidies, and even Social Security as manifestations of Americans' greed.*

PJO'R: The problem with Social Security is that people want to get more out of it than they put in. The problem behind the problem is the sense of entitlement that seems to be overwhelming our society. Things that used to be privileges have become rights. People feel entitled to free medicine, free retirement benefits, every kind of disaster relief, protection from bad luck and from bad weather, and on and on, never asking themselves, "What have I done for society that would make society want to do anything for me? What have I even tried to do?" It's one thing to talk about crippled war veterans, whose sense of entitlement is justified, but why must society fix things for teenage drug addicts? If members of society want to help others who have gotten themselves in trouble or have simply had bad luck, that's great, that's Christian charity. But what makes people think that the rest of society is obliged, or should be forced by law, to help them every time they screw up?

JW: *Well, what does make them think that?*

PJO'R: I don't know, but I think newspapers and magazines, the media in general, encourage people to think this way.

JW: *And lawyers?*

PJO'R: Lawyers certainly do. But with lawyers there's usually some measure of logic—much as I detest the abuse of litigation, especially in liability cases—there's some measure of logic in it, even though that logic is often strained. But there is no measure of logic in someone saying, "Well, I've got myself addicted to heroin, so the nation, the government, the taxpayers, owe me a program to get over my addiction."

JW: *Or "The government owes me a subsidy to operate my farm."*

PJO'R: Precisely. It's important to remember that most of these subsidies do not go to poor people; the majority go to the middle class. Our modern federal government is spending almost $5,000 a year on every person in America. The average American household of 2.64 people thus receives almost $13,000 worth of federal benefits, services, and protection per annum. These people would have to have a family income of $53,700 to pay as much in taxes as they get in goodies. Only 18.5 percent of the population has that kind of money. And only 4.8 percent of the population file income tax returns showing more than $50,000 in adjusted gross income. Ninety-five percent of Americans are on the mooch.

JW: *Is that how the federal budget deficit got so big?*

PJO'R: It got so big because in a democracy people can vote benefits for themselves and vote not to pay taxes for them. People simply want all this stuff for less than it costs. That's all there is to it. Lawmakers are doing nothing but responding to their constituencies.

JW: *The whores are us?*

PJO'R: The whores are us, although I must say that there are certain kinds of lawmakers—liberals, I call them—who egg those constituencies on: "Isn't there more stuff you would like? What have we forgotten? Dental care, that's it. Wouldn't you like some free dental care, too?"

JW: *And you've suggested that the growing number of old people are a big part of the problem.*

PJO'R: Yes! All of a sudden there are geezers and duffers and biddies everywhere you look. There didn't used to be this many old people. I remember when it was just the occasional coot on a porch rocker waxing nostalgic about outdoor plumbing. Now they're all over the place—arteriosclerosing around on the racquet-ball courts, badgering skydiving instructors for senior-citizen discounts, hogging the Jacuzzi at the singles apartment complex. They're even taking over pop music. I went to see the Who last summer, and a bunch of old farts were playing in the band.

JW: *But how do old people contribute to the budget deficit?*

PJO'R: About thirty percent of the federal budget is now spent on "older Americans." As the antediluvian segment of the population continues to grow, we'll be spending more and more on them. The over-fifty-fives are the only age group in the country that will get significantly larger in the next century. By 2030, a fifth of the nation will be old, and lots of the old will be ancient. In fact, the eighty-five-plus bunch, according to the Census Bureau, is the nation's fastest-growing group. There will be between 15 and 30 million of them by the mid-2000s. Yet though they may be alive, they won't be doing much living. Last year a Harvard Medical School research project examined thousands of geriatric Bostonians and found double the previously estimated incidence of Alzheimer's. Nearly half of those over eighty-five had signs of the disease. Medicare already costs taxpayers $100 billion per annum, with thirty percent of that money spent on treatment in the last year of patients' lives.

JW: *The future of the baby boom isn't pretty.*

PJO'R: The baby boom is rapidly turning into the Senescence Swell. Those of us born between 1946 and 1964 constitute one third of the total U.S. population. And we're already worse than our parents. We're the most vapid, screw-noodled, grabby, and self-infatuated generation in history. Imagine what we'll be like in forty years—wearing roller skates in our walkers, going to see Suzanne Vega in Atlantic City, grumbling that our heart-lung machines have gone condo, and buying Ralph Lauren cashmere colostomy bags.

JW: *You're not mad about Europeans, or "Euro-Weenies," as you've called them, and I gather that you don't enjoy traveling in Europe.*

PJO'R: Say what you will about "land of opportunity" and "purpled mountains majesty above the fruited plain," our forebears moved to the United States because they were sick to death of lukewarm beer—and lukewarm coffee and lukewarm bathwater and lukewarm mystery cutlets with mucky-colored mushroom cheese junk on them. Everything in Europe is lukewarm except the radiators. You could use the radiators to make party ice. But nobody does. I'll bet you could walk from the Ural Mountains to the beach at Biarritz and not find one rock-hard, crystal-clear, fist-sized American ice cube. Ask for whiskey on the rocks, and you get a single gray, crumbling leftover from some Lilliputian puddle freeze plopped in a thimble of Scotch (for which you're charged like sin). And the phones don't work. They go "blat-blat" and "neek-neek" and "ugu-ugu-ugu." No two dial tones are alike. The busy signal sounds as if the phone is ringing. And when the phone rings you think the dog farted.

The Europeans can't figure out which side of the road to drive on, and I can't figure out how to flush their toilets. Do I push the knob or pull it or twist it or pump it? And I keep cracking my shins on that stupid bidet thing. (Memo to Europeans: Try washing your *whole* body; believe me, you'd smell better.) Plus there are ruins everywhere.

I've had it with these dopey little countries and all their poky borders. You can't swing a cat without sending it through customs. Everything's too small. The cars are too small. The beds are too small. The elevators are the size of broom closets. Even the languages are itty-bitty. Sometimes you need two or three just to get you through till lunch.

JW: *Let me bring you back to a domestic issue: you've been critical of the War on Drugs. I assume you think we're losing.*

PJO'R: We've already lost.

JW: *Why?*

PJO'R: A modern arrest requires a stack of forms as thick as a Sunday *New York Times* "Arts and Leisure" section, and filling them out is as complicated as buying something at Bloomingdale's with an out-of-state check. A modern conviction requires just as much effort and tedium in court. The average D.C. cop, for example, spends twenty days of his month testifying or waiting to do so. The end result of the dangers, annoyances, delays, boredom, and paper shuffling that go into a bust is . . . nothing. The perp's turned loose. Mostly the perp is turned loose right there in the precinct house. Mere possession of coke usually gets you a citation, a ticket, like you'd turned left on red with your nose. Get caught selling to the UCs, the undercover policemen, and you might have to stay in jail until tomorrow morning.

You can't walk one block in any city in America without wackos and soaks spitting up in your pants cuffs and homeless vagabonds gnawing the tassels off your Foot-Joys. You can't stop at a stoplight without getting squeegeed in the kisser by practitioners of beggary—the most rapidly expanding sector of America's economy. One out of five American children are growing up needy, and fifty-three percent of those kids have nothing for a dad except a blind, microscopic, wiggle-tailed gamete that hasn't held a job since it got to the womb. Drugs are an improvement on some of these problems. Who wouldn't rather have a couple of plump, flaky lines on a mirror and half a disco biscuit than lead the life these people are leading? Drugs are the answer, after all, to the question "How can I get high as a kite?" or "How can I make money without working?"

JW: *Are you saying that drugs are just a symptom?*

PJO'R: Drugs are just a symptom. We all know that. "Drugs are just a symptom." Well, blindness is "just a symptom" of river fever. And having your genitals swell to the size of a Geo Tracker is just a symptom of elephantiasis. And death is just a symptom of AIDS. Even without reading *Time* or watching "Nightline," just with what I can see with my own eyes, I think the symptom is bad enough to treat. Consider the "mushrooms," for instance. "Mushrooms" is slang for kids and old people who get shot down under dealer cross-fire. When the poor, damn mushrooms have a nickname, that's a bad symptom—a symptom worth treating. And if we're serious about treating the symptoms, maybe we'll begin to get an inkling of what the hell disease we've got.

JW: *So what are we going to do about drugs?*

PJO'R: We can get hysterical about them. That's always been fun. I can remember the antediluvian age of drug hysteria, when the occasional bebop musician's ownership of a Mary Jane cigarette threatened to turn every middle-class American teenager into a sex-crazed car thief. This particular hysteria proved well founded. Every middle-class American teenager did try marijuana and did become sex-crazed, although no more car-thievish than usual.

Then there was LSD, which was supposed to make you think you could fly. I remember it made you think you couldn't stand up, and mostly it was right. The much predicted heavy precipitation of wingless adolescents—which caused many people to move their cars out from under trees near hippie pads—failed to materialize.

The early seventies heroin craze likewise petered out before emptying the nation's Scout camps and Hi-Y chapters. And by the time PCP came along to make kids psychotic, kids were acting so psychotic anyway, who could tell the difference? The only unifying theme in these drug scares seemed to be an American public with a strong subconscious wish to get rid of its young people.

Marijuana is self-punishing; it makes you acutely sensitive, and in this world, what worse punishment could there be? Heroin turns people into amoral scuzzballs. But a heroin addict who gets his fix is well behaved or dead—and you can't get better behaved than that. And a heroin addict who doesn't get his fix is helpless. I lived on the Lower East Side during New York City's smack phase, and one night a big guy with a knife tried to rob me. This would have been frightening if he hadn't been half a block away and shaking so badly he couldn't move. "Come here and give me all your money!" he yelled. "No," I shouted back. I left him to work it out on his own.

JW: *What about crack?*

PJO'R: I've smoked freebase, which is the couture version of crack. It felt great. Actually, it felt too great. It reminded me of that experiment that you read about in college psychology textbooks, about the rat that had the electrode inserted directly into the pleasure center of his brain, and then he pushes the little lever that activates the electrode, and he keeps pushing it and pushing it and pushing it—until you have to read about him in a college psychology textbook. I didn't feel like smoking freebase twice.

Crack is a drug for those who are already fucked up. In fact, getting fucked up is for those who are already fucked up. Crack-cocaine use has shown few signs of spreading to this nation's well blessed. County fairs will not be filled with bruised and bleeding Holsteins because 4-H members went into milking frenzies while smoking rock. There isn't going to be a sudden dearth of nuclear physicists because Asian kids are selling their homework to buy vials.

We're not serious about the drug trouble in this country. We're not serious about the trouble causing the drug trouble. We're not serious about anything. We've got a welfare system that pays you to have illegitimate children but takes away your medical benefits if you get a job. We've got big-city property laws where if you buy a piece of rental property, you're punished with a price freeze, but if you wreck a piece of rental property, no force on earth can evict you. When somebody screams obscenities at imaginary tormentors and takes a crap on your front steps, you can't get that person committed to a mental institution. But walk through the park after 8:00 P.M. and all your friends call you crazy. We are not a serious nation.

JW: *How do you regard the new generation of journalists?*

PJO'R: The journalists in my day, not even going back to *Front Page* times, were cynical, hard-drinking, often not very well educated people, but people who could write drunk or write sober

---

and write quickly. Now journalists have turned into a nest of do-gooders. They're a bunch of laptop-tickling, nonsmoking, non-drinking, macrobiotic-looking, twinkly little twerps. I see them all over the world. They were all over the place in the Gulf War. They're completely electronically plugged in, always playing around with modems and things. On the convoy into Kuwait, in the middle of the night, we ran over shrapnel and got flat tires, and it was wonderful to see these kids suddenly confronted with the material world. Something that they couldn't scroll up on, something that didn't have a password key. They didn't have the slightest goddamned idea how to change a tire. They couldn't tell gasoline from diesel oil. Useless in the real world. Kind of hard to equate these people with Mike Royko.

JW: *Why are they like that?*

PJO'R: It's the fault of *All the President's Men*. I had never met a journalist who had been to journalism school previous to about four years after that movie. And then all of them had been to journalism school. What goes on in journalism school? It takes ten minutes to teach somebody to write a pyramid lead. What else is there to know? Except everything in the world, of course, which takes twenty years of hard work. Whenever I speak to college journalism or writing classes I tell them, "I've only got two things to say to you. If you want to write, write. The only way to learn how to do it is by doing it. And the other thing is read." It's amazing how many of these kids you meet who don't read. If you want to write, you have to first read.

JW: *Are today's journalists representative of their generation?*

PJO'R: In general, no. When I lecture on college campuses, it's like going back to pre-1965 college. The kids are in fraternities and sororities, they sort of care about their classes and are a little worried about their careers, but not too much. They love to drink beer. They're nice. They're kids, not monsters from space like we were. I like them. But young journalists, especially television ones, are awful. Television has become the career of choice for extremely ambitious, talent-free individuals.

JW: *Can you explain the difference between Republicans and Democrats?*

PJO'R: It's really very simple: if you think about God, he's obviously a Republican. He's a middle-aged, even elderly, white male. He's quite stern, definitely into rules and regulations, very legalistic. He holds people responsible for their actions. He holds the mortgage on literally everything on earth. He's very well connected socially and politically—it's very difficult to get into God's heavenly country club. It's obvious from the number and condition of the poor on the earth that God is not terribly interested in their material well-being. He's a Republican.

Santa Claus is obviously a Democrat. Santa Claus is jolly, he works very hard for charity. He may know everything about everybody, but he never uses it. He's kind to animals. He gives everybody everything they want without thought of a quid pro quo. He's a great guy. But unfortunately, he doesn't exist.

P. J. O'Rourke is the Irrational Affairs Correspondent for Rolling Stone *and a regular contributor to the* American Spectator. *His books include* Modern Manners, Holidays in Hell, *and* Parliament of Whores.

ABOUT THE AUTHOR

JON WINOKUR is the compiler/editor of half a dozen books and a self-styled connoisseur of curmudgeons.